AMELIA

Amelia was afraid, especially since her violent father was determined that she marry into the powerful Culhane family. Though smooth, polished Alan was taken with Amelia's fragile beauty, Amelia was haunted by his dangerous brother. King Culhane could say more with a look than his brother could with a dictionary, but his temper, like his courage, was legendary in east Texas. But Amelia couldn't deny the raging need that could only be assuaged by King's embrace.

LACY

When Lacy Jarrett and Cole Whitehall are unwittingly compromised into marriage, her dreams of a passionate forever are met with cold, hard resentment. The boy whom she teased and flirted with not so long ago has been changed by the horrors of war. Their uneasy union bridles with torment that is made worse by the blatant desire that remains unquenched and unchallenged. However, Lacy's undying love for the handsome Texan is her destiny, and she vows to reignite the sensual fire dormant in their souls and unlock the secrets of Cole's stormy heart.

TRILBY

After months in the dust and grime of war-torn Arizona, Trilby longed for the cool, green bayous of her Louisiana home. If life was hard, Thorn Vance made it almost unbearable. The rough, sexy cowboy had somehow decided Trilby was the kind who gave freely of her charms, and he wanted his share. He frightened her, but she refused to give him the satisfaction of showing it. Although they tried to deny it, not even the wide expanse of the desert could contain the explosive heat that threatened to consume them both.

He felt her mouth tremble as she yielded. A soft sound came against his body, and he knew that she was lost, completely his.

It went to his head. He groaned, and his hands found her head, cupping it, his thumbs exploring her cheeks, the corners of her mouth, while the hard, hungry kiss went on and on.

She sobbed something against his mouth, and he lifted it just a fraction, his breath jerking out against his lips. "What?" he whispered, half-dazed by the sweetness of her in his arms after weeks of being haunted by the memory of her kisses.

"King . . . Alan . . . will come back soon," she choked.

"Kiss me," he said roughly, bending to her mouth again.

Also by Diana Palmer
Published by Ivy Books:

LACY
TRILBY

AMELIA

Diana Palmer

FAWCETT COLUMBINE • NEW YORK

A Fawcett Columbine Book
Published by Ballantine Books
Copyright © 1993 by Susan Kyle

All rights reserved under International and Pan-American Copyright Conventions. Published in the United States by Ballantine Books, a division of Random House, Inc., New York, and simultaneously in Canada by Random House of Canada Limited, Toronto.

Library of Congress Catalog Card Number: 93-90207

ISBN 0-449-91050-4

Manufactured in the United States of America

BVG 01

In Memorium
"Mama Alice" Milakovic

Chapter One

Date: 1900

AMELIA HOWARD LOVED THE DESERT COUNTRY OF west Texas. It might not be as green and lush as the eastern part of the state, and there were dust storms and coyotes, wolves and rattlesnakes to cope with, but it had a fascination all its own. Occasionally there were bandidos who raided across the Mexican border, which was just over the Rio Grande—Rio Bravo del Norte as the Mexicans called it—from El Paso. There were no Indian raids; there hadn't been any for twenty years or more. Still, something was always happening on the border, and Amelia worried constantly about her brother, Quinn, who was a Texas Ranger. Border problems often meant Ranger intervention.

It had been something of a shock for Atlanta-born and bred Amelia to find herself in west Texas. When her youngest brothers had died two years ago of typhoid fever, her father, Hartwell Howard, had suffered a head injury in a buggy accident trying to get the doctor to come and see them. After that, he suddenly changed. His personality became violent, and he had rages that were unbelievable.

Quinn had gone away to fight in the Spanish-American War and then had settled in El Paso. Left in

Atlanta with her failing mother and her abusive father, Amelia learned quickly that being docile and obedient was the only way to escape the physical violence that began to accompany her father's personality change. It was worse when he drank, and he had started doing that, too. Presumably he did it because of the worsening headaches.

Her mother had died of pneumonia just a year ago. Amelia felt her loss keenly, as did her father. A year ago, he had still had periods when he acted normally. Now, everything was different.

Hartwell had become suddenly impulsive and restless. Just a week after her mother's funeral, he took a notion to move to El Paso with Amelia, to be near Quinn, who had joined the Texas Rangers and was stationed in Alpine, Texas. Hartwell had abruptly seized an opportunity for dynasty-building in his friendship with a wealthy Texas rancher. The move to work in a Texas bank where the rancher kept some of his fortune was one step in that direction. That it had taken several months to arrange hadn't stemmed Hartwell Howard's enthusiasm, either. In fact, at times it had seemed to be the only thing that regulated his increasingly erratic behavior. The second step in her father's plan was trying to force Amelia into a romantic entanglement for which she had no taste whatsoever.

Her father had suddenly become a money-hungry tyrant. Nor was his cruelty flavored with regret or mercy. But in spite of it all Amelia had stayed with Hartwell. She was intelligent enough to realize that there had to be some connection between the head injury her father had suffered in the buggy accident and his radical personality change. She had loved the man he was. It was not in her to desert him now, when he needed her most.

She had always been Hartwell's favorite child, and her loyalty to him would survive anything, even his rages.

But even if she had been hard-hearted enough to desert him, she didn't know what she would have done. She had no source of income, and no way of getting one.

Their father had been so kind when she was a little girl, she reflected. He was forever bringing his children and his wife small presents—small, because his job at the bank as an accountant did not generate much income—but there was always affection and compassion from him. This man he had become was no longer recognizable as her father. But out of the love she had borne him in her childhood, Amelia stubbornly stayed with him, protecting him from the world.

That was becoming increasingly difficult. The rages were closer together and now were produced by the smallest things: ashes on his jacket or a misplaced paper.

Amelia was twenty. She had no experience of men. She was lovely enough to marry where she chose. But her father wanted to marry her to Alan Culhane, youngest son of the powerful west Texas Culhane ranching family. The Culhanes did not know what Hartwell was like away from the bank. There was always the risk that they would find out the hard way.

One time Amelia had been frightened enough to try to run away. One night in Atlanta, just before they moved to El Paso, he'd hit her viciously with a leather strap. She still shuddered, remembering what had happened. It was the only time she had reconsidered her decision to stick it out with Hartwell. But her father was in tears the next morning and she gave in and moved with him to Texas. Now, here in El Paso where

Quinn was nearby, she felt more confident about her choice.

Amelia had idolized Quinn when she was a little girl. She still did. For all that they were four years apart in age, they looked like twins. Quinn had blond hair, the color of her own, and the same deep brown eyes, although his eyes looked almost black in anger. He had a straight, regal nose, and he was enormously tall. Amelia was only of average height, but she was slender and well made.

Quinn had finished college at the same time as his friend King Culhane, who was five years older than he but who had started college quite late in life. Amelia had only managed to finish high school. Her father felt that women should not be too intellectual, and he'd refused to let her seek higher education. What he didn't know was that Quinn had schooled her in the classics and in languages, not only Greek and Latin, but French and Spanish as well.

She had a facility for languages, and she was fluent, but her father didn't know. There was a lot about Amelia that he didn't know, because she now kept one side of her complex personality carefully hidden. Her temper and spirit were submerged to prevent her father from flaring up when she displayed them. He seemed to grow worse daily. She had consulted a doctor about his headaches once and had been told that his mind might be permanently impaired and that he might even die one day of unseen injuries. The doctor had wanted to see Hartwell, but when Amelia gently suggested a meeting, Hartwell became so violent that she had to put a door between them. Since then she had been afraid to mention it again. Her father had high blood pressure in addition to his headaches, and she didn't want to risk killing him.

Nor had she told Quinn her suspicions. He had cares of his own without being asked to bear hers as well.

She could shoot a gun; Quinn had taught her. She could ride a horse expertly, from an English saddle or a Western one. She had a mischievous sense of humor that popped out when she was in young company and relaxed. She could paint. But the face she deliberately presented to Alan and the rest of the Culhanes was necessarily a dull and lackluster one. To all appearances, she was a rather blank young woman with an absent smile, lovely but introverted and not very bright. Most of all, she was calm and never argued, so that her father would be calm as well.

Hartwell had forgotten the mischievous, fiery Amelia of years past, which suited her very well. Except that Alan Culhane seemed to like her this way, and that hadn't been the idea of the masquerade at all.

In many ways, it was easier to cope with her father here on Latigo, the sprawling ranching empire owned by their host, Brant Culhane and his family. The Howards were in residence for a hunting party, and fortunately her father was more interested in sport than in his new passion for overseeing every aspect of Amelia's life. He was taking medicine for the headaches and drinking very little. He didn't want to alienate the man he was trying to lure into a business partnership, or the man he wanted Amelia to marry. So she was left to her own devices. Life was pleasant enough except for the one thorn in her side.

The friendship between the Howards and the Culhanes was a longstanding one, formed when Quinn was at college with the eldest son and heir. But it was the younger son, Alan, whom Hartwell Howard had chosen to marry Amelia. Alan didn't know it yet. Amelia hoped he wouldn't find out, because while she liked him, she had no desire to become his wife. Not when it would mean living in close proximity to *him*. The thorn. The serpent in paradise. She hated him. And loved him.

Amelia caught a movement out of the corner of her eye. As if she'd conjured him up, there he was. The thorn. He was approaching as she strolled quietly along the trail near the house, a small posy of wildflowers clutched in her slender hand. She winced with apprehension, because every encounter seemed more painful than the last.

His whole name was Jeremiah Pearson Culhane, but no one ever called him that. He was King Culhane, and all he lacked were the regal clothes and crown. He had the authority, the bearing, the menace of absolute power, and he used it. He didn't need the prop of his impeccable European background, although it included several cousins from half the royal houses in Europe. He was simply King.

Seeing him dressed as he was now, it was difficult to think of him as a wealthy man. He was wearing the same working clothes that his cowhands wore: faded, stained jeans with flaring batwing chaparreros—the leather chaps that cowboys wore to deflect the vicious chaparral and cacti. His hat was a Stetson, black, wide-brimmed, with a simple leather hatband. His boots were misshapen from use and thick with mud. He wore a crumpled blue bandana around his neck, over a faded and worn chambray shirt with mother-of-pearl buttons on the cuffs and down the front. He carried a Winchester repeating rifle in a scabbard on his saddle. Most of the men did. There were some savage creatures in the wild, some with two legs instead of four.

King didn't speak as he rode past Amelia. He didn't even look at her. The silent treatment had gone on for a week—the entire length of time Amelia and her father had been visiting. He contrived to ignore her completely, even when the family was all together in the evenings. No one else noticed, but Amelia did.

From the very first time she'd seen him, when Quinn had brought him home from college to visit with the Howard family in Atlanta six years ago, she'd adored him. She'd only been fourteen, and her big, dark eyes had followed him lovingly. After that one time Quinn mostly went to Texas with King for visits, because King was oddly reluctant to visit the Howard household.

Alan had come to Atlanta for the twins' funeral, but he'd gone on the train back that very day. King never came back again, because Quinn went to fight in Cuba and then moved to Texas.

Now of course by that time Amelia was the creature her father's mercurial rages had made her. When she and her father had arrived at Latigo for the hunting trip, King quickly made his utter distaste for Amelia known. She'd overheard a scathing inventory of herself from him the day before. It had wounded her. He was a sophisticated, worldly man around whom beautiful women revolved like planets. For a rural man, he had something of a reputation with city women of a certain sort. Amelia had been disturbed by Quinn's sometimes blatant stories about him after they left college. But one long look at him six years ago had been enough to change her life.

It hadn't changed his. He never looked at her. He never spoke to her. He simply pretended not to see her.

Amelia wasn't a violent woman, but she sometimes thought she would enjoy throwing a rock at him. Her own adopted persona had probably been her downfall where King was concerned. He took her at face value, as a nondescript woman with no brain, no personality, and no spirit, and he treated her that way. Nothing had ever hurt quite as much. Her soft eyes watched him ride away, tall and straight, almost a part of the horse. If only he could see past the mask she was forced to wear to keep peace with her father to the woman underneath. But there was no hope of that now. With a long, pained sigh, she turned back toward the house.

"You're so quiet, my dear," Enid Culhane prompted after dinner that evening. They were all sitting around the parlor, sipping coffee while they worked at new embroidery patterns together. The men had retired to Brant's study to clean their weapons and get ready for the next day's hunt.

Enid's dark eyes narrowed as she studied the demure Amelia. She often thought that there was much more to Amelia than anyone realized. There was a mischief in her dark eyes from time to time that was at odds with her quiet demeanor. And Enid also had her own opinion of the girl's father. Not a favorable one.

"Brant mentioned that we might go to a concert one night at Chopin Hall. Would you like that?"

"I love music," Amelia replied. "Yes, thank you."

"Have you a gown?"

"Oh, yes. I have two."

Enid finished the delicate embroidery of a flower, her eyes curious. "King is sometimes difficult," she said without preamble. "He has too much success with women. So much that I sometimes think he is in danger of becoming a cruel rake.''

"But he is not!" Amelia flushed furious at her own impetuous outburst and dragged her embarrassed eyes down to her own handwork. Not before her hostess had seen, and understood, the little flash of defense, however.

"You think highly of him, do you not?"

"He is . . . a striking man, in many ways."

"Striking, and thoughtless." She started on another flower. "Marie is getting the girls to bed. Would you ask if they need anything before I let Rosa close up the kitchen and go to bed?"

"Certainly."

Amelia walked down the long hall to Marie Bonet's room and knocked gently before she opened the door. The girls, aged six and eight, had Marie's dark hair and dark eyes. They were propped up in the spare bed across the room from Marie's, dressed in ruffled and laced cotton gowns. They looked like angels.

"How pretty!" Amelia laughed. *"Tres belles!"* she added in French.

"Tres bien. Tu parles plus bon, cherie," Marie praised.

"Due, I am certain, to your fine tutoring," she replied. "Mrs. Culhane asks if the girls need anything else from the kitchen before the cook leaves."

"No, they are fine. I was going to tell them a story, but they like yours so much better. Do you mind? I impose?"

"Not at all!" Amelia protested. "Go on, do. I'll get them settled for you."

Marie smiled. She was petite and dark, very kind and gentle. Her husband had died of a fever only a few months before, leaving a distraught widow to cope with two little girls. Fortunately, there was money in the family, so Marie wasn't left destitute. Enid Culhane was a cousin of Marie. The women had become close, and Enid had invited Marie and the children to stay at the ranch.

Once Marie had gone back to the living room, Amelia curled up on the bed with the little girls and opened the French reader of fairy tales. She struggled with some words, but the girls were eager to teach her. It was a learning experience for all of them, and she did love children.

She covered the little girls up to their necks when they were sleeping and kissed their rosy cheeks. She stood looking down at them with tender eyes, wondering if she would ever have a child of her own. The thought of being forced to marry Alan and bear his children made her ill.

She turned and tiptoed to the door, opening it very quietly. But as she closed it and slipped away down the dark hall, she collided suddenly with a tall, powerful figure and gasped as lean hands gripped her shoulders.

She knew before she looked up who had steadied her. When King was within a yard of her, she could feel the hair standing on end behind her nape. She had a peculiar kind of intuition that always recognized him, even before he spoke.

Her eyes lifted, curious and quiet, to the dark, lean contours of his face. He had silver eyes, deeply set under thick brows in a lean, square face notorious for its expressiveness. King could say more with a look than his brother could with a dictionary. His temper, like his courage, were legendary in this part of Texas.

He was wearing a dark suit, and against it his white

shirt emphasized the olive of his complexion. He was a
striking man. He didn't have Alan's good looks or the
craggy ones of his father. But there was something in
that face that made women want to crawl to him. Amelia
had seen them simper around him for years and hated
his arrogance and sensuality. She hated knowing that he
could have any woman he wanted; especially since
he made it so apparent that he didn't want Amelia.

"Watch where you're going, can't you?" he asked
curtly.

"Sorry," she said demurely and went to move away.

Surprisingly, his hands tightened on her soft upper
arms. "What were you doing in there?" he asked suspiciously, jerking his head toward Marie's bedroom.

She lifted both eyebrows. "Pilfering jewels?" she
suggested with a smile.

He scowled.

"I was reading the girls to sleep," she said quickly.
She hadn't meant to give voice to her sense of humor.

"They speak very little English."

He thought her a liar as well as a thief. What else
could she expect? *"Mais, je parle français, monsieur,"*
she told him. Mischievously she added, *"Je ne vous
aime pas. Je pense que vous êtes un animal."*

His head moved. Just a little. Just a fraction. Something changed in his silver eyes. *"C'est vrai?"* he replied softly.

Blushing furiously, she jumped away from him. He
let her go without protest, and she took to her heels,
running pell-mell down the hall to her own room. She
darted in it and closed the door, locking it as an after-
thought. Her face was scarlet. Why hadn't she realized
that such an educated man might have a knowledge of
languages past the requisite Greek and Latin? Certainly

King Culhane spoke enough French to understand that she'd said she didn't like him and that he was an animal. She didn't know how she was going to face him!

Of course she had to eventually. She couldn't hide in her room during after-dinner coffee. And while she might have betrayed a little knowledge of French, at least she hadn't disgraced herself by addressing him in the familiar tense. She adjusted her white lace blouse in the waistband of her long black skirt and tucked wisps of hair back into her high coiffure. She winced at her own pale reflection in the mirror and wished she hadn't been quite so forthcoming.

Enid and Marie and Hartwell Howard were nibbling on the delicate Napoleon pastries that had been served with their coffee when Amelia joined them in the parlor.

Her dark-faced, mustachioned father gave her a cursory appraisal. He had a glass of whiskey in his hand, and his cheeks were red—a dangerous sign. Amelia gave thanks that she wasn't alone with him. "Where have you been, miss?" he asked angrily. "Is this any way to behave in company?"

"I do beg your pardon," Amelia said softly, placating him as usual, keeping her eyes lowered as she sat beside Marie and Enid, almost trembling with nerves. "I was detained."

"Mind your manners," her father repeated.

"Yes, Papa."

Alan came into the room with King and their father. All three men were wearing dark suits, but King looked impeccably elegant in his, while Alan looked uncomfortable. Brant, as usual, was the picture of the country gentleman.

"Your father mentioned that you play the piano, Miss Howard," Brant addressed her, smiling. He was very like Alan, dark-haired and dark-eyed, with an olive complexion. He and Alan were tall, but King towered over them both. King's eyes were a light, silvery gray, deep set with thick lashes. His face was more angular and lean than those of the other men in his family, square-jawed with a straight nose and high cheekbones. He had a lithe, predatory way of walking that made Amelia's heart race.

"Of course she plays," Hartwell answered for his daughter. He gestured toward the spinet. "Play some Beethoven, Amelia."

Amelia got up obediently and went to the piano. She couldn't look at King as she passed him, but she felt his eyes on her every step of the way. Disconcerted by the unblinking scrutiny, her slender hands trembled on the keyboard as she began to play, and she made one mistake after another.

The sudden slam of Hartwell Howard's fist on the flawless finish of the cherry side table made Amelia jump. "For God's sake, girl, stop banging away at the wrong keys!" Hartwell roared, disconcerting his host and hostess, not to mention Amelia. "Play it properly!"

She took a steadying breath. Her father's temper had a visible effect on her. But behind it, she knew, there was something much worse than temper. She shot a quick glance at him. Yes, his eyes were glazed, and he was holding his head. Not tonight, she prayed. Please don't let him die here . . . !

"Well, what are you waiting for?" her father raged.

"Possibly for you to stop, so that she can concentrate on her music," King remarked. His voice was pleasant enough, but the look that accompanied it made Hartwell stiffen.

As if he realized that he'd overstepped himself, Hartwell sat back on the sofa. He touched his temple and frowned as if he were trying to think. He glanced at Amelia. ''Go ahead, daughter, play for us,'' he said, and for an instant he was the kind, sweet father she'd adored.

She smiled and let her hands rest on the keys. Then she began to play. The soft, building strains of the ''Moonlight Sonata'' filled the room, swelled like the tide, ebbed and flowed as she let the music become an expression of the turmoil and pain and longing in her own heart.

When she finished, even her father was silent.

She looked up into turbulent silver eyes that were far too close. She hadn't heard him move.

''You have a gift, Miss Howard,'' he said quietly and with faint surprise. ''It was a privilege to hear you.''

''Yes, indeed,'' Enid enthused. ''I had no idea you were so talented, my dear!''

Other praise fell on deaf ears. Amelia had heard nothing past the soft words King had spoken. But beyond that was the darkness growing again in her father's eyes as he finished his drink and his host rose to refill his glass. Her heart raced with fear.

''May I be excused, do you think?'' Amelia asked Enid quickly.

''Nonsense,'' Hartwell said coldly. ''You'll stay and be sociable, my girl.''

''Papa, if you please,'' she tried again, her dark eyes wide with apprehension.

''I do not please,'' he replied. His eyes were growing glassier. ''Remember your promise to obey me, Amelia,'' he added with a soft warning, and his face tautened.

She could hardly forget when the promise had been made and the fierce blow which had prompted it. But now, Quinn was nearby. She had to remember that. If she were careful, and smart, she could circumvent her father's violent outburst. She'd done it before, many times. She knew of only one way.

"Alan, you promised to show me the roses, did you not?" she improvised with a shy smile in the younger man's direction. No one could see, in her position, the desperation in her eyes.

"Indeed," Alan replied. "Shall we, my dear?" And he proffered his arm.

She took it with cold, numb fingers, smiling as she followed him blindly from the room, dreading the impact of her father's voice if he objected. But she was betting that he would not. This was what he wanted.

And miraculously, he did not object. He turned and began discussing the weather with his host. He wanted Amelia to become involved with Alan. He had in mind a merger of families. Naturally he didn't protest.

"I'll join you, if you don't mind," King said lazily, and fell into step beside them.

He pulled an imported cigar from his pocket and struck a match to light it. In the glow, his face had a hardness that Amelia had never encountered in any other man. But patently, he didn't approve of her friendship with Alan. Perhaps he sensed her father's plan and intended to put a quick end to it. Certainly, his opinion of her was made evident at every turn.

"Where did you learn to play like that, Amelia?" Alan asked gently, glaring at his brother.

"I had a private tutor," she replied. "Papa feels that young women should be artistic."

"And mindlessly obedient, obviously," King added carelessly.

"King!" Alan snapped. "Pray keep your opinions to yourself."

"Since Miss Howard is so obviously the obedient slave of her parent, suitors must be in short supply." He took a draw from the cigar and in the semi-darkness of the patio with its surrounding rose gardens, there was a cold glint in his silver eyes. "Not so, Miss Howard?"

Amelia despised him. The two small confrontations with him this evening had softened her toward him, and now when he sensed she was vulnerable, he decided to attack. How could she have forgotten his opinion of her?

"You must think what you like, Mr. Culhane," she said with quiet dignity.

"Really, King, hasn't she endured enough tonight?" Alan asked impatiently.

"If she hasn't, then I certainly have," King replied with faint contempt. He made her a brief bow. "Good evening, Miss Howard."

She stared after him with bloodless lips, so tightly compressed that she thought she might never again be able to open them.

"He is impossible at times," Alan said gently. "Don't let him upset you, Amelia. He likes to bully people. It appeals to his sense of humor," he added coldly.

Amelia glanced at him covertly, reading the resentment and dislike in his expression. Alan was the youngest son and the last to be considered. King was the eldest, and the middle brother, Callaway, was off prospecting in east Texas. Alan stood in King's shadow and knew that he always would. Amelia felt a kind of kinship with him, because certainly she would always stand in her father's. She would never have a moment's peace or independence or freedom while her father drew breath. Not, she thought, that she would wish him dead. She only wished that things were as they had been when her little brothers were alive. Had her father been in a better condition, or absent, she was certain that she'd have lobbed a big rock right at King's arrogant head.

She forced her busy mind back to Alan and listened with every appearance of interest to his stories about the ranch. But inside she was dreading the end of this visit when she would have to return to town. Right now they were living in a boardinghouse where the presence of other people protected her. But her father had been talking of buying a house for himself and Amelia. If he did that Amelia would have no protection. Quinn lived in the Ranger barracks. There must, she thought frantically, be something that she could do to prevent such a move. She had to keep calm and think!

A desperate solution to her predicament came creeping into her mind. If she married, she thought, her father's hold on her would be broken. She would be free, and surely Alan would be kind to her. But then her father would be alone, and he might hurt himself or someone else. Could she live with her conscience if tragedy resulted from her urge to get away? He had been the best father in the whole world. Had their situations been reversed, he would certainly not have deserted her in her time of need.

She looked up at Alan with soft brown eyes and smiled sadly. No. She could not run from her responsibility. And even if she did, it would not be fair to use Alan in such a way. He was much too nice.

Alan forgot what he'd been saying and smiled back. Odd, he thought as they continued along the path between the fragrant roses, that he hadn't noticed how pretty Amelia was in the moonlight!

══ Chapter Two ══

A MELIA HAD MANAGED TO GET TO BED THE NIGHT before without having to confront her father. He hadn't appeared when she came to the breakfast table.

Surprisingly King was there, dressed for work, and so was his father, Brant, and his mother, Enid. Alan wasn't. Neither were Marie and the children.

"Am I too early?" she asked, halting in the doorway. Her hair was in an upswept hairdo, pulled into a loose topknot on her head, and she was wearing a neat blue-striped pinafore over her gray dress. Her button-up gray shoes were just barely visible below her skirt as she hung there, uneasy. For all her shyness and lack of so-phistication, she was the very picture of innocence and beauty in glorious bud.

King looked at her with cool disdain. He was used to women fawning over him. His wealth and family name made him desireable to women, a fact he had long accepted. He was cultured and well bred and had all the right connections. But this woman got under his skin. Perhaps it was because he knew that she disliked him. Or perhaps it was because her cowardice made her contemptible in his eyes. Nevertheless, she was delight-ful to look at. If only there was more to her than beauty. She played the piano well, and she spoke a few simple

19

words of French, but she had no real intellect and no backbone.

King was not a genteel city man. He was rough and he could be cruel, and this child-woman would need a very gentle man. No, she was not for him. Besides that, she thought he was an animal. That thought amused him and his lips curved. It had been a long time since he'd wanted anyone with the fervor he felt for Amelia. How ironic that he had to pretend distaste for her to hide it.

"Of course you're not early," Enid was telling Amelia with a laugh. "Sit down, child. The others are sleeping in."

"Including your poor father." Brant chuckled. "We had a rather late evening. I've insisted that he not be awakened, because I'm taking him out on the hunt today, he and Alan. We may be gone for several days. I have my eye on a nasty customer who's been bringing down cattle hereabouts—a rogue mountain lion."

Amelia sat down at the table without looking at King. He didn't return the compliment. His silver eyes cut at her with pure cold mockery. He looked at her as if the sight of her offended him even as it amused him in some cruel way.

"What will you have, my dear?" Enid asked as she put a platter of biscuits on the table, fresh from the warming tray in the gas oven.

"Just eggs and bacon, please," she replied. "I never eat a large breakfast."

"Pass the eggs, dear," Enid asked her husband. "Coffee, Amelia?"

"Oh, may I?" Amelia asked with a guilty glance at the doorway. "Papa does not approve. . . ."

"Papa is asleep," King replied with faint sarcasm.

"You have a full day, do you not?" Brant asked his son curtly.

King shrugged. "When do I not? Enjoy your trip. Mother and I will see that Miss Howard does not become . . . bored," he added with an enigmatic look.

His parents stared after him curiously when he left and exchanged equally enigmatic glances with each other. His hostility toward Amelia had puzzled both of them. Like Alan, they sympathized with her because of her father's callous treatment. King acted as though he felt she deserved it.

"Roundup is often difficult for King," Brant said slowly, smiling at Amelia. "Perhaps he will mellow when it is over."

"Of course he will," Enid added.

Amelia only smiled. She knew that King's attitude had nothing to do with his duties around the ranch. They stemmed from a peculiar dislike of herself. She had looked forward to her father's absence, even while she worried about what might happen to him on the hunt if he were overtaxed. Now she dreaded the certainty of King's presence over the next week or two.

At least, she told herself, Marie and the children were here, along with Enid, to provide a buffer. Her heart lightened. It would not be so difficult after all.

The hunting party was provisioned and outfitted and ready to ride by late afternoon.

"We'll camp in the hills tonight and set out for the Guadalupe Mountains tomorrow. We'll be near a telegraph office, so I can cable you of our progress," Brant told his wife, and bent to kiss her cheek and embrace her tenderly. "Take care. King is here, and he can contact the Ranger post in Alpine if there are any dirty dealings on the border while we're away.''

Enid nodded solemnly. There had been a few isolated incidents, and a murder on a nearby ranch in recent years. Border gangs operated. So did Mexican rustlers. Civilization might abound in El Paso, but this far out of town it was sidearms and careful watch that kept the peace. Not to mention the Frontier Division of the Texas Rangers; although there was much talk of disbanding that, since the Rangers had very nearly worked themselves out of a job here.

''Have you enough ammunition?'' Enid asked worriedly.

''Enough, and still more,'' her husband said, smiling. His head lifted at the sound of a horse's hooves, and his eyes beamed with pride as King bore down on them astride his coal black Arabian. The horse was a stud sire and a champion in his own right. Only King could, or would, ride him. Nor was he a working horse. King exercised him twice a day. He did, too, usually ride him to the neighboring Valverde estate when he paid court to Miss Darcy.

For the week that Amanda and her father had been in residence, Miss Darcy had come one evening for dinner. It had been a cold occasion, during which Miss Darcy had been condescending almost to the point of rudeness, while clinging limpetlike to King. She seemed to sense Amelia's helpless attraction to King, because she deliberately played up to him, making Amelia feel more inadequate than ever. Lovely she might be to an outsider, but Amelia's surviving parent had convinced her that she had nothing to offer a man save her domestic skills. Not that they were ever quite adequate to suit him these days. . . .

"Are you off, then?" King asked, leaning over the saddle horn.

"Off and running, my boy," Brant said with a smile. "Wish us luck."

"I'll wish that you corner that vicious calf-killer and score a deer or two as well," King agreed.

"In the higher altitudes, game may be more plentiful, since the weather there is still quite wintery this early in spring," Alan put in. "Will you be all right, truly, Amelia?" he asked softly.

She was touched by his concern. "Certainly I will, Alan. I'll think of you while you're away."

"See that you stay in the house," Hartwell Howard told her sharply. "No dillydallying!"

"Yes, Papa," she agreed readily.

"Practice your piano, while you're about it," he added indifferently. "You play clumsily."

"Yes, Papa," she said again. She went close to fix his collar with gentle hands and worried eyes. "You will be very careful?" she asked uncertainly.

He glared at her. "I shall be fine! Stop fussing over me!" He jerked on his gloves and mounted his horse with little concern for the bit in the poor animal's mouth. It reared, and he brought the quirt down on its flank viciously.

King swung out of the saddle with blood in his eyes, before his brother or his father could say a word. He jerked the quirt out of Hartwell's hand and slammed it to the ground.

His silver eyes met the other man's with honest dislike. "Our mounts don't feel the spur or the quirt," he told the man in soft, dangerous tones. "You can walk to the mountains if that doesn't suit you."

Hartwell eyed the younger man warily, his cheeks

red. He wiped at his temple under the hat he was wearing. "Of course, dear boy," he said with a hollow laugh. "The animal is rather unruly, you must have noticed."

"Only when the bit tears at his mouth in clumsy hands," came the blunt reply.

Hartwell looked down at the quirt and seemed to be debating his next move. King made it for him. He put his booted foot squarely over the quirt and calmly began to light a cigar.

The gesture was enough. Hartwell gathered the reins, gingerly this time, muttering under his breath about such consideration for a silly dumb animal as he moved away.

Amelia's fingernails had made crescents in her palms. She had looked for her father to go crazy at the rebuke, perhaps to even grab a gun and start shooting. He was unpredictable. But King didn't know that, and she couldn't tell him. He probably wouldn't believe her anyway.

But Brant saw the anxiety on Amelia's face and knew that something was amiss. "King," Brant began warningly.

The younger man looked up at him without blinking, his silver eyes still flickering dangerously.

"We should go, Father," Alan prompted, wary of explosions. The two older men were both rash and hot-tempered. And often they didn't see eye to eye on issues.

"Yes, I suppose we should," Brant said finally, shifting restlessly in the saddle. "Watch your back," he told King.

"You watch yours," came the curt reply.

Brant smiled at his wife, nodded to Amelia, and

turned his mount. Alan followed suit, glancing back until he almost fell from the saddle watching Amelia.

"Young idiot, he'll break his neck. Must you encourage him so, Miss Howard, or are you just following Papa's commandments?"

She turned, shocked at the vehemence in his voice.

"Really, King," Enid clucked, glaring at him. "You were on your way to see the Valverdes, were you not? Pray, don't let us keep you."

"How could you, when such a charming and fashionable young woman sits waiting for me in her parlor?" he asked with a contemptuous glance at Amelia in her simple homespun dress.

Amelia felt the whip of that comment like a rope burn. The Howards had been a respected family in Atlanta but not a very wealthy one. Amelia had never had elegant clothes or a rich life. Neither did she covet it, but King seemed unconvinced.

"Shall I help Marie with the girls, Mrs. Culhane?" Amelia asked her hostess with a pale smile. "She likes to bath them about this time, I notice."

"Certainly, if you like, my dear. Marie will be leaving in the morning for home, so I'm certain she'll appreciate your help with the packing as well."

"She's leaving?" Amelia couldn't know how upset she sounded.

King arched an eyebrow. "You sound as if you feel she is deserting you in the face of doom, Miss Howard," he mused.

"I don't feel that way at all, Mr. Culhane," she assured him. "I'll just get back to the house," she added quickly and, sidestepping King, lifted her skirts and ran toward the house.

He watched her with cold, narrow eyes.

"What is wrong with you?" his mother demanded icily. "Why are you so cruel to her?"

He shrugged and moved to swing into the saddle, pausing to relight his cigar. "I won't be away long," he said carelessly.

"What you see in that Valverde woman is beyond me," she told him. "She's cold and calculating and the most mercenary human being I've ever known."

He leaned over the pommel. "You left out honest. She has the virtue of being exactly as she appears. She wants me for the ranch and my lineage, just as every other woman has," he added with a cold smile. "I admire her cold-blooded approach. It appeals to my sense of irony."

"I know what caused this cynicism, but you were very young when it happened," Enid said softly, "and even such a deep scar should fade in time. It is not her death you can't forget, anyway, it is the fact that she had deserted you." He didn't speak. He looked explosive. "King, there are many women who look for qualities in men which bear no relevance to wealth."

"Indeed? Women such as our fleeing guest?" he asked, watching Amelia's dash onto the porch. "She's still little more than a child; a rough hand would destroy her," he said, almost to himself. "She is drawn to Alan's smooth profile and parlor manners. Her father," he added, glancing at her, "is much more drawn to the possibility of a partnership through marriage, don't you think?"

"Alan should marry," she returned curtly. "And Amelia is a lovely, sweet girl."

"A spineless jellyfish with no spunk and no grit," he said shortly. "She lacks the nerve to speak back even to her father, despite his deplorable treatment of her.

You ask me to admire such spinelessness? The girl may have a pretty face, but she is a coward. I had rather marry an ugly wild mustang than a broken pretty filly.''

"Women are not horses,'' Enid reminded him.

"They yield to the same treatment,'' King said carelessly, with a last glance at Amelia's retreating figure. "A sugar cube and a soft word, and the wildest of them will submit,'' he added as he gathered the reins.

Enid still stared up at him quietly. "She fears her father. It is not the sort of fear that is engendered by a loud voice, King.''

"And how would you know?''

"I am a woman,'' Enid replied simply. "There is an unspoken language that we share.''

"And the tendency to look for drama where none exists,'' he murmured with a chuckle at her glower. "I shan't be long.''

Enid watched him canter away with impotent rage. Sometimes he and his father maddened her with their arrogant manners. She knew all too well how brutal a man could be, and how overpowering, when he took to drink. Amelia's fear the night before had not been of her father's voice, she knew it. There had been something more there, and this afternoon she was certain of it when she saw the girl's look of relief mingled with anxiety as her father left the ranch. Perhaps during his absence she could draw her out and discover what the problem was. If she could help, she decided, she would, men or no men.

Amelia helped bathe the girls and then sat in the parlor with Marie and Enid, chatting, while she worked the intricate crochet pattern Enid had taught the women.

"Did your mother not do handwork, Amelia?" Enid asked curiously.

"Mama was much too busy trying to watch the children and keep house and cook," Amelia said gently. "As I was."

"King mentioned that you never seemed to rest when he visited Quinn those few times," she added.

"I wonder that your eldest son even noticed," she replied colorlessly. "He never looked at me."

Enid lifted a quick eyebrow, but she didn't say anything. Alan had gone with King on one visit to the Howards while the youngest boys were still alive. King had come home brooding and austere for days. He seemed to find nothing to relate about Amelia, but Alan must have seen a different side of her. He let slip little glimpses of Amelia's life. A particular one came to mind, that of Amelia playing Indian with two little boys in the backyard late in the afternoon, laughing and radiant in the sunset. Alan had told King about it, and King had made the cold remark that Amelia was hardly the type to roughhouse with children.

Enid recalled that the little boys had died only a few months later, of a vicious bout of typhoid. The family had grieved and grieved. Alan had gone back with Quinn for the funeral. King had told his mother, and no one else, that he refused flatly to stay in the same house with Amelia. So Alan had gone instead to represent the family. He had noticed a change in Hartwell Howard, a violence in his manner and a building affinity for hard liquor that seemed to grow by the day. His wife, Amelia's mother, had quickly begun to fail.

"How is your brother?" Enid asked.

"Very well. Quinn writes to us," she said with a smile as she finished a row and turned the piece she was working on. "Isn't that unusual, for a man? But he writes a very elegant and literate letter. He is in New Mexico, searching for a man who killed a banker in El Paso. Imagine, my brother, a Texas Ranger."

"And a very good one, for all we hear," Enid replied.

"Your brother is a Ranger?" Marie asked, aghast. "Oh, but how delightful! And I will not get to meet him. My father was employed with the police in Paris. I am certain that they would have had so much to discuss, if they met!"

"Indeed they would," Amelia said, smiling. "Perhaps you will come to visit again and Quinn will be in town."

"*Certainement,*" Marie agreed. "But for now, alas, I must return home, must I not, Enid?"

"As you say, my dear," Enid replied with a twinkle in her brown eyes, "*certainement!*"

The women said good night to Marie, and she went to settle down with her children.

"I will lock up before I come to bed," Enid told Amelia. "Good night, my dear."

"Do wake me before Marie leaves," Amelia pleaded. "I wouldn't want to miss seeing her off."

"Of course you don't. Sleep well."

"And you."

Amelia closed the door of her bedroom and changed into her long, cotton gown. It had a pretty row of pink lace around the high collar and lace at the wrists as well. She took down her long, blond hair and sat before the vanity mirror, combing it with long, lazy strokes.

She was twenty. As she watched her arm lift and fall, watched the brush pull through the silken skeins of hair, she wondered if she would ever marry and have children, like those of Marie. It would be nice to have a husband. The brush poised in midair, and her brown eyes grew cold and fearful. Or would it?

What if she chose badly? Her father had seemed so kind and good, and then he had changed. What if Amelia unknowingly chose a man who liked to drink or gamble or had no control over his temper? What if she married a brutal man who thought of her as a piece of property and proceeded to use and abuse her. Marriage now seemed to Amelia like a very real threat, not a promise of happiness. Downplaying her assets kept men from being attracted to her, and she was glad of it. She was certain that she never wanted to marry, even if children would have been a delight. Besides, there was her father to consider. He might yet live a long time. There was no one else to be responsible for him, except perhaps Quinn. But Quinn had to work. That left Amelia. And Hartwell wasn't going to rest in his efforts to get her married to Alan.

She put the brush down slowly and felt her body grow cold. She really must speak to Quinn when he came home again, she decided. Surely he would come back by the time her father's hunting trip was over.

She felt her arms break out in goose bumps. Silly, she thought, to worry so. She was a God-fearing woman. She had to believe that she had the hope of a settled, less terrifying life than she had enjoyed so far. She was no coward, even if she had been forced to act like one in her father's best interests.

Her hand lifted the brush, and she forced it through her long, soft hair once more. You must have courage, she told her reflection. You will be free one day, and

Papa will be, too, from the pain that makes a savage of him. If only he would see a doctor. But he would not even admit the need.

Meanwhile, she thought ruefully, she had a more immediate problem. Marie was leaving. Now Amelia would have only Enid's company for protection against the thorn in her flesh. How would she cope with King without the buffer of other people? It seemed she was trading one rough man for another.

But Enid would be her buffer, she told herself. It would be all right.

Finally, she put down the brush and climbed in between the thick white sheets and covering quilt. It was late March, but the nights were cool here on the fringe of the desert. The cover felt nice.

She closed her eyes and soon fell asleep.

King was already gone when she went to see Marie and the girls off the next morning. She had said more good-byes in two days than in the past two years, she thought as she waved them off at the train station in El Paso.

It was, she thought, a good thing that Enid had asked old Mr. Singleton down the road for a lift to town that morning and a ride back as well. There had been no explanation or apology for King's absence, and Amelia reasoned that there might be something about it that Enid didn't feel comfortable telling her.

Mr. Singleton took her arm and Enid's, shaking his head. "Those trains," he complained. "They lay more track and more track. The blessed things set fires, don't you know?"

"Progress, Mr. Singleton, is to everyone's advantage," Enid chided the old man.

"Not so, madam," he lamented. "Ah, for the days when the ranges were still wide and a man could be himself without censure."

"Mr. Singleton saw a gunfight once," Enid whispered to Amelia. "He actually saw John Wesley Hardin shot down by John Selman!"

"Here in El Paso?" she exclaimed.

"Indeed," came the reply. "And not so long ago, either. Only a few years back."

"Oh, I've seen more than that little scrape in my time," the old man recalled, his blue eyes misting with memory. "I've seen buffalo cover the plains and wild Indians riding on the warpath to glory. I've seen covered wagons rush the horizon and the first telegraph wires strung." He glanced down at Amelia. "Just about your age, I were, when I came here and settled with my brothers. My, my, Amelia, them was hard days. Real hard days. Comanche wars hadn't ended then. There were a man burned alive on this very ranch. . . ."

"Mr. Singleton!" Enid hissed.

He stopped, remembered himself, and cleared his throat as he saw Amelia's wide, shocked eyes. "I do beg your pardon, Amelia. I forget sometimes."

"Oh, that's . . . that's quite all right," she faltered.

"Come along, Amelia, we'll let Mr. Singleton buy us a nice ice cream soda, and we'll talk about some pleasant things!" she added with a meaningful glance at their companion.

"Yes, ma'am," he said obediently.

On the way to the soda parlor, they passed the city's famous alligator pit, and Amelia had to stop and watch the creatures as food was tossed down to them by various passersby.

"Dangerous varmints," Mr. Singleton muttered with

evident disapproval. "Ate Don Harris's foot off, they did, and the city fathers had the gall to say he asked for it!''

"He certainly did," Enid said with a jerk of her head. "He took off his shoe and sock and stuck his foot in there, didn't he?''

"Weren't no call for that gator to bite it off," Mr. Singleton argued.

"Perhaps it hadn't been fed," Amelia ventured, watching the strange dead eyes of an alligator that seemed to be looking back at her.

"Ate two chickens that very morning," the old man argued. "Wish they'd close that thing down.''

"Just make sure you don't wander too close to it," Enid cautioned Amelia. "Now, let's get some ice cream. It's very warm out here today!''

They were late getting back, because Enid had wanted some new patterns and cloth. There was a fiesta coming up at the end of the week, she told Amelia, and they'd have just enough time to sew new dresses for it.

Enid had insisted that Amelia choose a bolt of fabric for herself, and when the younger woman leaned toward pearl gray, Enid had immediately insisted on a gay lavendar.

"But this is more than I can afford," Amelia had protested.

Enid had gently but firmly had her way. The cloth was cut and wrapped, matched with thread, and taken out of the shop.

"You'll look lovely in it," Enid chided. "It's little enough recompense for all your help with Marie's children this week. You've been constantly watching them.''

"I've enjoyed it, and Marie hasn't felt well at all.''

"She's been frail since she lost her husband," Enid replied. "We all thought this would be a good holiday for her, and it has been. You've brought her out of her depression. I'm very grateful. Marie has been like a daughter to me."

"She's very sweet."

"Will you mind if I tell you that you're very sweet, too, my dear?" Enid asked gently. "I'm enjoying your company."

"And I yours," Amelia replied. She gnawed on her lower lip. "This fiesta, is it going to be here?"

"Why, no. It will be at the Valverdes," Enid said. "But we're all invited. We don't stand on ceremony when there's a party. Everyone comes."

Amelia hesitated. She didn't like the Valverde heiress, and the woman certainly didn't like her.

"Don't worry so. You'll have a good time. Hurry, now, and change for dinner. Rosa made her famous fried chicken. Can't you smell it? It's my favorite!"

Amelia didn't argue. She went to dress, already dreading the party she could see she wouldn't be able to avoid attending. It would be torment to watch King dancing with the other woman, rubbing his distaste for her in her face.

═══ Chapter Three ═══

At dinner King sat at the head of the table looking unapproachable. Enid did her best to keep the conversation going, but her son made no remark unless prompted. He ate his food and drank his coffee and then retired to the study to smoke without asking anyone's permission.

"Something's happened," Enid muttered, watching as the door closed behind him. "He's always like that when he's upset. He never rages, as Brant does. He simply goes quiet and closes up."

Amelia helped her clear away, wondering what could have upset him.

"No, no, I'll wash these few. Rosa's already gone for the night. Dear, do take King a second cup of coffee before I drain the pot, will you? No cream or sugar. He likes it black."

"But . . ." Amelia hesitated, panicked.

"He doesn't bite," the older woman assured her with a smile. "Go on. It's all right."

Amelia hated herself for being persuaded. It was bound to lead to disaster, but it was hard to say no to Enid.

She carried the full cup in its saucer to the door of his study and knocked, grimacing as the coffee threatened to overflow the cup.

"Come in!"

His voice didn't sound at all inviting, but Amelia gently opened the door and entered the room. Her heartbeat was unnaturally heavy as she approached the desk with her eyes on the cup instead of King.

He was lounging in the burgundy-colored leather chair behind the desk, his big, booted feet resting on the thick pad that covered the surface of the big oak desk. Smoke from his cigar wafted to the ceiling.

She felt his eyes as she put the cup down on the desk. Her gaze glanced off the brandy snifter in his hand and, higher, the speculative look in his glittery silver eyes.

"Your mother asked me to bring your coffee," she said quickly, turning to beat a hasty retreat.

"Close the door and sit down, Miss Howard," he said curtly, stopping her in her tracks.

She turned, hesitating uneasily. "It's rather late. . . ."

"It's barely six."

Still she didn't move. The thought of being closeted with her worst enemy was disconcerting. She didn't want him to see how vulnerable she was to him.

"I said," he added very quietly, holding her eyes, "close the door."

She tried one last time. "It's improper," she said.

"In this house, in the absence of my father, I decide what is and is not improper. Do as I say."

His look was calculating. Amelia almost rebelled. But she was tired and worn. She gave in and gently closed the door.

Something flashed in King's eyes before he averted them to the ashtray in which he flicked ashes from his long cigar. He'd hoped to prod her temper, to see if she had reserves of that spunk he'd seen only once, when she was with Marie's children. But he couldn't make it happen. Perhaps she really was the weakling she appeared to be when her father was close by.

Amelia sat down in the chair facing the desk, on its very edge, with her hands clutched together in her lap.

"I went into town today. I met an acquaintance of your father who asked if Alan's engagement to you had been announced."

She was shocked. "What?"

"It seems that your father has in mind inciting my brother to marry you," he said without preamble. "And that he has advertised this intention to certain of his acquaintances in banking."

Her lips opened to protest, but she saw the uselessness of it. "Whatever my father's intentions, Alan is only my friend," she said. How could her father have been so indiscreet?!

King's eyes flashed dangerously. "Be his friend, by all means, if it pleases you. But marriage is out of the question," he added deliberately. "I strongly advise you to repulse any attempt my brother may make to form an alliance with you."

She worked at composing her face. "May I ask why?"

"My brother needs a strong woman," he said simply. "You have hidden talents, I admit. But you are hardly my idea of the modern woman. Your father tells you how and when to breathe, Miss Howard," he added coldly, leaning forward to spear her with his gaze. "A woman who is so easily led by a parent will be quite unable to cope even with a man as genteel as my brother, much less with life on a ranch the size of this one."

He seemed to think nothing of piling insults on her head. She could hardly believe what she was hearing.

"Mr. Culhane, your brother and I are friends," she emphasized. "I assure you that he no more wants to marry me than I want to marry him. As to the other, my father has said nothing of this to either of us, I assure you!"

He was watching her with that steady unblinking stare that made her fidget nervously. "And if he had, what would you have told him?"

She went very still and averted her face.

He saw the faint movement of her body. "Why are you afraid of your father?" he asked curtly.

The question rattled her. "You are mistaken," she faltered.

"Am I?" He lifted the cigar to his firm mouth, still holding her gaze. "My mother tells me that she has invited you to the Valverde fiesta Friday evening."

"Unless you object . . . ?"

"It would be dangerous to leave a young woman here unattended. Of course you will accompany us." His eyes narrowed speculatively. "Perhaps we can find a suitable young man to escort you."

She stood up very calmly. "I do not require an escort, but thank you, Mr. Culhane, for your consideration." Let him chew on that for a while, she thought with faint triumph.

He leaned back in the chair again, watching her. He always seemed to be watching her, she thought.

"Quinn said that you never kept company with a man," he remarked abruptly.

"There was no time for such frivolous behavior," she replied as she moved to the door. "I had younger broth-

ers to take care of, until they died, and the house to
keep.''

''Your mother did very little.''

''My mother was an invalid,'' she said with a faint
sharpness to her tone. ''She was unable to care for the
house.''

He was silent. The cigar sat smoking in his lean hand.
Her carriage was very proud, he noted. She had an
innate dignity about her that sat oddly beside her cowardice.

''You are twenty. It is time you married.''

''So long as my choice falls short of Alan,'' she
agreed.

He glowered, looking for sarcasm in her lovely face,
but it was calm and quite composed.

''I have plans for Alan.''

''So he tells me,'' she replied. ''You and my father
are two of a kind, Mr. Culhane.''

''An insult, Miss Howard?'' he asked.

She turned to the door. ''You must apply your own
interpretation.''

She left him without waiting to be dismissed, closing
the door quickly behind her. Her heart was hammering
as she went to rejoin Mrs. Culhane in the kitchen. The
odd little exchange left her breathless and exhilarated.
No man of her acquaintance had ever had the effect on
her that King Culhane did.

The week passed slowly. Amelia and King's mother
sewed, worked in the kitchen garden, and did the rou-
tine chores, like washing clothes. Wash day was a long
and drawn-out chore that took almost a full day every
week. It involved some heavy lifting, so assistance from
two of King's men had to be requisitioned. They had to

fill the huge wash tubs with water for washing and rins-
ing, and the big black kettle on the fire had to be re-
plenished with water and bleach for boiling the white
things to get them clean.

At least twice a week, chickens were killed and
cleaned and cooked, not only by Enid but also by the
small, wizened man who cooked for the cowboys in the
bunkhouse. A calf was often butchered for the men,
with some for the household kitchen as well. Other
meats, from hogs butchered the past fall and made into
sausage and hams, and steers, hung in the smokehouse
until they were needed. Breads and canned vegetables
from last summer's harvest constituted the major part
of meals. That would be true until the garden that had
been planted earlier in the month was yielding fresh
vegetables.

King spent long hours in the saddle and away from
the house, to Amelia's eternal gratitude. She was very
relaxed when she didn't have to worry about the sharp
side of King's tongue.

In fact, without her father's fearful presence, she was
like a different woman. She was relaxed and gay. Enid
noticed the sudden change with sly interest, but she
never said a word.

Amelia took a few minutes late one afternoon to
gather some early spring flowers in the meadow under
the mesquite trees. It was a lovely March day, just the
right temperature, with the sun making soft shadows on
the ground. She felt free as she gazed at the high peaks
of the mountains in a chain around the horizon. If only
she could jump on a horse and ride away, far away, and
never have to worry about her father's health again!

But at least he wasn't here now, she told herself. She was free. Free!

She laughed and spread her arms, dancing around in a circle to an imaginary waltz, her heart so full of the beauty of her surroundings that she felt near to bursting.

The sound of horse's hooves startled her and froze her in an awkward position with her skirts flying around her ankles. She stopped so suddenly that she almost fell over.

King reined in under a big mesquite limb and stared down at her from under the shadowy brim of his black hat.

"Have you gone mad in the sun?" he asked politely.

"Perhaps I have," she said. She felt cold even in the hot sun with his icy eyes biting into her.

"I wanted to warn you not to stray far from the house," he said solemnly. "A couple of Mexicans have shot a rancher just over the mountain from here. They haven't been apprehended."

Her hand went to the high lace collar at the throat of her green gingham dress. "Oh, my."

"There's no need for immediate concern. My men will watch the house. But don't go far."

"I won't." She noticed the sidearm he was wearing. That was new to her, the old black gun belt with the nickle-plated .45 Colt swinging from it, its worn black handle speaking of use.

His eyes followed her gaze. "My father gave it to me when I turned eighteen," he informed her. "It went with me when I joined Colonel Wood and Colonel Roosevelt in Cuba in '98 and we charged up Kettle Hill to route the Spanish."

"Yes, I remember. You fought in the Spanish-American War. So did Quinn, in the same volunteer cavalry.'' She remembered how worried she'd been, for both of them. Alan hadn't gone. College had been much more important to him than fighting a war.

"Quinn enjoyed soldiering," he told her. "Probably that's why becoming a Ranger had such appeal for him. We had two Texas Rangers in our immediate outfit. Quinn became pals with them."

This was the first time he'd ever really spoken to her as a person instead of a nuisance. She found herself smiling.

"Our uncle was a peace officer in Missouri," she said. "He was killed by outlaws in a bank robbery."

He nodded. Quinn had related the story often in their college days. He leaned over the pommel, and his eyes went to the bouquet in her slender hands. "What are those for?"

"The dinner table," she said. "Enid asked me to pick them."

"My mother loves flowers." His eyes lifted to hers. "Do you?"

"Oh, yes. Back home I had a rose garden," she told him. She looked around with patent disappointment. "I don't suppose roses live out here. . . ."

"Some do," he said. "But other kinds of flowers do better. I'll take you out on the desert one day, Miss Howard, if you survive a west Texas summer, and show them to you."

"Would you?" she asked with undisguised pleasure, her soft brown eyes lighting up as she looked at him.

Those eyes made him uneasy. The old, familiar turbulence that he didn't understand tugged at him and made him vulnerable. He'd avoided Amelia for years to stay them, but now she was captivating him all over again. At least Darcy didn't manage to drain his resolve. He found her attractive and even desirable, but he wanted her only with his mind, not with his emotions. Amelia made him feel as if tender fingers were stroking his heart. He wanted her until it was painful.

"I have to get back to work," he said abruptly, sitting up straight. "Remember what I said." He wheeled the horse gently and trotted off the way he'd come.

Amelia watched him go, enthralled by the picture he made in the saddle, long and lean and elegant.

As if he sensed her rapt stare he pulled the horse to a halt and abruptly turned in the saddle to look back at her.

She made a pretty picture in the setting sun, with her golden hair haloed by the fiery colors on the horizon. She looked fragile somehow, and lonely. He looked at her for a long moment before he could force himself to move on.

Amelia, having seen that unexpected stare, was touched by it and vaguely discomforted. She sincerely hoped that King wasn't going to start anything. The last thing in the world she needed was to find herself involved with a man as domineering and overbearing as her father—whom she was desperate to escape.

Friday arrived. Amelia and Enid had taken two days to sew their respective dresses on the Singer treadle sewing machine in the parlor. Amelia's was made of crisp lavender taffeta with puffy sleeves and an overlay of rich lavender chiffon. Appliquéd lace adorned the bodice and hem in a copy of a Charles Worth design that featured a narrow waist with a gored skirt. It looked very feminine and elegant, and she wore her upswept blond hair in a small tiara of artificial white roses.

"How lovely you look," Enid told her with genuine affection.

"Oh, so do you," Amelia said, smiling. And the older woman did look very elegant in her own gown of green taffeta.

Both women wore long, opera length white gloves and carried purses decorated with seed pearls. Amelia's had belonged to her mother. How fortunate, she thought, that she had it in her cases.

King joined them in the parlor, resplendent in a vested dark suit and a four-handed tie. His black boots were highly polished, and his immaculate dark hair was topped by a new black Stetson.

"My, how handsome you look," his mother said warmly.

His eyebrow jerked at the flattery. His silver eyes went to Amelia and slid over her with something approximating distaste. He made her feel inadequate and dowdy, unusual feelings for a woman whose beauty had not gone unnoticed despite her lack of a social life.

She moved a step away from him, pretending interest in smoothing her dark cloak. The cloak would be needed, because it was still cool at night.

"I'll bring the surrey around," he said curtly and went off to fetch it.

"I prefer the buggy, but these dresses won't ride comfortably if we're packed in like sardines," Enid said, laughing. "We'll let King sit in front, and we'll ride behind."

Amelia smiled, but secretly she was relieved. It didn't make her feel particularly secure to have to sit beside King and try to make conversation. Especially when he made his dislike of her so evident.

"Come along, my dear." Enid motioned to Amelia.

There was an ominous rumbling outside, and the older woman grimaced. "Oh, dear, I do hope the rain holds off until we arrive. I don't want to get my skirt muddy before the first dance!"

A sentiment which Amelia echoed fervently.

It didn't rain the whole long, bumpy way to the Valverde estate, several miles down the winding dirt road. The sandy trail was firmly packed, but Amelia didn't like to consider how treacherous it would be when rained upon. She and Quinn had once been in a buggy that mired down in Georgia when rains badly muddied the road to church. Even the strong horse Quinn had hitched to the buggy couldn't pull it out. They were forced to ride the horse home, pillion, and Amanda's dignity and her legs felt the strain of it that night. Fortunately in the dark, she hadn't been seen.

King pulled up in front of the porch and helped the women out before he went down to the stable to leave the horse and surrey with the stable hand.

The house was well lighted, its broad front porch full of costumed people drinking punch and conversing, while inside a small band played gay music.

"You'll enjoy this," Enid assured her. "Come. I'll introduce you to our host and hostess."

Enid had told Amelia before that the Valverdes were descendants of Spanish settlers who had been granted a huge tract of land here before the war with Mexico. After the Spanish were driven out of the territory, American settlers were invited in by Mexico. Soon afterward however, the American settlers demanded their independence from Mexico, and war broke out. The Valverde descendants had, by that time, been accepted by American settlers and were part of the independence movement. They retained their huge land grant mainly, Enid said, tongue-in-cheek, because they had enough cowboys to fend off interlopers.

Horace Valverde and his wife Dora were short, dark, and rather reserved. Dora welcomed them with more warmth than her husband, motioning for Darcy to come and join them.

"Have you met our daughter, Darcy, Miss Howard?" she asked Amelia.

"Yes," Amelia said with a quiet smile. "It's nice to see you again, Miss Valverde."

"We're glad that you could come," Darcy said carelessly. She beamed at Enid. "My, you do look lovely!" she added, toadying to the older woman. "Did you buy that gown?"

"You know that I sew my own clothes." Enid chuckled, flattered. "Amelia made hers as well. She's quite accomplished at copying designs she likes."

"Why, yes, your gown does remind me of one I saw in New York," Dora agreed, giving Amelia's gown a second look. "It's a Charles Worth design, isn't it, my dear?"

"Yes, it is," Amelia said, flushing as King joined them, catching the tail end of the conversation.

"King! How dashing you look!" Darcy enthused, taking his arm prisoner with no attempt at formality. "Everyone's ignoring my lovely Jacques Doucet original from Paris," she added with pouting lips.

"You know you always look lovely to me, whatever you wear," King said with a warm, genuine smile.

Amelia felt chilled. Darcy's gown, while it might have flattered a taller woman, made the short, dark Darcy look like an ice cream sundae. The woman was attractive but hardly a beauty. And expensive designer gowns made little difference. Perhaps King loved her and saw her with the eyes of the heart. Imagine him in love, she thought wildly, and had to force herself not to laugh. He seemed the last man on earth to succumb to a woman's charm.

"Well, who is this vision?" a pleasant male voice enquired, and a tall, blond man with a mustache came up to stand beside King. But it was Amelia, not Darcy, at whom he was staring appreciatively.

"Miss Amelia Howard," Dora said, "this is Ted Simpson, our friend from Boston."

"I'm delighted to meet you, Miss Howard," he said formally, bowing.

"And I, you, sir," she returned, making him a slight curtsy. She smiled up at him unreservedly, because he reminded her of her brother, and she liked him immediately. He wasn't broody or mercurial, and at least he made her feel attractive.

"Would you care to dance?"

"I should be delighted," she told him, and immediately took the arm he proferred. "If you'll excuse me," she said to Enid.

"Certainly, my dear."

King watched them walk away, chattering animatedly, with silver eyes that were positively grim.

"Don't they suit?" Dora asked innocently. "She's very pretty, your houseguest."

"I suppose she's stuck up," Darcy said cattily. "Most pretty women are. Helpless, too, I imagine, and not much use around the house. Can she ride?"

"I don't believe she does," Enid said, taken aback by the criticisms.

"Can you see her on a horse?" King asked with cold sarcasm, shocking his mother even further. "She's a

chocolate box beauty with no spirit and even less imag-
ination."

"You seem to know her rather well, to make such
easy comparisons," Darcy probed.

King shrugged. "Her brother and I have been best
friends for many years. I know Miss Howard only from
the vantage point of an infrequent visitor to their
home."

"I see." Darcy moved closer to him. "You don't like
her, then?"

"Darcy, really, what a question!" Dora laughed nervously.

"No, I don't like her," King replied bluntly, one
corner of his wide mouth curling up with contempt as
he stared at her and Ted on the dance floor. "She won't
last long out here."

Enid started to speak, her angry eyes eloquent, but
King forestalled her.

"Shall we dance?" King asked Darcy, and, nodding
to his mother and Darcy's, he escorted her inside to the
living room with the other dancers.

Amelia found Ted to be as undemanding and kind as
she'd first thought. He had a bright personality, uncom-
plicated. As they danced, they talked of the East, because he was a frequent traveler there on business for
his father's banking firm.

"I know Atlanta very well," he told her. "It is going
to be a major city one day, you know. It has the poten-
tial for greatness."

"I find it maddening to live in," Amelia replied. "I
enjoy the spaciousness of this vast land, although El
Paso is no small town either! One can become lost there
in no time!"

"I don't doubt it. Miss Howard, may I call on you?"

"I am staying with the Culhanes at present," she said reluctantly, "and my father is away on a hunting trip. I do not feel comfortable asking you to call on me there. It would be best if you wait until my father returns. We live in El Paso, in a boardinghouse."

"I see." He glanced toward King and Darcy. King was glaring at them openly.

"Mr. Culhane doesn't like me," Amelia said abruptly. "My father has decided that I would make a good match for King's brother, Alan. King does not share this sentiment. He feels that I am unsuitable."

"Does he really?" Ted, who had known King for many years, had never seen him hostile toward a woman—especially a beautiful woman like this. It was unexpected, to say the least.

"I should not have spoken so openly," Amelia said quickly, shocked at her own forwardness. She flushed. "Please forgive me. It has been a trying week."

"There is nothing to forgive," he chided gently. "You dance divinely, Miss Howard."

"Thank you. I haven't danced in many years, and only then with my brother. The band is very good, is it not?"

"It is, indeed. The man playing the violin is my brother, and the flute-player is my sister's husband."

"I am impressed!" she said. "Are you musical, Mr. Simpson?"

"No, sadly. Are you?"

"I play the piano, a little," she confessed. "It is my only real accomplishment." She wisely kept the rest of them secret. This man knew King. She didn't want her enemy to know that she was anything but his image of her—dull and not very bright and totally spineless. The last thing in the world she coveted was King's interest. Let Darcy have him, she thought in panic, feeling his eyes on her even across the room. Why was he always watching her?

"I cannot believe that such a lovely woman has only one accomplishment." Ted chuckled. "I must get to know you, Miss Howard, and see what others you possess."

"If my father agrees, I should enjoy receiving you," she said demurely.

His hand around her waist contracted and pulled her almost imperceptibly closer. "No more than I shall, Miss Howard," he replied. He smiled down at her, and across the room, a tall, silver-eyed man had to fight down a sudden murderous impulse.

==== Chapter Four ====

King didn't ask Amelia to dance. His mother approached him just as the party was winding down and bluntly asked why.

He was sipping punch, watching her dance again with Ted Simpson. "I have no desire to dance with Miss Howard," he said. "Isn't it obvious?"

"You make it so obvious that the other guests are speculating about the cause," Enid said shortly. Her dark eyes narrowed. "You might bow to tradition long enough to give the appearance of civility toward her."

He cocked an eyebrow. "Do I strike you as a man who gives a damn about tradition?" he asked with some of her own bluntness. "I have no affection for or interest in your guest," he added coldly. "I came here to spend some time with Darcy, whom I shall most likely marry one day soon."

Enid had to bite her tongue not to say anything. "She will be a match for you," she said finally.

"Indeed she will. She has spirit, and she is fearless."

"She is also cold-hearted and an utter . . . witch!" she added fiercely. "And you are blind."

She turned and walked back to the other side of the room to renew an acquaintance with some of the other women present.

King glared after her. He wasn't about to be swayed

51

by his mother. Perhaps she liked that docility that clung
to Amelia. He did not. In fact, it infuriated him. So did
the look of her, radiant in Ted's arms, laughing up at
him as she danced.

A picture of her in a green gingham dress, dancing
under the mesquite trees with a bouquet of wildflowers,
flashed unwelcome into his mind. Amelia, her blond
hair flying in the wind, her brown eyes laughing, as they
were now. . . .

His hand contracted in his pocket, and he felt his
anger grow as he watched the way Ted handled her. She
should not allow such familiarity to a man whom she
had only met, he told himself. She was silly and stupid
to let his flattery affect her so!

He almost walked over and took her away from the
other man. It was an impulse so unlike him that he
deliberately turned away from the temptation and went
back to dance with Darcy.

She walked out onto the shadowed end of the moonlit
porch with him, noticing his preoccupation.

"What troubles you, King?" she asked.

"Roundup," he muttered. He lit a cigar without asking her permission and hooked his boot on the lower
rail of the porch to smoke it.

"I hate the taste of cigars," she said haughtily.

He glanced down at her with an amused smile.
"Shouldn't I kiss you, then?" he chided.

She moved closer, almost purring. "If you like."

He threw the cigar down with little appreciation for
its age and cost and drew Darcy roughly against him.
He noticed the flicker of her eyelids and her fixed smile,
and he wanted to curse her. Darcy pretended to be en-
slaved by him, but her distaste of intimacy with him
was all too visible. Darcy's people had been well-to-

do, but that was no longer the case. Darcy liked high living, and with her father facing bankruptcy, King was her best bet. How he hated knowing that she barely tolerated his embraces for the security marriage to him would offer!

He kissed her roughly and felt her hands go against his chest, pushing, almost at once.

"King!" she laughed, drawing back. "How impetuous! We aren't even engaged," she added suggestively.

He let her go and calmly lit another cigar. She wasn't the first woman who suffered him for gain. He could only remember one woman in his life who'd welcomed him in intimacy. But she'd only been hoping to marry him for his fortune. When she thought he was at risk of losing it, she'd run away with a tinker. Ironically, the two of them had been killed by a band of renegades led by a Mexican devil who made a habit of raiding up into Texas. The Rangers were after him even now, although he was like a will-o'-the-wisp to catch. One day, he promised himself, he'd see Rodriguez swing from a rope or stand in front of a firing squad. He was sure that Alice would have come back to him, that she had truly loved him. She had panicked at the thought of being poor, that was all. She would have married him. But Rodriguez had killed her before she could see her mistake in running away. Alice had welcomed him into her bed time and time again, and he still woke sweating, remembering her quicksilver response. He had mourned her deeply, just after her death. But over the years, the sting had faded somewhat. Not that he forgave Rodriguez. Oh, no.

He smoked his cigar quietly, lost in his thoughts, and decided that Darcy's reluctance didn't affect him. Per-

haps if he had cared about her as he had cared about
Alice it would have.

Quinn Howard had settled himself down for the night
in a small canyon of the Guadalupe Mountains in New
Mexico. He had a smokeless fire and over it he was
roasting a rabbit. The critter was mostly skin and bones,
but it would fill empty space. He was sick to death of
hardtack and jerky.

He settled back against his saddle with his rifle loaded
and ready on the colorful but faded serape beside him.
His blond hair was sweaty and full of dust from the
day's hard ride, tracking the outlaw Rodriguez. The man
had actually robbed a second bank while Quinn was
trailing him, down in El Paso. He'd struck down a bank
president and badly wounded a young employee. Quinn
had doubled back, almost to the city, and then caught
the trail back up into New Mexico again. He felt as if
he were going in circles.

As he chewed the tough, sinewy rabbit meat, he
wished he had a good tracker with him. It wasn't his
best skill. His expertise with a pistol and rifle was that.
But he did well enough, he supposed.

He hoped Amelia was all right. Their father drank
too much these days, and he could be violent. Quinn
had tried to find a way to get Amelia away from him,
but it wasn't possible just yet. He slept in the Ranger
barracks when he was in town, which wasn't often, and
he was stationed at Alpine, not El Paso. It would take
a better rank and a better posting before he could offer
her any alternative.

Poor Amelia. Her life had certainly been no bed of
roses. Quinn grieved for her. Only he knew the agonies
she suffered and the danger she faced. He had to do

something soon, he determined. The drinking was
worse, and so was its aftermath. One day Hartwell
Howard would go too far. His blood pressure would
shoot high enough to kill him during one of his outbursts, or he would hurt Amelia. Quinn knew that he
could never live with a tragedy if he'd done nothing to
try and prevent it. The problem of Amelia had to be
solved, and soon. He wished he knew what had made
his father change so drastically, and he decided that it
was probably grief for the loss of his wife and two little
sons.

If only Amelia felt a tenderness for Alan Culhane,
he decided. A marriage between them would be a good
idea, and it would put Amelia under King's protection.

King disliked her, but he wouldn't allow her to be
harmed. King was always controlled, and he would
never lay a brutal hand on her.

Now there would have been a match. If Amelia had
been her old self she would have been perfect for King.
Quinn was sorry that she'd changed so.

He laughed at his own folly in entertaining such
thoughts of matchmaking. They were enemies, and it
was better so. Better to let King cling to his miscon-
ceptions about Amelia and steer her toward Alan, who
would be kind to her even if she never reached any great
and passionate heights with him. He finished his rabbit,
and without having solved the problem of Amelia, finally leaned back and drifted off to sleep to the crackle
of the fire and the distant wailing of coyotes.

Amelia had seen King go out on the dark porch with
Darcy, and something inside her grew small and withdrew. Nevertheless, she pretended gaiety, and Ted responded to her charm with every scrap of his.

By the end of the evening, he had promised to call on her the moment her father was back and they were home again. He didn't realize how Amelia dreaded her father's return and the certainty of violence when they were back at the boardinghouse. The one point in her favor she reminded herself again was that it was a crowded boardinghouse at the moment, and her father was forced to be more circumspect than usual.

But his job at the bank meant that soon they would be able to afford a small house, and that would place Amelia at his mercy as his pain and rage grew. And inevitably, soon, he would die. . . .

She was standing alone at the drawing room door while Ted went to get her a cup of punch, and her face and eyes registered the panic she felt.

"Are you all right?" King asked suddenly.

Shocked by his silent approach, she looked up with wide, wounded eyes and heard his breath catch at the vulnerability in her flushed face. Their eyes held, and Amelia felt new and shocking sensations tingling all along her slender body.

"Amelia?" Darcy called sharply, and rapidly moved close to hold onto King's arm with a look of pretended concern. "You do look ghastly, my dear. What is it?"

Amelia felt patronized, unsettled, and afraid. She looked around with blind apprehension for Ted, and relief flamed on her features when she saw him waving to her from the punch bowl, where he was waiting to be served.

"Oh, you're thirsty, is that it?" Darcy dismissed the incident at once. "Ted will look after her, King. Do come and meet Mr. Farmer. Amelia will excuse us, won't you?"

"In a minute, Darcy," King said coldly.

Darcy looked taken aback, but she forced a smile and moved reluctantly away.

Amelia's wide brown eyes met King's, and she colored again, having lost the rescue she was certain of having.

King eyed her with speculation and renewed interest. The electricity that had flashed between them was shared. He knew she'd felt it, from the fear in her eyes and the color that was flooding her cheeks. He liked the sense of satisfied pleasure it gave him, to know that her reaction to him was violent and unpretended. It had been a long, long time since a woman had been attracted to him physically and not financially. It made him feel strange.

He moved closer, deliberately. Not blatantly closer, but enough that she could feel the heat from his body and smell the cologne he used. He could see her bodice move more rapidly as her breathing changed.

"What is it, Amelia?" His voice sounded different. Husky. Deep. Smooth, like a flow of molasses.

She could barely get enough breath to answer him. "As your . . . as Miss Valverde said, I'm . . . I'm only hot."

His big, lean hand came up unobtrusively to lie against her bare arm where the sleeve of her gown was separated from the long, white opera gloves she wore with it. The touch of him was electric, frightening. Her pupils dilated wildly as she met his eyes.

"Your skin certainly is," he said quietly, frowning. "Are you feverish?"

"No! I mean, no. It's just the crush of people, I'm sure it is, so many in one room . . . !"

"You're babbling," he said gently, and a quizzical half-smile touched his firm mouth as he looked at her.

Her bow lips parted, and his eyes fell to their soft pink perfection. He saw the faint tremble of the full lower one and knew a hunger so violent and unexpected that it made his muscles contract all over his tall body.

Her hand went to the jacket over his broad chest, as much for support as for protest. "King," she whispered in a soft plea.

He watched her lips move and wanted to take them under his, to part their softness and ease between them, to feel her body yield to his and her arms slide around him. He wanted the softness of her breasts against his bare chest. . . .

Her eyes lifted to meet his, and the silver glitter in them made her heart stop. She hadn't dreamed of an emotion so sudden and shocking. She hadn't known that she was capable of this violence of need. She certainly hadn't expected King to react like this to her, when he'd as much as told her he was engaged to Darcy. She felt, and looked, all at sea.

"Do you want my mouth, Amelia?" he asked very softly, his eyes relentless.

The words shocked, appalled. "Mr . . . Culhane!" she gasped.

She started to jerk away, and his lean hand snapped around her wrist, staying her hand on his chest.

"Don't struggle, or you'll draw attention to us," he said roughly.

"What are you doing?" she asked frantically, her eyes drawing away from his finally to search the room. But, incredibly, no one was looking at them.

"Insane, is it not?" he asked in a low whisper. "We can feel the world spinning around us and not one other person seems to be aware of it."

Her shocked eyes levered back up to his, finding his

steady, glittery gaze intimidating even while it excited her.

"Oh, yes," he said on a curt laugh. "I feel it, too. What a joke that is, Miss Howard, when my mind finds you nothing if not contemptible!"

She struggled for composure. She'd fallen right into his trap. It was another method of tormenting her, that was all. He'd discovered that she was vulnerable to him, and now he was going to use that against her.

"Your opinion of me will not keep me awake, sir," she said with as much pride as she could manage.

"Your hunger for me will," he shot right back. He smiled slowly, mockingly. "Have you been kissed, Amelia, by anyone who knew how?"

"You are impertinent," she bit off.

He moved imperceptibly closer, so that she could almost feel the tips of her breasts under the taffeta brushing his suit coat. "I have a knowledge of women that would shock you," he replied quietly. "And of a certainty, you would allow me to kiss you. In fact," he said, breathing, letting his gaze wander to her trembling mouth, "you ache for it!"

She had never expected this kind of blatant cruelty from him. She should have known that it was inevitable. Like her father, he was adept at torture.

With a soft cry, she whirled away from him, hurting her wrist as she dragged it from the steely grip of his fingers. She made a path toward Ted, her expression more revealing than she knew in her shaken state.

"You poor thing," Ted exclaimed when she reached him. "Here, I'm sorry it took so long." He handed her the punch and watched solicitously as she held it with trembling hands to her mouth. Some spilled on her immaculate white gloves, and she knew that they would be stained. Stained, like her mind from King's harsh words, his humiliating accusations. She finished the punch and looked around for Enid.

The older woman saw and recognized her desperation. With a puzzled frown she excused herself from her friends and went to see about Amelia.

"It is rather late," Enid said gently. "Are you tired, Amelia? Would you like to leave?"

"Oh, yes, please," Amelia said shakily. "I'm sorry, Ted, I'm having a wonderful time, really I am. I'm just very weary."

"And unused to such late hours, I suspect," Enid said with a smile, although her eyes were watchful. "I'll find King and ask him to get the surrey. Will you stay with Amelia, Ted?"

"Of course!" he said at once, beaming at her.

Out of the corner of her eye, Amelia saw King speaking to his mother. He shot a cold glance in her direction and abruptly turned on his heel and left the room.

"He isn't pleased to be dragged away from Miss Valverde, I see," Ted mused. "I'm sorry, Amelia. I should have offered to drive you and Enid home. . . ."

"That's all right," she assured him. "After all, he can return if he wishes, can he not?"

"Certainly. Would you like some more punch?"

She shook her head. "I'm fine. Really."

But she wasn't. Her mind was whirling with new terrors. She didn't want to go home with King. She didn't want her father to return. She wanted to run away, fly away, escape, flee . . . !

"My dear, you look very strange," Enid said, suddenly interrupting her thoughts. "Come along. We can wait for King on the porch. Perhaps the cool air will refresh you. Come with us, won't you, Ted?''

"I'd be delighted, Mrs. Culhane. As I told Miss Howard, I should like very much to call on her when her father returns from his hunting trip.''

Enid stared at him warily. She knew of King's antagonism for the man and her own husband's distaste for him. On the other hand, she had no right to forbid Amelia to see anyone.

"I have told Mr. Simpson that it will have to wait until my father returns,'' Amelia said quickly, sensing Enid's discomfort. "My father is extremely strict about my callers.''

"I see. Then we must both adhere to her father's wishes, Mr. Simpson,'' Enid said with a pleasant smile. "I'm sure you understand that I am responsible for her welfare while her father is away.''

"I do understand,'' Ted said with a slow smile.

Enid laughed. "Well, then.''

He escorted them onto the porch, where they talked idly until a disgruntled King returned with the surrey. Ted helped the women into the back of the conveyance after they had said their good-byes. King spoke not one word until they were back at the ranch house, having left Enid and Amelia to converse.

When he pulled the surrey up in front of the house, he shouted for one of his men. Amelia escaped out of the other side while he was assisting his mother to the ground. She was on the porch before he knew it.

"Go ahead, Amelia,'' Enid told her. "I'll be right along to unlock the door.''

"I'll unlock it,'' King said curtly.

He was beside Amelia in two long strides, but she abruptly moved back to where Enid was standing,

avoiding any attempt at conversation with a panic that
was almost tangible. She wouldn't look at him, not even
when he opened the door and stood holding it for the
women.

Disregarding convention in her surge of fear, she
dashed ahead of Enid into the house and, calling a muffled good night behind her, ran down the hall to her
bedroom.

"My dear," Enid said, turning to King, who was
oddly pale and out of sorts. "Have you said something
unpleasant to her?"

"Good night, mother," he said curtly.

He turned and went out, closing the door loudly behind him. He wandered out to the barn and supervised
the cowboy who was unhitching the horse and bedding
it down for the night. His presence was unnecessary,
but he couldn't face any more questions from his
mother. He didn't want to think about what he'd said to
Amelia or remember the look on her face. Hurting her
was indefensible. He hardly understood himself. He
only knew that he'd never felt quite so low in his life.

Amelia was deliberately late getting up the next
morning, so that she wouldn't have to see King. She
didn't escape Enid that easily, however. The older
woman watched her with renewed interest, even while
she carried on a casual conversation about the beautiful
morning.

"What did King say to you last night, Amelia?" she
asked abruptly.

The younger woman's face flushed. She dropped her
biscuit and had to scramble to get it back in her fingers.
"He only emphasized his dislike of me," she lied. It
was impossible to tell his mother what had really been

said. "I regret his hostility, but it isn't unexpected, you know. Some people . . . simply can't get along."

Enid's sharp eyes saw the telltale signs of sleeplessness. There had been more to it than that. She knew there had! Her gaze went to the slender arms in the long-sleeved blouse and held, shocked.

"Amelia, what has happened to your poor wrist?" she exclaimed at the bruise there.

The shocked gasp and attempt to hide the abrasion told her all she needed to know. "I saw the argument you had with my son and the way you moved away from him so suddenly. King did that, did he not?" Enid demanded hotly.

"I did what?" came a slow, rough voice from the doorway.

King lounged there in his working clothes, his chaps rustling as his long legs moved, bringing him into the room.

"Look at Amelia's wrist," Enid said shortly.

His expression changed. Amelia tried to hide it, but he went down on one knee beside her chair and captured her hand, gently but firmly turning her arm so that the deep purple of the bruise was visible.

His intake of breath was audible.

"I have very delicate skin," Amelia muttered, pulling it away from him. This time he let go at once, rather than risk marking her again.

"How could you?" Enid asked with sadness in her eyes as she looked at her son.

"Indeed," he said, his voice quiet and subdued. He looked at Amelia from his close vantage point, his silver eyes turbulent on her distressed face. "Forgive me, Miss Howard," he said, without his usual self-possession. "My loss of temper was regrettable."

She moved her chair back, away from him. He was like her father. He was brutal. She didn't want to be near him, to have to look at him, to talk to him. She wanted him to go away.

Her withdrawal pricked his temper and made him inflexible. He got to his feet smoothly and glared down at her.

"Was there something you needed?" Enid asked pointedly.

"I came to ask Miss Howard if she'd like to see the flowers I mentioned to her the other day," he replied tightly. "Obviously, she does not, if it means suffering my company."

Amelia closed her eyes. Please go, she thought. Please go away. You remind me of him. . . .

Enid got to her feet and took her son's arm, almost dragging him out of the room.

"What the hell is the matter with her?" he demanded hotly, glaring at his mother. "Did you see? She acts as if I have leprosy!"

"You treat her as if she does," she replied unflinchingly. "I wish Alan were here. He is gentle with her. Which is probably why the two of them are so compatible."

He glowered down at her. "And I know nothing of tenderness."

"That is so," she agreed curtly. "You have hardened your heart since Alice died. The sort of woman you seek these days has no need of tenderness. Why do you not take your precious Miss Valverde to see the flowers, King?"

"She has no interest in such things."

"Only in the money that pays for the land on which they grow," his mother said with faint venom. "Go and tend to your business. Amelia wants no part of you. Nor can I blame her. Surely her father is enough of a trial. It is no surprise to me that her life has been singularly lacking in male suitors. Probably she will live and die a maid for want of a little kindness from anyone!''

She turned and left her son standing there.

He didn't move for a long moment. That bruise on Amelia's arm made him feel like the lowest sort of desperado. Only a coward used brute force against a woman. He hadn't meant to hurt her. His emotions, always under impeccable control, had loosed the chain last night in the grip of the most insane desire he'd ever known. His hunger for Amelia had made him cruel. Now he felt guilty, but he had no idea what he was going to do about it.

Damn women, he muttered under his breath. Damn it all! He stomped down the hall and out the front door, banging the screen door behind him. Disguising his pain in bad temper, he went out to supervise the branding of the new calves. By the end of the day, more than one cowboy had evinced the opinion that who was getting their hides burned today was the men!

Chapter Five

A MELIA HEATED WATER AND POURED IT IN THE SINK, adding cold water from the hand pump to regulate the temperature. Then she washed the few dishes, while Enid did the sweeping. Dust came in through the doors and screens despite all Enid's precautions. Here in west Texas, she told Amelia, it was something that couldn't be changed, so it might as well be tolerated. Amelia couldn't help but think the same sentiment might be applied to King. But he was barely tolerable even on good days.

Roundup went on. King worked his men until late Saturday night, after which most of them got roaring drunk and began shooting up the desert behind the bunkhouse. The gunshots made Amelia nervous.

"I'll have King speak to them," Enid said. Both women had gotten out of bed at the clatter and were standing in the hall in their gowns and long, warm robes.

A door opened, and King came out into the hall. His dark hair was disheveled, and his jeans and boots had obviously been thrown on rather hastily, because his shirt was only half-tucked-in. As he moved closer, Amelia got an all too vivid look at a broad, bronzed chest covered with thick black hair.

"You aren't going out there without a gun?" Enid asked when he reached them.

"Why do I need a gun?" he asked with a glare. "They're only drunk."

"But they might shoot you," Amelia spoke up, her dark eyes wide and worried.

He stopped, surprised at the obvious concern. When he looked at her, his eyes lingered on her face in its frame of long, beautifully unruly blond hair. Her complexion was rosy from sleep, and in the lacy, ruffled layers of her nightclothes, she looked like a flower in bloom. He had to struggle to get his mind back where it belonged.

"I won't be long. Stay in the house," he told them.

He moved to the front door with long, angry strides. Amelia's dark eyes followed him, lingering on the powerful lines of his tall body in the close-fitting jeans. He was elegant, she thought wonderingly, and he made her feel so safe when anything threatened. If he only didn't remind her so forcefully of her father at his very worst. . . .

The night swallowed him up. The women went to the curtained windows and stared down toward the bunkhouse. It was brightly lit, and loud noises echoed from it. A minute later, King moved onto the porch, throwing a drunken man roughly to one side when he was accosted. He went into the bunkhouse, and the women heard his voice, unfamiliar in its loudness, because Amelia had never before known him to raise it.

The results were immediate. The noise stopped. Then there was a challenge, and a minute later there were several thuds and a crash. Amelia looked at Enid worriedly.

"I have to tell you, my dear, that this is, sadly, a

familiar occurrence," the older woman said softly. "Men will be men. Of course, King can handle them. They respect him, you see."

Amelia shivered. "Because he's good with his fists," she said dully.

"In these parts, a man must be. And not only with fists but with guns when the occasion calls for it. There is a lawless element here on the border and all too few peace officers. In order to hold a property, one must still be prepared to defend it when the occasion warrants."

"So violent," Amelia murmured, shaken.

"Life often is, even in the most civilized city."

"I suppose so." Amelia strained her eyes, because there was no sign of King. "Is he all right, do you suppose?" she asked nervously.

"My son is quite capable of handling his men. Don't worry so." Enid's dark eyes narrowed. "You are concerned for him."

"Of course," she faltered. "I mean, one is bound to be concerned for anyone whom violence threatens."

"I see."

Amelia hoped not. She didn't want her feelings to be quite that evident, as confusing as they were.

She pushed back her wealth of long, blond hair and watched with quiet desperation until finally, King came out of the bunkhouse and stood speaking to the man he'd motioned outside with him. The cowboy nodded, made some conciliatory gesture with his hands, and King turned and walked back to the house.

"I'll pour him a brandy," Enid murmured. "I think he may need it."

She left Amelia standing there and went toward the

parlor with her kerosene lamp, leaving Amelia the one she'd lit beside the door.

King came in, brooding and unsmiling. There was a cut on his lower jaw.

"You're hurt!" Amelia exclaimed softly.

He turned toward her. The compassion in those dark eyes made him feel warm inside, touched him in ways he'd never been touched.

"I'm all right," he said slowly.

But she came closer to peer up at him through the softly lit darkness with concern. Involuntarily, her fingers lifted to touch his lean jaw. "Does it hurt very much?" she asked.

His breath felt trapped in his chest. "No." His voice was curt, because her unexpected tenderness unsettled him. She was lovely, he thought, with her hair loosened like that and her body gently outlined by layers of frilly lace. Faint perfume drifted up from her warmth into his nostrils and made his head spin.

He caught her slender hand in his fingers and held it gently while his narrow silver eyes studied her uplifted face. His jaw clenched, and suddenly he turned his head and, pulling her hand up, pressed his mouth to the bruise he'd made on her soft white wrist the night of the fiesta.

The feel of his mouth disconcerted her. Her lips parted breathlessly as she met his eyes, and the touch of his mouth on her skin made her knees go weak.

Her heart was throbbing. He could see it at the side of her throat, see the lace jumping as she breathed. Incredible, that a woman so lovely could find him disturbing. It was no act, either. She was all but trembling from just this light touch. His eyes fell to her soft mouth, and he had to fight to keep from dragging her body against him and taking those pretty lips roughly under his own.

The look in his eyes made Amelia nervous. Her gaze dropped to his chest, and that made it all worse, because in all her life she'd never seen a man with his shirt open like that. It was terribly exciting to see the play of muscles under so much thick hair. It must feel faintly rough against soft skin, she speculated, and her cheeks went red at her renegade thoughts.

He saw that reaction, and it made his body go taut. He imagined how it might be, to have her bare breasts pressed to his skin, and his pulse began to throb at his temples.

"Amelia," he said huskily, and pressed his mouth to her soft palm.

His eyes closed as he savored the faint scent of her cologne that clung to it, and he knew that she was as helpless as he was. His own vulnerability made him angry even as it stirred his senses to their limit. His teeth nipped at the skin on the heel of her palm, and he opened his eyes and looked down into hers to watch her reaction.

She was stunned by the sensation the rough caress produced in her body. She knew that her eyes betrayed her by mirroring everything she felt, and she made a soft sound of protest deep in her throat.

The rattle of a bottle brought them both back to reality. King abruptly dropped her hand, but he was breathing heavily, and Amelia gave silent thanks for Enid's presence when she came back into the room.

Keenly aware of the atmosphere in the room, Enid quickly softened it by handing King the brandy snifter and asking about the crew in the bunkhouse. The question gave a shaken Amelia the opportunity to compose herself. But she couldn't help noticing that the big, lean hand holding the brandy snifter was faintly unsteady.

King saw her eyes on it, and his own flashed dangerously.

"Shouldn't you go back to bed, Miss Howard?" he asked icily.

Amelia shivered under the whip of his voice. "Yes, I believe so. Good night."

She beat a hasty retreat into her room and closed the door behind her. She wasn't surprised to find herself shaking.

"You are very unpleasant to her," Enid remarked quietly.

King finished his brandy and set the glass down with slow deliberation. "She has no nerve."

"Perhaps there is a reason."

"Even if that were the case, she is not my concern. I have no wish to saddle myself with a pretty little piece of fluff with no backbone."

With that curt remark, he went back to his own room.

Amelia, unfortunately, had heard every word. She bit back tears of pure rage as she made her way in the darkness to her bed. The dreadful man, she thought furiously. He knew nothing about her, nothing at all! He simply took her at face value and believed her worthless. She wasn't spineless! She wasn't a piece of fluff, either!

She wondered what King would say if he knew the real reason she gave in to her father so easily.

She remembered the night she'd run from her father. He had been drinking until he was almost senseless. Amelia had made some gentle remark about taking the liquor bottle. He had whipped off his belt and started bringing it down on her arms and back. She had escaped from the house. But the elderly policeman at the nearby station had laughed at her when she sobbed out her complaint, adding that it did a woman good to have the meanness beaten out of her from time to time. And he'd sent for her father. That had been the worst night of her life. Hartwell, having been drinking heavily again, had taken her home and put more welts on her lovely white skin for the embarrassment she'd caused him.

She had spent several days in bed, and a friend's daughter had come to look after the housework and cooking. Quinn, by that time, was fighting in Cuba, and there was only Amelia and her father in the small clapboard house on Peachtree Street. No one knew what had happened. She had no hope of rescue.

That was still the case. Quinn, even if she dared tell him the true scope of their father's incredible cruelty, could offer her no help. He lived in barracks. And if she told him, what then? How could she show to any man, even her own brother, the proof of her accusations? Her own modesty protected her father as much as her fear for his health and well-being.

Men were such brutes sometimes, her mother had said once when Hartwell had been in a fight over a political race. She had smiled, though, and Hartwell had chuckled at her comment. They had been so happy. . . .

She looked at the bruise on her wrist and remembered trying to snatch it from King's ruthless, steely grip. But it was his mouth that she felt when she touched her wrist. What an odd thing for him to have done, to kiss the hurt he'd inflicted. Her skin tingled, her heart leaped, with the memory of his shocking tenderness. It had angered him, that lapse. Perhaps it was why he had said such terrible things about her.

She had to remember that her father had been kind and pleasant until the death of her brothers. How could she ever trust her life to a man, knowing what she did about their dark side? And in marriage there would be much worse than a male hand wielding a riding crop.

A distant cousin and her husband had come to visit only once, at Christmas while her mother was still alive. Amelia had awakened one night to pitiful, wrenching sobs and pleas, followed by a muffled scream coming from the bedroom her cousin was using. The violent sounds had shocked and then frightened Amelia. The scream had terrified her. It had been followed by more sobbing, but by then Amelia had the pillow over her head, shivering. It had convinced her that a man's brutality was not limited to a lifted hand, and she was terrified of what would happen in marriage, in the darkness behind a closed door.

Her lack of suitors was due as much to her own repugnance of men as to her father's watchfulness. She remembered King's mouth on her wrist and palm, though, and wondered vaguely at the pleasure it had given her, at the sensations it had produced in her virginal body.

King had felt that same pleasure, she was certain of it. She had, after all, seen his hand shake. Amazing, she marveled, that he despised her but could still be attracted to her. Not that he wanted to be, she realized. He'd made that very plain to his mother. She turned her hot cheek into the pillow. A minute later, she pillowed it on the wrist that King had kissed and went to sleep.

* * *

The trail had grown cold for Quinn. He lost it in the Guadalupes and had just started, reluctantly, back down to the valley below, when he spotted three riders with pack mules in the distance.

In the wilderness, it paid to be careful. He withdrew his rifle from its saddle sheath and urged his mount slowly down the path, his keen dark eyes never leaving the distant riders. He worked his way down and around behind them, using all his skills not to be detected.

When they stopped and dismounted, he did, also. He moved quietly through the underbrush in a stop/start motion like that of an animal. Only man, he knew, made rhythmic footsteps.

He hesitated just at the edge of their camp with his rifle ready. But there was something familiar about those men, especially the eldest.

When he realized his mistake, he laughed out loud. The sound brought the three men around, the oldest one reaching for his sidearm before he recognized Quinn.

"For heaven's sake!" Brant Culhane chuckled, holstering his pistol. He went forward to shake the Ranger's hand. "What are *you* doing way up here?"

"Tracking Rodriguez," he told Brant. "Hello, Father. And you, Alan."

"Rodriguez is dead, they say," Brant Culhane mused. "Or invisible."

"He is neither, I assure you," Quinn said wearily. "I grow tired of pursuing him however. How is Amelia?"

"Very well," Hartwell said curtly. "She is staying with Enid while we're away."

Quinn frowned. "And King?" he added.

"Certainly, and King," Hartwell muttered. His dislike of King was apparent. "Your absence of late has been felt. Have you lost all interest in your family?"

Only in watching you browbeat my sister with no recourse, he almost said. He stared at his parent with quiet hostility, wondering as he did a great deal these days at the shocking change in their father's personality over the past few years. "My duties require a great deal of travel," he said noncommittally. "King is well?"

"Disgustingly healthy, as usual," Brant said with a smile. "Roundup is in full swing. He'll be cursing when I get home, but we were losing a lot of cattle to a mountain lion. I hope to bag him while we're up here."

"Good luck, then. I have to move along."

"You could spend the night, surely," Hartwell complained.

"I could not," Quinn countered lazily. "I have to make a stop in Juarez on the way back to confer with the Mexican authorities. I'll see you soon, Father, in El Paso."

"As you say."

Quinn said his good-byes, and when he was riding back toward Texas, he thought bitterly that his father got worse by the day. The man who had once been congenial and tolerant was now inflexible and contemptuous of everyone he considered his inferior.

Quinn pitied Amelia. Something must be done about her situation. She had changed since his removal from home, first away to war and then into the Rangers. The bright, happy girl he remembered from her childhood had gone forever. She was somber and quiet and frightened. He wished she could talk to him, tell him what troubled her. At least she was safe for the moment at Latigo. King might not like her, but he would take care of her.

He crossed the Rio Grande eventually and rode down through the mountains toward Juarez. It was dark now, and he camped for the night, his guns ready. A sound caught his attention, a movement in the rocks as if someone had stumbled and fallen.

His pistol in hand, he moved carefully around the boulders to see what the source of the commotion was. He found a dark-haired young boy in worn jeans and sandals and a stained gray poncho lying in an awkward position at the bottom of a small incline, groaning.

"Are you all right?" he asked in English.

"No hablo," he murmured painfully.

"¿Usted es Mexicano?" he asked immediately in Spanish.

"Sí," he replied. *"¿De donde es?"*

"Estoy de los Estados Unidos," he replied. "El Paso."

"Ah. El Paso del Norte," he said, grimacing. *"Puede ayudarme? Mi pierna . . . pienso que es quebrado."*

He thought that he had broken his leg, did he? Quinn didn't think so. He examined it and found no breaks. A sprain, probably, but it wouldn't hurt any less. He explained that to the boy and asked if he was alone. There was an odd look in his eyes.

"Mi compañero va allá," he said, gesturing toward Juarez. *"No sé cuando está."*

He could derive no more information. The more he questioned the boy, the more belligerent and frightened he became, as if he had something to hide. He was amazingly reticent.

"Here, then," he murmured, falling back into more comfortable English, "let's get you to the fire."

He holstered his sidearm and lifted the boy. He needed a bath, he thought wryly.

"God, you stink," he murmured.

Amazingly, he understood him. His lips pulled into a shy smile. "I have a run-in with a, *como se dice*, a polecat," he told him in broken English.

"A skunk!"

"*Sí*. It no come off, yes?"

"It no come off, no." He shook his head. He appeared to be stuck with the boy for the time being. He hoped his nose would survive.

"Do you have a name?" he asked when he put the young man down at the small camp fire. "*¿Como se llama?*" he added.

"*Me llamo Juliano Madison,*" he replied. "*Soy de Chihuahua.*"

"*Con mucho gusto,*" he said gallantly, wondering at the boy's last name. His eyes were very light. He might be a mixture of Mistizo and white.

"*El gusto es mio,*" he returned politely. "I would die for a cup of coffee," he added on a groan.

"Aren't you a bit young to drink it?" Quinn asked, puzzled.

"I am sixteen, *señor*," the boy replied tersely. "Not a man yet, *es verdad*, but not a boy. *Dios mio*, if only I had been a man . . . ! Papa, he will kill me."

"Oh, I see. You snuck off from home, is that it?" He chuckled. "Well, fathers aren't so bad, sometimes. He's probably worried." He knelt by the camp fire. "You can have the coffee. And a nip of brandy to help the pain," he said, fishing out his brandy flask.

"*Señor*, you have saved my life. When I lost my horse, I thought I would surely die, bumping about in the dark." His face hardened. "Manolito will die, of a certainty, for what he has done this night. My papa will slit his ugly throat!"

"You have family in Mexico?"

"Only my papa and my three uncles," he said.

"I think they need to take better care of you, if you don't mind my saying so," he mused dryly.

"I failed my papa," he said heavily, grimacing as he shifted his hurt leg. "Manolito got drunk in Del Rio and didn't want to leave. And, *Dios*, what he did to her . . . ! Papa will kill him, or I will! They ran me out of town, so I was going home to bring the others. And this has to happen!"

"Where are you bound?"

"Chihuahua," he said reluctantly.

Quinn was wary of the boy's reticence. His profession made him that way.

"Here. See if this doesn't help your leg."

The boy took the cup he offered and sipped. "Why, it is good coffee," he said, surprised.

"One learns to make it so, eventually."

"Why are you down here, *señor*?" he queried after a minute.

He hesitated. It wouldn't do to tell the boy who he was or why he was here. Most Mexicans loved Rodriguez. "I have to see the Mexican authorities on some financial business."

The boy studied him, his huge pale eyes unblinking on the blond man's face. "You mean, money matters?"

Quinn pulled back his vest closer over the five-pointed silver star under it. "Yes. I'm in banking in Texas."

The boy's hands trembled around the cup, and he winced.

"What is it?" he asked.

"My leg . . . it hurts me," he added, rubbing it.

"How about a spot of brandy?" he asked, smiling.

He poured some into a cup and handed it to the boy, who took it gratefully. Quinn fixed a place for him to sleep, deciding that it would be as well to leave the boy at the nearest village and let him rest before continuing all the way home. But the one thing he was not going to do was turn his back. He'd sleep with his gun in his hand tonight, just in case. The boy had shifty eyes, forever looking around as if he was being chased. Quinn didn't want to risk having his throat slit in his sleep by that grimy hand holding the tin coffee cup.

King was badly out of humor Sunday morning. He drove the women to church and sat stoically beside them while the sermon was delivered.

Amelia was as aware of him as he seemed to be of her now. It was nerve-racking to sit next to him, so close that she could feel his powerfully muscled leg against her thigh in the crowded pew. His arm was over the back of the seat, and when the man on her other side crossed his legs, Amelia found herself right up against King.

His silver eyes slid down to catch hers and hold them, and for a moment the whole congregation disappeared. Her eyes widened, softened as they searched his lean, craggy face.

He forced his gaze back to the pulpit, but the arm around the back of the seat moved down, and he slowly crossed his own legs, the action pressing his thigh close to hers.

She didn't know how she was going to bear it. Her mind was thinking thoughts far removed from the minister's sermon, and the feel and smell of King's long, fit body was making her tremble and weak all over.

Abruptly, as if the contrast disturbed him too much, his arm moved back to his side. Then, incredibly, his lean hand felt between them for Amelia's and captured it roughly. His fingers edged between her gloved ones and contracted.

He never looked at her. His eyes were fixed on the minister. But his jaw clenched, and he looked a little frightening. Amelia's eyes sought the newness of his hand locked with hers, and she couldn't help the surge of longing it engendered. Helplessly, her thumb smoothed over the back of his big hand, feeling the muscle and strength and warmth of it with quiet fascination.

The sermon was very short that morning, and Amelia was grateful. The last hymn required King to let go of her hand, but he shared his songbook with her, standing much too close to let her look on with him.

Enid couldn't help but notice the attraction which was slowly overcoming her son and their guest. But it delighted her to see King disconcerted like this. She smiled to herself, glancing over at the pew the Valverdes occupied. Darcy was watching, too, and she didn't like what she saw.

As soon as they left the pew, Darcy moved in, appropriating King's arm on the way out of the church and involving him in conversation with herself and her parents.

"She is very persistent," Enid said, watching the girl. "But King's interest in her is dynastical, not romantic. I daresay she leaves him completely cold. Her major interest at the moment is joining the Valverde ranch to ours in marriage. Her father shares it."

"She is a handsome woman, and intelligent," Amelia said quite fairly. "I don't doubt that King finds her attractive."

"Possibly." Enid was noncommittal. She drew Amelia over to speak to some of the women in her ladies' circle group, which occupied them until King was able to extricate himself from the Valverdes and announce his intention to leave.

This time they had a passenger. Miss Valverde had wrangled an invitation to lunch. She climbed in beside King and chatted to him animatedly until they arrived back at Latigo.

Amelia was out of the surrey by the time King helped Darcy and his mother alight, her white lacy dress gathering dust at the hem as she walked quietly to the front porch with the group.

"I'll just keep King company while you get everything on the table, Mrs. Culhane," Darcy said with a faintly superior smile, resplendent in a suit of blue taffeta with black trim and buttons and matching hat. "I'm just hopeless in the kitchen, my mother says."

Amelia didn't doubt it. She smiled back and followed Enid inside, removing her pert veiled hat on the way to her room.

"You needn't change, Amelia," Enid told her. "Everything is ready. Rosa cooks for me on Sunday. She'll have it on the table by the time you freshen up."

"Oh. I don't mind helping."

"I know that, my dear," Enid said with a gentle smile. "You're a lot of company for me and certainly no burden on the household." She glared toward the front porch, where the soft creak of the swing chains could be heard. "And you do at least have good manners!"

"I'll be right along," Amelia said, escaping from what she knew was coming. Mrs. Culhane's dislike of Darcy was apparently growing by the day.

On the porch, Darcy was watching the horizon while King smoked his cigar.

"I do wish you wouldn't smoke," she muttered irritably. "I hate the smell of those nasty things!"

"Sit somewhere else," he invited lazily, smiling at her impatience.

She settled herself like a martyr. "I shall simply have to bear it for the pleasure of sitting close to you."

If that was pleasure, he'd have hated to see pain. She was as stiff as a board, obviously finding him as distasteful as the cigar but determined to put up a good front. It had disturbed her to see him holding Amelia's hand. She was jealous and determined to show him that she was a better bet than the other girl in the matrimonial stakes.

King knew that already, and he was certain that he didn't want to marry Amelia Howard. But on the other hand, Amelia's hand felt just right in his. There was strength in it, but softness as well. He remembered her soft little palm under his mouth and the look of compassion in her brown eyes when he'd been hurt. It disturbed him to remember it.

He caught a glimpse of Amelia coming toward the door, to call them in to the noon meal, no doubt. Did she think she had him in her grasp, he wondered? Was she seeing him as a possible matrimonial prospect? He couldn't risk that, not when he was so vulnerable toward her.

Without counting the cost, he flipped the cigar out into the dust and abruptly bent, dragging a shocked Darcy up to him. He kissed her with every indication of true passion for the benefit of the woman standing, shocked, in the doorway. He felt absolutely nothing, but that wasn't how it looked to Amelia, or to Darcy when he lifted his head.

"Why, King, how impetuous you are! You'll rumple me!" she complained coyly.

His eyes had flashed to the doorway in time to see Amelia turn and move quickly back the way she'd come. That should get the message across, he thought.

He got to his feet and pulled Darcy up. "Come. They must have it on the table. I thought I saw Miss Howard at the door."

"Did you, indeed?" Darcy was smiling coldly. "I hope she wasn't too embarrassed," she lied.

King didn't reply. He took her arm and led her into the house. His face was as unreadable as stone.

Chapter Six

I T WAS THE WORST SUNDAY AMELIA COULD EVER RE-
member. Darcy stayed late, so that it was after dark
when King drove her home. Amelia made a point of
sticking to Enid when he came back, and very shortly
after that she went to bed without even looking at him.
Witnessing that kiss had destroyed some fantasies in
bud. If he wanted to kill her interest in him, he was
doing a good job. Amelia was cut to the quick by his
attitude. She withdrew into herself and made a religion
of staying out of his way.

Instead of placating him, however, her pointed avoid-
ance made him wild. He hated having her look past him
or stare at his shirt instead of meeting his eyes. He
knew that he'd brought on her shy withdrawal. He'd
thought it was what he wanted. Now, he wasn't sure
anymore. Every time he looked at her, his heart ached.
If only her father would come back and take her home,
take her out of his life, so that he could come to grips
with the temptation she presented! He wanted no part
of such an unaccomplished, dull, spineless woman!

Two nights later, he finished early on the ranch and
came in to have supper with the women. It was a quiet
meal, and afterward he joined them in the parlor while
they did needlework. He rattled his newspaper as he
read it. The front page was full of news about the Boer

War and how it was progressing. There was another
story about a man who was scheduled to be hanged
soon in New Mexico territory for shooting a man
in a drunken spree. He could hardly keep his mind on
the paper with Amelia sitting across from him, her slender body in its lacy garment making him hungry for the
feel of it in his arms.

"Your father should be home soon," Enid remarked
to King. "He said two weeks, and it's been almost
that."

Amelia's face paled. She hadn't realized, in her fool's
paradise, that it was so close to the time of her departure from the ranch and a resumption of her father's
tyranny. She missed the stitch she was putting into her
embroidery pattern and hit her finger accidentally. She
winced and stuck her finger in her mouth to stem the
flow of blood.

"Are you looking forward to being in your own home
again, Amelia?" Mrs. Culhane asked.

"It isn't a home so much as a suite," Amelia confessed. "Father is going to buy a house soon, but we
have three rooms in Mrs. Spindle's house right now.
It's very nice. She cooks for us as well, and her rents
are very reasonable."

"I've lived here all my married life," Enid recalled.
"When Brant and I were first married, his father had
just finished building this house. We had the rooms that
King occupies now." Her eyes sparkled in memory.
"Half the people in the territory came to see us married, in the same Methodist church we attended this
morning." She glanced up at her son. "You'll be married there as well, I assume."

"When I marry," he said stiltedly.

"Darcy wants a big church wedding, does she not?"
she persisted.

He didn't want to talk about Darcy. He put his paper
aside. "I haven't any definite plans," he said firmly.

Enid lifted an eyebrow. "I thought it was all settled.
Darcy speaks as if it is. She had some very firm ideas
about how she wants my home remodeled," she added
without looking at him.

King let out a rough breath. He'd suspected that Darcy
had upset his mother. He glanced at Amelia, but her
impassive face gave away nothing of her inner feelings.
Whatever Darcy had said to her, if anything, it had
made no apparent impression. He wondered if anything
ever did. She was almost completely without emotion. Until he touched her, he thought arrogantly.

"We can discuss such things later," King murmured.
He glared at Amelia, then stood up. "Come for a walk,
Amelia. You can do needlepoint anytime. I want to
show you something."

She didn't move. After the explosive attraction between them had flared Saturday evening and then again
Sunday morning, she had no wish to be alone with him.

"Do go, Amelia," Enid prompted without looking
up from her needlepoint. "The exercise will do you
good, and the first roses are blooming. I think the darkness heightens their fragrance."

"Very well." She put down her embroidery and went
along with King, aware of his tall presence beside her
as she'd rarely been aware of anything.

The garden was full of flowers, and two of the rose-
bushes were in bud. One rose had just bloomed out. It
was white and easily seen in the darkness that was lit
only by the windows of the house and a crescent moon.

"You have avoided me since Sunday," he said without preamble.

"Mr. Culhane . . ."

He caught her arm, firmly but not hurtfully, and brought her to stand in front of him. His silver eyes searched her face in the dim light. "Say my name."

Her breath was strangling her. His touch unsettled her. "King," she whispered.

"My name, Amelia," he emphasized gruffly. "You know it, don't you?"

She swallowed. It sounded strange in her mouth as she forced it out. "Jeremiah," she said softly, looking up.

Ripples of pleasure made their way through him. He'd never liked his given name until he heard it on Amelia's lips. It sounded different.

"Is Amelia your only name?" he asked curiously.

"Amelia Bernadette," she whispered.

"Amelia Bernadette." He pictured a little girl with blond hair and big brown eyes as he said it, and his thoughts made him restless. He was only thirty. Why should he suddenly think of a family?

"Shouldn't we go back in?" she asked quickly.

"Not until you tell me why I frightened you," he replied quietly.

"You are like my father," she blurted out. "You must have it all your own way, yet you have no respect for any creature that you can grind under your heel."

"Yet you allow your father to make such a creature of you, do you not?" he asked mockingly. "You are the very picture of an obedient child in his presence."

"You do not understand," she said in a haunted tone.

"I know that you dislike your father," he replied. "And while he is overbearing, and not very kind to

animals, he is nevertheless your father. You owe him
respect. I only object to the way you cower when he
speaks to you. Have you no courage? No spark of will?''

''I daresay your Miss Valverde has sufficient for us
both,'' she replied coolly.

He arched an eyebrow and smiled. ''Indeed she has.
I appreciate spirit in animals and women.''

''Why, because it amuses you to break them?''

He was very still. ''You think of all men as brutes,
is that it?''

''Some men are,'' she said huskily.

''Some women invite it,'' he returned.

She tried to pull away from him, but he refused to let
go of her shoulders.

''Stand still,'' he said quietly.

She desisted, fatigued and depressed as she considered that her father would soon return.

''Is there no inclination in you to fight?'' he asked.
''Suppose I had in mind dragging you into the bushes
with lewd intent, Miss Howard?''

''I should scream.''

''And if I covered your mouth with mine,'' he whispered, bending, ''and prevented it?''

She felt his breath on her lips. She wanted to run.
She wanted to stay. She remembered how he looked
just awakened, with his hair rumpled and his shirt open.
She remembered the touch of his mouth on her wrist
and how it had made her feel. All those thoughts paralyzed her in his grasp. When his hard mouth came
closer, all she could do was watch its approach without
even the appearance of protest.

His lean hands came up to frame her oval face. They
were warm against the faint chill of evening, and just

slightly callused. His pale eyes met her dark ones, almost with speculation.

"Your mouth has the shape of a Cupid's bow," he said, his deep voice smooth and low in the silence of night. His thumb moved across it in a teasing, exploring caress. "It trembles when I touch it. Is it fear that you feel with me, I wonder, or something more?"

She grasped at sanity. He was going to marry Darcy. Surely, this was only another taunt, another effort to make her vulnerable and then laugh at her weakness.

Her hands grasped his shirt and pushed, but he was immoveable.

"Shhh," he whispered gently. The hands framing her face became caressing. His eyes fell to her soft mouth, and he began to bend toward her. "In the parlor Saturday night," he said roughly, "and in church Sunday, there were fires burning between us. I want to see how deeply they burn, Amelia. I want to take your mouth under my own and taste you like a ripe apple. . . ."

As he spoke, his lips began to fit themselves to hers with what she dimly recognized as expertise. He hesitated when she protested, renewing his efforts very gently when she stopped resisting him. He felt her hands tauten on his shirt and then slowly relax as his lips probed delicately between her own.

"I will not hurt you," he whispered into her mouth.

His hands moved, catching her arms and guiding them gently up, around his neck. They moved again, his lean fingers touching her back, burning through the thin lawn of her dress as they pressed her to him. She could feel the muscles of his broad chest, its warmth and strength as his arms slowly enfolded her.

It was new and frightening to be held so closely and feel so empty, as if life suddenly depended on the mouth

slowly invading her own. She felt the hardness of his
lips as they began to move insistently, trespassing beyond the tight line to touch the dark inner recess of her
mouth.

She stiffened, because this new intimacy was causing
sensations that made her knees go weak.

He lifted his dark head and looked at her. He wasn't
teasing, or mocking, now. His eyes were half-closed,
glittery in the dim light.

"Your mouth has the softness of a flower petal," he
whispered. "And you taste of innocence, Amelia. Innocence and virginal terror."

"Please, you must not, . . ." she began breathlessly.

"Why?"

"There is . . . there is Miss Valverde," she managed
huskily.

"One chaste kiss is hardly a proposal of marriage,"
he murmured. "And it will be chaste, if that makes
you less afraid to submit to me. Come here, Amelia."

He kissed her again, but not insistently or boldly. His
mouth was tender, coaxing hers to respond. She tensed,
but her lips yielded to the slow stroking of his mouth,
and with a jerky sigh, she let him have her mouth without restraint.

The submission, unexpectedly sweet, made him
reckless. His hand went behind her head and gently
cupped it, pulling her mouth upward, even closer, so
that the pressure of his kiss increased and grew demanding, ardent. His arms swallowed her up, but so
tenderly for all their strength that she forgot her misgivings. Her hands tangled in the thick hair at his nape,
savoring the softness and coolness of it under her fingertips.

She felt his hand at her throat then, sliding hungrily

up and down it, and he turned her, so that his ardent mouth forced her head back against his broad shoulder, imprisoned. The kiss went on and on, and she felt near to fainting when his hard lips finally lifted.

Her eyes opened, misty and startled. She was still clinging to him, her heart beating madly against his chest.

He looked totally impervious to any emotion. A faint smile touched the mouth that had ravished hers.

"Will you fall if I put you from me?" he asked with quiet amusement.

She couldn't answer him. It had been earthshaking. But to him, it appeared, there was no such uniqueness. He wasn't even breathing hard.

After a minute, she pulled against his hands, and he loosened her at once. While she stood dragging in air, he calmly lit a cigar and stood smoking it, his eyes on the distant horizon.

She was a fool. She wondered why she could never see through his tricks. Perhaps this latest lesson would teach her restraint.

With a heavy sigh, she turned and walked back toward the house without another word. But he fell into step beside her, tall and elegant. Cigar smoke drifted down into her nostrils, harsh after the faint and delicate perfume of the rose.

He hadn't spoken, but when she started to go up the steps, his hand came out and prevented the movement.

"Your mouth still holds the evidence of my kisses," he said quietly. "Unless you want my mother to make unwarranted speculations, it might be wise to wait a bit before going inside."

The lazy observation was the last straw in a basket of them. She went up onto the porch and sat down in the porch swing, expecting him to go elsewhere. But he didn't. He eased down beside her and rocked the swing into motion.

Her stiff posture said more than any words could. He slid an arm over the back of the swing and studied her with interest, until her face flamed and her hands clenched in her lap.

"Darcy Valverde enjoys the gifts I buy her and the wealth and position of my name," he said quietly. "But she loathes the touch of my mouth on hers."

She couldn't speak. Her throat felt choked.

"In time," he added coldly, "she will learn to respond to me. Her family is one of the original ones, from the days of the old Spanish land grants. Like my own family, she is born to this country. You will not last the year, Miss Howard. You are too soft, and far too docile, to manage the rigors of this sort of life."

She felt her teeth clench. "Perhaps you are right," she said stiffly.

"There is, after all, more to a relationship between a man and a woman than kisses," he continued, forcing the words out. "Similar backgrounds and common interests are necessary. Darcy can ride like a cowboy and shoot like a Ranger. Despite her sharp tongue, she is accomplished as a hostess."

"She will be exactly what you require in a wife, Mr. Culhane. I knew that."

"I wanted to know what it would feel like to kiss you," he said flatly. "I think you had the same curiosity about me. It was best indulged before there were any formal ties to be broken by such an action. You have a sweet mouth. But it was only curiosity. Nothing more; Not on my part."

"I knew that, as well," she said without looking at him.

He stared at her hard for a moment, trying to read her expression. But it never wavered. She was untouchable on the surface. If he didn't remember so well how her arms had clung, how her mouth had answered his, it might have fooled him. It had been folly to give in to his hunger. Now he was faced with the task of pushing her away and making her aware that he wanted nothing more to do with her.

She was a child in many ways. He should never have touched her. The impulse had been building for days. Weeks. Just as well to have strangled it at birth, but his feverish desire had clamored for expression. It was going to be hard to forget her ardent response. Every time he touched Darcy for the rest of his life, he would mourn the eager submission of Amelia's soft mouth.

"So long as you understand the situation," he said curtly.

She got to her feet. "Indeed I do," she replied brightly. "Good evening, Mr. Culhane."

She didn't look back as she went into the house. In case her mouth was still swollen—and it felt so—she called a soft good night to Enid from the doorway and went quickly down the hall to her room. She throbbed from head to toe with frustrated passion and temper, and she knew she would never sleep. But to have to look at King Culhane again tonight would cripple her heart! Why, why, could he not leave her alone?

Quinn helped the Mexican boy into Juarez, to the barrio where he said he wanted to be taken. His people would come for him, he promised. So Quinn left him with two women who apparently knew him and then began the long journey down to Del Rio, from whence the boy had apparently come when he was hurt. As soon as he rode into town, he went along to the commandant's headquarters, where he discussed the bandit Rodriguez.

The Mexican officer was sorry, but they could give him no help in locating the man. It was said that some of Rodriguez's cohorts had been in Del Rio just recently. However, he promised, every effort would be made to cooperate if Quinn cared to stay in Del Rio for a day or so.

Quinn agreed gratefully. That would give him some time to catch his breath and heal his saddle sores, he added, tongue-in-cheek. He left the military commander's office and went to find a telegraph office. He sent word to the Ranger post in El Paso that he was going to conduct a search in Del Rio before returning.

He was tired to death. There was a small cantina where he'd found lodging the last time he was in town. It offered a little something extra: the best girls on the border. It had been a long, dry spell between women, and Quinn needed something soft in his arms for a night. It was an urge he disliked giving rein to, but a man had his needs.

He bought himself a small whiskey and beckoned the wife of the owner to his table, discreetly inquiring if she had a girl for him.

She grinned from ear to ear. Oh, yes, she said with faint malice. She did, indeed have a girl, one who was sure to please the *Americano*. The girl was very pretty. It would cost him a lot for this one. At least five American dollars.

Quinn was intrigued. He'd never seen a pretty woman in a place like this. She must be Mexican, all the others were, but it would be worth the price if what the woman said was true.

He gave the money to the buxom woman, and she showed him to a small room far down the dirt floor of the hall.

"Allá," she told him, pointing to the door. *"Buenas noches, señor,"* she added with a cruel smile.

Quinn frowned. It sounded as if the woman disliked the girl. He began to wonder if something was amiss here.

He opened the door and went inside, closing and locking it behind him. It was a sparse confinement, with only a chair and a bed and a tiny window. The sounds of music from the cantina drifted in the open window along with voices murmuring in Spanish.

Quinn took off his hat and tossed it onto the chair. He ran a hand through his thick blond hair and moved to the side of the bed.

A girl was lying on the serape that covered the rudely made bed. She had long, black hair that laid around her oval face like a fan. Thick black lashes laid on cheeks that were faintly flushed. Her skin was almost translucent, her lips red, a natural red, not colored. She was wearing a peasant blouse that revealed breasts like pert little apples, firm and beautifully shaped. Her waist was small, and her hips gently rounded above long, elegant legs that showed where her colorful skirt had ridden up to her thighs. Her feet were bare. Pretty feet, he thought absently.

He sat down beside her and gently ran his big hand up her waist and over her breasts. They felt as firm as they looked. She was wearing nothing under the thin blouse, and as he touched her, her nipples hardened. He could see them stand erect. She made a sound and moved on the serape, but her face was drawn as if in pain.

"Wake up, pretty girl," he said softly, and shook her gently. "She was right, you know. You are pretty."

She groaned and shifted. A minute later, her long eyelashes lifted to reveal eyes so blue that for a moment the shock of color startled him. He'd never seen a Mexican girl with blue eyes and white skin, and he frowned.

She stared at him. Her dry, parched lips separated, and she tried to swallow, but her throat was as dry as her mouth.

"*Agua?*" she whispered.

He looked around and found nothing to drink. There was only a tin cup on the bedside table. He took out his brandy flask and poured a little into the cup. He took it to her.

She had to have help to sit up. "*Mi cabeza me duele,*" she moaned.

Her head hurt. She spoke perfect Spanish. Her coloring was odd, but she must be what she seemed.

"Drink that," he told her. "Don't talk."

She took a sip and choked, but then she took another and another. She laid back down, breathing steadily as she looked up at him. "*¿Donde estoy?*"

"*Está en una cantina en Del Rio,*" he returned.

"*¿Por qué?*"

He lifted an eyebrow and smiled lazily. How could she not know? He put the cup aside and leaned over her, his big hands framing her face. "Don't you know?" he asked softly.

He bent and laid his mouth over hers. She stiffened and pushed at his chest, but he was hungry, and she obviously belonged here, or what would she be doing in this room?

Her struggles didn't bother him. He'd known prosti-
tutes who felt obligated to put up a fight at first. It never
lasted, and they were usually the most ardent ones. He
kept on, his experienced mouth slow and sensual on her
soft lips, until she relaxed into the covers and submit-
ted.

It was interesting that she stiffened when his hand
smoothed over her breasts again. She started to protest,
but his mouth opened hers and probed gently inside.
Her fingers bit into his hard arms, but she stopped fighting the minute his hand slid under her bodice and over
her pretty breast.

"You feel like apples," he whispered into her mouth.
"Your breasts are perfect. I want to take them inside
my mouth and feel them with my tongue."

She understood English. She must, because the words
made her moan.

He untied the string that held the bodice together and
slowly pulled it down, baring her to his eyes. He caught
his breath audibly at the sight of her white skin. Her
nipples were a dark, soft pink, tight and thick against
the elegant rise of flesh.

"Sweet Jesus," he whispered, touching her with his
fingertips. "I've never seen anyone like you!"

Her voice failed her. His eyes were eloquent. He just
looked at her for a long time, his dark eyes fascinated.
Then he began to touch her, his fingers slow and gentle,
tracing every line and curve of her, making her untried
body yield without any effort at all.

"Sit up, little one," he whispered huskily.

He brought her into a sitting position and slid the top
away. "I'm going to take a very long time with you,"
he said as he bent to suckle at her breasts. "I'm going
to make it last all night long. . . ."

She felt his hand in her hair as he arched her and began to kiss her body. The sensations were frightening, but not unwelcome. Her legs felt heavy, and there was an unfamiliar tingling in her lower belly. She loved his callused hands on her silky flesh, loved the way he was touching her. He was a stranger. She should not permit this. But just as she thought it, his hand trespassed under her skirt, under her drawers, and found her where she was untouched.

She made a jerky cry at the shocking intimacy and would have captured his hand, but the throb of pleasure his movement there kindled paralyzed her. Her eyes flew open, along with her mouth, and she gaped at him.

"Here?" he asked quietly, and did it again.

She had never dreamed that it would be like this. He touched and stroked and probed, and her body was his, owned by him, possessed by him. He made her reach a pinnacle almost at once, watching her arch and sob and cry out to him. And even as the pleasure began to fade away, he kindled it again and again and again.

By the time he undressed and came to her, she was beyond any sense of reason. He stripped with quiet efficiency and pushed her back onto the bed, sliding between her legs and spreading them wide to admit his tall, muscular body.

She was so ready for him that the first hard thrust was immediately pleasurable, despite the shock of his entry and the faint sensation of tension there. He guided her, moved her under him, whispered to her, tutored her, as the heated minutes gathered speed. She thrilled to the quick, sharp movement of his hips, to the shocking, feverish words he whispered into her ear while he moved on her yielded, burning body.

She clung to him, and when the pleasure bit into her

body, she cried out harshly. His mouth covered the sound, muffling it, while he drove furiously for his own fulfillment. She felt him reach it, felt his body cord and jerk helplessly while he groaned into her open mouth.

He collapsed onto her finally and lay there, inert, trying to breathe. There had been women over the years, but never one like this. Her body had been a revelation to him. He had to force himself to withdraw from it, to roll onto his side. Even then, he couldn't let her go.

He pulled her against him and wrapped a long, heavy leg over her hips to keep her there.

"*Señor,*" she began unsteadily.

"Go to sleep, little one," he whispered roughly. "Don't ask me to let you go. I couldn't if my life depended on it. You are exquisite," he murmured, brushing her mouth with his. "You are my woman."

She didn't argue. It was all too new, and she was tired. She closed her eyes and pressed close into his muscular body. At once, she slept.

Quinn opened his eyes the next morning to harsh sunlight and a hangover. He hadn't realized the whiskey would hit him that hard. He moved his arm and felt a weight on it.

Frowning, he turned onto his side and looked down. The sight that met his startled eyes knocked the breath right out of him.

She was nude. Her body was perfectly formed from the top of her black hair to the tip of her pretty toes. She lay vulnerable to him on the white sheet that had come away from the serape in the night. As he looked, he knew at once that she wasn't Mexican. She was white. And he understood now, too late, why the woman in the cantina had charged so much for her.

═══ Chapter Seven ═══

IT HAD BEEN ONLY TEN DAYS SINCE ALAN, BRANT, and Hartwell Howard left the ranch when they returned. Amelia, sitting on the porch with Enid, saw the dust and three horsemen and knew that her brief respite was over. She would have to leave now, to go away from King and back to the uncertainty of life with her father.

But it was just as well, she thought with resignation. She couldn't even meet King's eyes after last night. Not that it seemed to matter to him. He was cold to her, quite obviously making sure that she didn't read anything into last night's ardor. But at least Enid was kind to her.

Now she was going to have to pack her things and go back to the boardinghouse, where her father would drink too much and there would be only the threat of strangers overhearing to protect her from him. It had been successful so far; but he drank more and more. When he bought them a house—which he'd already decided to do—there would be no protection at all.

Her face reflected her terror.

"Oh, my dear," Enid said gently. "Is it so bad at home?"

Amelia, shocked, had to fight down tears and panic. She forced a smile to her face. "It is only that I have

100

enjoyed staying here so much," she lied. "I have missed my father, of course."

"Of course." Enid nodded, but she hadn't missed that look on Amelia's face. Something was wrong. If only the girl had talked to her! Surely she could have helped. But now it would be too late, and King's behavior hadn't made it easier for Amelia. He was openly hostile again, just when Enid had thought he was becoming interested in their pretty guest.

The men dismounted at the steps. Two of the cowboys came along to stable the horses, while a beaming Brant unloaded the game and carried it into the kitchen, where the women would deal with it.

"We had some good luck," Brant told his wife, kissing her cheek warmly. "I cured out the skin for King."

He indicated a yellow fur hide, and Amelia knew without asking that it was the mountain lion Brant had been after.

"You look very fit, so you must have found plenty to eat," Enid teased.

Hartwell looked tired and half out of sorts. He put a hand to his head and winced. "I missed my shots," he muttered angrily. "All I have to show for the expedition is saddle sores and a headache."

Brant and Alan exchanged quiet glances. Hartwell's headaches, and the powders he took for them, had been quite noticeable on the trip, along with his vicious humor. "We saw your brother up in the Guadalupes," Brant mentioned to Amelia. "He was trailing a Mexican outlaw. He looks good. I think the life of a Ranger suits him."

"It certainly seems to," Amelia replied. "Hello, Father."

"I hope you've been pulling your weight here," he

said to her, austere and very pale. He removed his saddlebags to the porch. "I wouldn't want Enid to think I
raised a lazy girl."

"She has been a great help to me," Enid said rather
stiffly. "You are fortunate, Hartwell, to have such a
compassionate daughter."

He gave Enid a sharp look, but he didn't reply. "We
shall be leaving for home this evening," he announced.
"I must be back at my job tomorrow."

"Couldn't you stay, since it is the end of the week?"
Enid asked.

"I think not," Hartwell replied. "I will need to see
to my correspondence and such. I have a very responsible position at the bank, you know. It is fortunate for
my daughter that I do, as she spends money unwisely
and frivilously when I do not contain her impulses."

Amelia's hands clenched. It was untrue, as most of
the criticisms her father made about her to other people
were. His eyes were glassy, his face pale. She knew
these moods and how dangerous it could be to speak to
him until they passed. She kept her silence, swallowing
the insult.

Enid looked at Amelia and felt sick for her. The girl
had already assumed the personality forced on her by
her father: quiet, unresponsive, and painfully obedient.
What did the man do to cause such a reaction in his
child? she wondered. All her gentle probing hadn't elic-
ited one single enlightening comment from Amelia.

Hartwell dominated the conversation for the rest of
the afternoon, muttering about all the discomfort and
hardships he'd had to endure and cursing the impudence
of an Indian who'd stopped by the camp fire for coffee
one night. The Culhanes listened politely, but they

weren't sympathetic. Amelia wanted to tell her father to shut up; she wanted to apologize for him. Of course, she could do neither.

"Ted took quite a shine to Amelia," Enid announced after the women had dealt with the meat and provided lunch. They were sitting in the parlor with the men to have cake and coffee.

"Ted?" Hartwell asked suspiciously.

Enid explained, while Amelia sat rigidly in her chair with her hands folded in her lap.

"I don't approve of him," Hartwell said stiffly. "His family is at the low end of the social scale, and, I suspect, also at the low end of the evolutionary scale." He found his own sally amusing and laughed heartily. It didn't seem to occur to him that the others didn't join in.

"Ted is a man of bad reputation," Alan had to admit. "I should prefer that you have no social contact with him, Amelia," he said gently. "You are too tender a flower to entrust to such rough hands."

She smiled at him warmly. Alan was so likeable. So . . . unlike his brother. "You flatter me," she said demurely.

"Indeed he does, and you be properly appreciative," Hartwell told her firmly. "Alan is more your sort. He's the kind of young man I like to see you associating with."

Amelia flushed at the impropriety of the remark, but Alan only grinned.

"Good for you, sir," Alan replied. "In that case, may I call for Amelia on Saturday evening and take her to the concert at Chopin Hall? I promise to treat her with utmost courtesy and return her to your residence at a respectable hour."

"Certainly, you may escort her," Hartwell said, ignoring Amelia entirely.

It would have been nice if someone had asked her if she wanted to go, Amelia thought. But one look at her father told her not to ask the question.

"And now, we really must go," Hartwell said, rising. "Thank you all for your hospitality. Amelia, do likewise."

"Yes, Papa," she agreed, and quietly added her thanks to his.

"Do come back and see us, my dear," Enid said worriedly, trying not to let her sympathy show too much.

"I should like to," Amelia said in a subdued tone.

"Come along, come along, we don't have all day, girl!" her father snapped on his way out.

Amelia cringed, and inwardly so did Enid and the others. It was terrible to hear the way Hartwell talked to the girl. No wonder she was so withdrawn and fearful around him. What a different person she'd been while he was away, Enid thought curiously. Hartwell was an unpleasant man at best. How much worse must it be when he and Amelia were alone. . . .

She forced a smile to her face and saw them off, hoping that Amelia would feel close enough to her to ask for help if ever she needed it.

King still hadn't come in from the range when Amelia and Hartwell left. She tied her bonnet around her head to keep it from blowing off in the buggy and waved good-bye to the Culhanes as her father snapped the buggy whip against the horse's flank. The animal jumped violently, and Amelia's teeth clenched. It was a hired carriage and horse, paid for by the Culhanes, to her father's delight.

He was in a better humor as they headed back toward El Paso.

"Young Alan does seem to have a case on you," he said. "You encourage him, young woman. I have some far-reaching business plans that involve the Culhanes. Having a son-in-law among them could hardly hurt my chances. You're old enough to marry, and I'm of the opinion that Alan is by far the best you're likely to be able to catch."

Amelia's hands clenched in her lap as the buggy lurched along the road.

"Yes, Father," she said demurely.

He grimaced suddenly, with a hand to his temple. Suddenly, he gave her an angry glance. "I gave you no permission to attend a fiesta!"

The sudden mood swing was familiar, frightening. She swallowed. "Papa, everyone else went. I had to."

He wasn't convinced. "How did you come to be hounded by this man Ted?"

"He only danced with me," she said softly. "He is a very nice man. Not as nice as Alan, of course. I like Alan."

He moved his piercing gaze back to the dirt road. "King accompanied you and Enid?"

"Yes. He is all but engaged to Miss Valverde," she added quickly.

"Just as well. I find him offensively arrogant. You would never suit such a man. I am certain that spineless women have no appeal for that sort."

"Yes, Papa," she said obediently.

"Brant has told me of a house going cheap," he added suddenly. "I plan to look at it tomorrow and if it suits, buy it on the spot. You may begin to pack tonight."

Amelia felt a wave of nausea wash over her. "But
the boardinghouse is very convenient," she began hesitantly.

"So, you dislike the idea of having to work at cooking meals and cleaning, is that it?" he demanded
harshly. "You have grown lazy living a leisurely life at
the Culhane place?"

"That is not true! I did my share of work. . . . Oh!"

His hand had left a faint mark on her cheek, bringing
stinging pain and tears to her eyes. "Do not talk back
to me," he said with cold contempt. "No child of mine
is going to be allowed to do that!"

She glared at him through a mist of tears, fearing him
and hating him all at once. No more, for God's sake,
no more! she thought. It was unjust to have to live like
this for fear of endangering his life!

Her chest rose and fell heavily with the force of her
inner turmoil, but she didn't raise her voice. "If you
strike me again, I shall have nothing to do with Alan,"
she said deliberately, knowing his one weakness. Her
voice shook, but there was sudden resolve in it. Adren-
aline poured into her veins, making her oblivious to the
danger of his reply.

Her father was surprised. He hesitated, frowned as if
searching for words, thoughts. "Well, then, you . . .
you keep a civil tongue in your mouth when you speak
to me!"

She didn't reply. Brushing her hurt cheek, she kept
her eyes to the road ahead. She didn't know how she
was going to bear this for much longer.

"It is my head, Amelia," he said confusedly, wincing as he looked at her. "I fear that I am going mad,
you know, there are such terrible headaches, and I cannot . . . oh!" He caught his head in his hands and

dropped the reins abruptly. "Oh, dear God, it hurts
. . . so!"

"Here. Let me drive." She took the reins from him
and urged the horse forward. He was worse, all right.
She had to get a doctor to see him. She simply had to!

The Howards were long gone when King came wearily in the front door. He scowled as he looked around
the parlor and, instead of Amelia, found his father and
brother sitting with his mother.

"Welcome us back, boy," Brant said, rising to shake
his son's hand. "I brought you a present." He pointed
to the lion skin lying over the arm of the chair in which
King habitually sat.

"You got him, then," King replied with a smile. "I
thought you would."

"Dad got him, all right," Alan murmured sheepishly, "after I missed him twice."

"If you'd wear those spectacles instead of keeping
them in your jacket pocket, you might have better
luck," King chided, but not without affection. "It's
good to have you both home."

"Aren't you going to ask where Amelia is?" Enid
asked demurely, with her eyes carefully on her cro-
cheting.

"Obviously she and her father went home," he replied, unperturbed. "I'm famished. Is there anything in
the kitchen?"

"I'll dish it up."

"Alan and I will finish our brandy while you eat,"
Brant said, after a warning look from Enid, who often
seemed to read his mind.

"You do that, dear," Enid murmured. She led King
into the kitchen with a lighted lamp and then lit another

to give her enough light. "I pray for the day when we have gas lights, as they do in El Paso," she muttered while she went about punching up the fire to reheat the meat and potatoes in her stew. "There's coffee on the warmer, dear."

He poured himself a cup, quiet and uncommunicative.

"Amelia is afraid of Hartwell," Enid mentioned quietly.

He glanced at her. "Her problems are no concern of ours."

She stirred the contents of the big iron Dutch oven. "They might become so. Alan is taking her to a concert on Saturday evening."

King went very still. "Her father, of course, countenances such a match," he replied after a minute, his voice dangerously low. "I do not. I would not wish such a woman on my worst enemy, much less on my own brother."

"She is not what she seems," Enid said firmly. "You see only the image she projects for her father! I am certain that she has spirit and intelligence."

"She speaks a little French," he returned. "Barely enough to make herself understood, and probably Marie taught it to her."

"I wish you had been kinder to her," Enid said solemnly. "She has a tragic face."

"Many women are able to cultivate one to catch unsuspecting men in their webs."

"Women like Miss Valverde?" she asked sweetly.

"She is my concern."

"I shall move out of the house if you attempt to install her here as your wife," she informed him tartly, and her dark eyes sparked at him.

After a minute, his expression lightened, and a corner of his disciplined mouth curved up. "I wonder that my father has not taken a tree limb to you in the past."

"Oh, he did, once. I took it away and hit him with it." She chuckled.

King shook his head, amused. "Whomever I marry, it shall have to be someone like you, I think. A quiet, docile woman would be the ruin of me."

"I agree," she replied. "But do be sure before you take that step, my dear. Be very sure."

He didn't reply. He finished his coffee and poured himself another cup, just as she dished up his beef stew and set it on the table.

Amelia couldn't go downstairs to have supper at the common table in the boardinghouse. Her cheek showed the blow her father had dealt her, and it was too embarrassing to advertise it to the world.

It was unthinkable for a person with any honor at all to display her family's dirty linen for all to see. A woman, or man, who would betray their own flesh and blood, regardless of the reason, would certainly not hesitate to betray anyone else.

She went to her own room in the suite they occupied and locked herself in. It was as well that she had, when her father staggered up the steps two hours later, having imbibed heavily with some acquaintances. But this time, fortunately, he was too soused to cause any trouble. She heard him fall onto the sofa in their sitting room and closed her eyes gratefully. At least tonight she did not have to fear the violence that strong drink worsened in him.

He had a hangover the next morning and barely spoke

to Amelia, even at breakfast. But as he went out, he paused to remind her to pack.

"For by this afternoon, I expect that we shall have a house," he said stiffly, carefully keeping his eyes from her cheek. It wasn't swollen or obviously damaged, but he looked guilty and morose.

"Very well," Amelia said gently.

He hesitated, but only for an instant. He left, and Amelia went upstairs to gather their things, mentally hoping that he would relinquish the idea and that they would not have to move. Perhaps the house he found would be too expensive. Yes. The thought cheered her, and she went about cleaning the suite in a little less melancholy mood.

Her mind went homing to King, and she wondered that she couldn't stop thinking about him. He was certainly as bad as her father, with his cold eyes and contemptuous voice. But she couldn't help but ponder on his slow, hungry kisses. The emotion in them was hardly pretended. Certainly, he felt something for her, even if only an unwilling attraction. But her father despised him. And, of course, King despised her. He'd made sure she knew that it had only been curiosity that had caused him to kiss her in the rose garden. She knew that there was no hope in mooning over him. But all the same, it was very difficult to get her mind on another subject.

That evening her father came home in a rare good mood, and Amelia felt apprehensive.

"I have found the perfect house. It is furnished, and because of my friendship and business dealings with Brant, the man is willing to let it go for a pittance! Monday morning the arrangements will be final, and we shall move on Tuesday."

Amelia tried not to show her fear. "Shall it be large enough for Quinn to live with us?" she asked hopefully.

He frowned. "Why should Quinn wish to live with us? He is quite happy in the Ranger barracks. It is a small house, Amelia, not a mansion, and will barely be sufficient for the two of us. However, there is a large parlor. I expect to do a great deal of entertaining in future. You will be my hostess, and I hope you will not disgrace me with any shows of belligerence such as you presented yesterday. I do not enjoy striking you. However, a child should respect its parent."

She stared at him coolly, without blinking. "The newspaper featured a story which advocates public stocks for men who beat women."

He drew himself up to his full height. "You know very well that I was drunk that night I hit you with the leather strap," he said shortly. "And you promised never to speak of it again!"

Her hands locked together shakily. "You were not drunk last evening when you struck me."

"You were belligerent and disrespectful! I had every right to punish you!"

He was going white in the face, and his voice was raised, loud, threatening. Her strength of will began to dwindle under the force of it. He looked wild. His eyes were those of some savage animal, and she was afraid that she might have provoked him too far.

"Shall I tell the landlady that we will be down to supper directly?" she asked in a softer tone.

He glared at her, his eyes fixed, glassy. He blinked, then, and touched his temples, wincing, as if in pain. "What? Supper? Yes, go ahead, tell her."

Amelia left the room quickly but not with noticeable speed. She didn't want to incite him again.

Once in the hallway, with the door shut, she leaned
back against the wall, shaking. She could not bear to
let him humiliate and persecute her further, but she was
afraid to push him and risk more violence. He was less
controlled than ever these days, a condition which alcohol precipitated but did not seem to cause. He had
not been drinking the day before when he struck her
without apparent reason. His eyes then, too, had been
glassy and unfocused.

Now it seemed that he would never revert to the kind
man he had once been. Every day, he grew worse. The
headaches, too, came more regularly, and his personality seemed to deteriorate. He had been rude to King
and testy with the other Culhanes. He had humiliated
Amelia in front of them all the night he chided her
about her piano playing. That lack of manners had never
been a fault of his before the boys died. She had blamed
alcohol, but it seemed to Amelia now that he drank
only when the headaches were very bad. There were
also powders that he took, strong sedatives that he had
gotten from someone—not, she remembered, from a
doctor, either.

She went downstairs to speak to the landlady, feeling
morose and miserable. Whatever the problem, it was
not going to do her any good to brood about it. Her
father was getting worse all the time, and there was
nothing she could do. Least of all could she run away,
because she had nowhere to run. Quinn had no place
for her. She was truly a prisoner.

The one bright spot in her life was Alan. He was
kind and gentle, and she liked him. She had no plans
to marry him; it would be unfair to involve him in her
life when she had no love to give him. But it would be
nice to get away from her father for an evening and hear

some music. And if Alan were willing, they might pretend to be more than friends, so that her father would be kinder to her.

King had said that he wouldn't allow any alliance between herself and Alan, but she'd worry about that later. Brant would encourage it, and so would Enid. For the time being, King could be kept in the dark. But it would spare Amelia so much violence to have her father believe in an alliance between herself and Alan. Temporarily, at least, it would keep her safe. Her one real terror was the thought of living alone with her father in that house. She mustn't think about it. Perhaps something would happen to prevent it. She had hope, if nothing else.

As the morning sun of Del Rio filtered in through the dirty window glass of the cantina, the girl was crying, great huge sobs that wracked the slender white body that Quinn had possessed so hungrily. He threw a blanket over her before he got up and dressed. The tears upset him. He didn't know why a woman who'd chosen a life like this would be so hysterical at spending a night in a man's arms. Certainly she wasn't an innocent, even if for a few minutes he had thought her one. She must have known what she was getting into when she agreed to work for the madam. It was odd, though, for a white woman to work in a Mexican brothel.

"*Mi padre* . . . he will kill you!" she choked, looking at him with venom in her blue eyes.

"If he valued you so much, why did he allow you to work in a brothel?" he demanded hotly, spurred by his own guilt into striking back.

"Brothel?" Her lovely face went blank, and she

stared at him with sudden, horrifying comprehension. "A brothel? *¿Una casa de putas?!*"

"That's about the size of it," he agreed, nodding. "How could you not know?"

She bit her lower lip, and the tears came again with great, wrenching sobs. "I am dishonored!" She sobbed. "Disgraced. Padrecito took such care, he and my uncles, to protect me. . . . And Manolito's mother was jealous of it. I went to Juarez to help him bring my little brother home, because he had an accident. But he deserted my brother on the trail. He had put peyote in my food, and I knew nothing. He must have brought me here. I only half remember it." She wiped her tears and shook back her long, black hair. "You bought me?"

"I bought you," he replied coldly.

Her lower lip trembled, but she lifted her chin and stared at him proudly. "I hope that your pleasure was worth my life, because I refuse to live in such disgrace. You have made a . . . *puta* of me," she choked.

He moved to the bed and sat down beside her, hating the way she flinched back, shivering.

"Don't be stupid," he told her bluntly. "There's no need for that. Only you and I know it even happened, and I swear to God, nobody will hear it from me. Do you think I'm not shamed by it? I had no idea you weren't like the others! I would never have touched you if I had known!"

"You . . . would not?"

He searched her wan face and felt a great surge of pity and regret. She was so young. And very, very pretty. She spoke Spanish like a native, but no way was she Mexican.

"I'm sorry," he said softly. *"Lo siento."*

She grimaced, wiping the tears away with the backs

of her hands like a child. "What will I tell my papa?"
she whispered. "That . . . that woman out there, the
one who sold me to you, she will tell!"

"She will not," he said shortly, and meant it. "I'll
speak to her. She will tell no one."

"You cannot make her be silent, *señor*," she said
sadly. "She is not the sort of woman to be frightened
of a gringo, except one of the dreaded Texas Rangers,
and you are not one of those, *es verdad*," she said,
unaware of his quick glance. "My papa, though, everyone is scared of him. I will tell her who is my papa,
and she will be too afraid to speak of this!"

He hesitated. "Who is your papa?"

"Why, Emiliano Rodriguez, of course," she said
proudly.

Quinn didn't move, didn't flinch, didn't dare give
away anything. He was a Ranger and after Rodriguez,
and he'd had the luck to find the outlaw's daughter. He'd
have to keep that star hidden for the time being, and
perhaps he could get the girl to take him right into Rodriguez's camp. He couldn't believe his good fortune!
He hadn't known that Rodriguez had any family here.

"We have to get you out of here and back to your
home," Quinn said. "Where is it?"

"A little village, in the north."

"What little village?" he probed carefully.

"Malasuerte." She smiled at his look of ignorance.
"It is all right. I will lead you to it."

"Why do you live in Mexico when you're as white
as I am?" he asked. "And how can you be Rodriguez's
daughter?"

"But, I am Mexican," she replied. "I mean, I was
raised here, in Mexico, after *mi padre* saved me from

my stepfather. I have lived here since I was ten. Six years, *señor*."

"So you're his adopted daughter," he mused. "And you're sixteen. Who would have thought it?" He touched her hair, gently. "You're very pretty."

She lowered her eyes, shamed.

He got up abruptly. "Get dressed," he said. "I'm taking you out of here."

=== Chapter Eight ===

AMELIA DRESSED IN THE SAME PRETTY LAVENDER dress she'd made for the Valverde party for Alan. It was a new dress, she thought, and surely no one who'd seen her at the Valverdes would be at the concert. The family budget was still too small to stretch to party dresses, even if Amelia did sew her own. She had a treadle machine, but it was old and temperamental. Besides, she couldn't afford fabric. Her father didn't give her an allowance, and he felt that it was shameful for a woman to work, so she couldn't take in laundry or sewing to make any money. That's why it had been so cruel of him to tell the Culhanes how frivolous she was.

The dress would have to do. And Alan never noticed what she wore. Friends didn't.

Alan called for her promptly, and her father was sober and even congenial.

"I'll have her back at a respectable hour, sir," Alan promised. "How did you fare with the house?"

"I have bought it. We will move Tuesday."

Amelia seemed oddly unenthusiastic, Alan thought. "I'll bring some of the boys, and we'll help, if you like," Alan offered.

"That is very kind of you, sir," Hartwell said. "I will accept your offer with gratitude."

"Shall we go?" Alan asked, offering Amelia his arm.

117

They rode in the comfortable buggy to the theater, and he smiled at the elegant picture she made in that dress. "You look lovely," he said.

"Thank you. Your mother bought this material for me," she added. "It was so kind of her."

"Yes, King took you to the Valverde fiesta, didn't he?"

She froze up. "He escorted your mother and me."

"I understand. King can be difficult at times," he said slowly. "Perhaps it might help you to understand him a little better if I told you why he is so antagonistic toward you."

"That isn't necessary," she said quietly. "He explained it to me quite vividly."

He frowned. "He did? How odd, because I've never known him to speak of Alice to anyone. I only know because mother told me."

They were at cross-purposes, Amelia decided. "He said nothing of any woman except Miss Valverde, to whom he is all but engaged."

"Darcy," Alan muttered darkly. "He'll regret it for the rest of his life if he marries that cold woman. He is determined not to risk his heart again, that much is obvious." He turned the buggy toward the street that led to Chopin Hall. People were milling about on the sidewalks nearby, dressed in their Sunday best for the concert.

"He had an unfortunate experience?" she asked, hoping Alan would elaborate before they reached the stable, where he would leave the horse and buggy.

"A very unfortunate one. He fell in love with a girl named Alice Hart. She found him quite unattractive except in a material way, but King was too smitten to realize it. She played up to him, promised to marry him. Considering the depth of his attachment to her, I cannot help but believe their relationship was more indiscreet than their families knew. Just about that time, the family suffered a financial setback. Texas cattle fever almost wiped us out. The lovely Alice, realizing that King could well end up penniless, abruptly turned her attentions to an English duke who was visiting El Paso. Within a week they had both been killed in a buggy accident." He pulled into the stables. "King took it badly. Perhaps he felt that she would have turned to him again, in time, because he would never blame her for leaving him. But in some ways, it made Latigo what it is today. It was his single-minded determination to succeed that gave us our wealth. Father was ready to give up. King wouldn't."

"This Alice . . . she was pretty?"

"She was an angel," Alan said honestly. "The most beautiful woman I've ever seen. You're lovely, Amelia, really lovely. King has reason to distrust beauty. He's determined to wed Darcy but only with his mind. She suits him as a wife." He shook his head. "But she'll never suit his heart, and Mother detests her."

"Still, it might be a good marriage," she said quietly. "One never knows."

He didn't reply. He helped her down and left their transportation with the stable owner. There were plenty of people waiting to enter the concert hall. Some of the women were wearing very expensive clothing, and Amelia was glad she was wearing a pretty dress.

"You'll enjoy this orchestra," Alan told her. "I'm told they've played in the north quite extensively. And the score is a favorite of mine: Beethoven's 'Ninth Symphony.' "

"Oh, yes, the one that includes Schiller's 'Ode to Joy,' " she added eagerly.

Alan's eyebrows arched. "Why, Amelia, I had no idea you were conversant with the classics!"

"I know just a little about classical music," she confessed. "Quinn taught me. Father wouldn't allow me to go further than high school, and he even tried to stop me from finishing. He thinks it is silly to educate women."

"And you do not."

"I think a woman's brain is the equal of any man's," she replied, looking up at him. "And that it is a crime to impose limits on knowledge."

"I tend to agree." His eyes narrowed. "King mentioned that you spoke a few words of French?"

It was a question. She moved uncomfortably. "Actually, I read it quite well. I rarely understand much if it is not spoken slowly. Marie helped me to refine my accent."

"You are a creature of hidden talent, Amelia," he said. "What other accomplishments are you keeping concealed so carefully?"

"I am not so talented," she replied.

"What else did your brother teach you?" he persisted.

"A little Latin and Greek," she had to confess. "And I can understand Spanish."

He caught his breath. "And you think of that as a small accomplishment?"

"I have a facility for languages, that is all," she said firmly. "And please do not repeat this conversation. My father would be furious if he knew what Quinn had done."

He noticed her hands clasping and unclasping. Beauty

and brains, he thought. He could do much worse than court Amelia for himself. There was no real competition, unless he counted Ted. Speak of the devil, he thought, when he saw the tall blond man with a lovely brunette on his arm nearby. That wasn't all he saw. Elegant in evening clothes, his brother King was standing at the opposite side of the lobby with Darcy Valverde.

"Let's go in, shall we?" he asked quickly, before she saw the others. He clasped her hand in his, feeling its soft strength, and smiled at her as they walked into the auditorium.

He led her to a chair, still possessing himself of her hand as he sat beside her.

Amelia felt nothing at his touch. It grieved her, because she had to agree that Alan would make her a good and kind husband. But it wasn't the same as when King had touched her.

King! Why should she be thinking of him? she wondered irritably. She smiled at Alan and allowed him to retain her hand as other people began filing into the room.

"Well, look who's here!" Darcy's shrill voice caught everyone's attention as she saw Alan and Amelia, pausing with an unfriendly King at her side. "How nice to see you again, Miss Howard, and how very pretty you look! I have to confess, I did so admire that dress when I saw you wearing it at our party last week. Isn't it flattering to her complexion, King? Your mother was so kind to buy the material for her."

Amelia could have gone through the floor with humiliation. But she didn't flinch. She simply stared at Darcy without speaking, her face composed, her dignity quietly intimidating. Her dark, unblinking eyes made the girl laugh nervously and begin to fidget.

"Shall we sit down, King? Nice to see you both!"

Darcy pulled at King's lean hand. He was watching Amelia, his expression one of faint curiosity at her composure. She was red-cheeked from Darcy's venomous comments, but she was a trooper. That wasn't cowardice in those dark eyes, it was a dignity beyond her years. He fought down a skirl of admiration for the way she'd handled the insult.

"The dress does indeed suit you, Miss Howard," he said quietly, and without malice. Then he saw her hand resting in Alan's, and the contempt in his silver eyes heightened her color. "Do enjoy yourselves. Good evening."

He walked away briskly to join Darcy.

"I'm sorry about that," Alan said, tightening his grip on her hand. "Darcy is a spoiled brat, isn't she? How can King be so blind!"

"She isn't rude to him," Amelia mused with faint humor. "Don't worry, Alan. I've endured worse." She had indeed, at the hands of her father in public places, back in Atlanta just before they moved to El Paso. Her ability to field insults was almost legend by now. She turned her head toward the stage, where the orchestra was tuning up, and schooled her eyes not to turn one inch in King's direction.

The program was broken by a brief intermission, during which Alan escorted Amelia into the lobby and went to purchase sarsaparilla for them both.

While she waited for him, King, having left Darcy with two women friends, joined her by the doorway.

"It promises to rain before the evening is over," he said.

"I expect so." Clouds were low overhead, and there was an ominous rumbling. She ran her gloved hands up and down her arms, already feeling the chill. At home, her father would be waiting, probably drunk. . . . "Oh!"

King had touched her shoulder, and she jumped helplessly, her dark eyes wide and fearful.

He withdrew his hand at once, his face glowering angrily. "You have no nerve. Are you afraid even of storms?"

She lowered her eyes and moved away from him.

"Miss Howard!"

Her head turned. Her dark eyes accused, detested. "Your future wife is staring at you, Mr. Culhane," she said in a chill tone. "I have no desire to become her victim a second time in one evening. I would appreciate being deprived of your company."

He put his hands in his pockets, and his eyes searched hers in a static silence, making it impossible for her to tear her eyes away. The electricity outside was nothing compared to the current that was running between them. Amelia was alarmed by the growing strength of it.

"Fate plays cruel tricks on the senses, does she not?" he asked curtly.

"As you say."

"If Alan asks for the pleasure of your company again, deny him," he said bluntly. "I do not want my brother involved with you. Is that clear?"

He turned on his heel and went back to Darcy. Amelia had a terrible impulse to pick up one of the spitoons and fling it at the back of his head. Her thoughts unnerved her. She turned and began looking for Alan just as he came back with two bottles of sarsaparilla.

"The last two bottles left." He chuckled. "Here."

It was tepid but rather tasty, and she drained the bottle of its fruity contents just in time to hear the orchestra tuning up for the finale.

After the concert was over, she followed Alan outside, careful to keep a distance between herself and King. It wasn't until they were in the buggy and driving away that she relaxed. Wherever Alan's big brother had gone, she hadn't seen him again after they seated themselves in the concert hall for the end of the concert. It had been a relief not to find those silver eyes damning her again.

"There is a lovely spot on our property where a hill overlooks the cattle in the valley below," he mentioned as they raced the rain back to the boardinghouse where Amelia and her father lived. "I would like to take you there for a picnic next weekend."

"Your brother has warned me not to accept further invitations from you," she said, smiling gently at his shocked look. "You know that he doesn't approve of me, Alan. It is folly to risk his displeasure. There's no future in it," she added miserably. "You're my friend, and I'm very fond of you. But there can never be anything more. I . . . do not want a relationship of any sort with a man."

"My brother doesn't tell me how to live my life," he said curtly. "I enjoy your company, and I hope that you enjoy mine. Amelia, I have no desire for marriage now," he added with a smile. "But we're both young, and it can do no harm for us to spend time together. King can mind his own business."

"And you know that he will not," she replied. "He is like my father. . . ."

"He is nothing like your father," he corrected gently. "Amelia, you don't know King. You see only the face he presents to the world, not the man beneath it. He is not what he seems. Least of all is he a bully.''

"He has been to me," she said stiffly.

"Yes. It has puzzled us all, his odd attitude toward you. Mother thinks it is an attraction which he does not want to own," he added with a smile. "That may well be the case. You are a lovely woman."

"I am a milksop," she said curtly. "That is what he believes. That I am dull and uninteresting and a jellyfish. Oh, and I am stupid as well."

"Has he said this to you?"

"He said it, and I overheard," she replied. "I know what your brother thinks of me, and I do not care! His opinion is of no consequence whatsoever to me!"

It was the first time Alan could ever remember hearing Amelia's voice so brittle and full of anger. He wondered if King was the only one who was fighting an unwanted attraction.

"Come on the picnic with me," he said. He looked at her out of the corner of his eye. "Or are you too afraid of King to risk displeasing him?"

That was a challenge. Amelia took a deep breath. "Very well, then. If you are willing to risk it, so am I. If my father approves, of course."

"Your father will approve." He hesitated, turning the reins in his hand. "Amelia, he has odd turns of mood, did you know?"

"I knew," she said flatly.

"And periods of utter violence," he added. "He took a buggy whip to one of the pack mules. My father had to wrestle it away from him and pin him to the ground until he came back to himself." He looked at her white face. "You know about these incidences, do you not?"

"It is worse when he drinks and takes those powders

that are meant to help the headaches,'' she said with sick fear. ''I think that one day he may kill me, Alan. . . .''

''Amelia!''

She put her gloved hand to her mouth. ''I did not mean to say such a thing. Of course, he will not harm me, it is only that he is so frightening when he gives vent to his temper,'' she said quickly. ''Please, do not think of it again.''

He didn't want to give it up, but she looked terrified. ''Of course, if that is your wish.''

''You must not speak of it, either, least of all to your family! If it should get back to him. . . .''

''It will not,'' he promised. ''Here, Amelia, I will walk you to your door.''

She let him help her down. It had been a disastrous evening. She only prayed that her father wouldn't be drinking.

And, glory of glories, he wasn't. He was, in fact, congenial. He offered Alan a brandy and spoke to him with real affection. Alan left convinced of the man's sanity.

Once he was gone, however, Hartwell turned to Amelia with cold eyes. ''See to it that you give him no cause to break off this growing relationship,'' he warned her. ''It is my wish that you will marry him.''

She started to tell him that it was impossible, that she didn't, couldn't, love Alan in that way. But his eyes were gaining that familiar gaze.

''I find him very pleasant,'' she said. ''He is taking me on a picnic next weekend. With your permission, of course, Papa.''

''He has it. Go to bed.''

Grateful for the respite, she went quickly to her room

and closed the door. Her hands, she noticed, were like
ice.

Alan and the cowboys came Tuesday to help the
Howards move, which was accomplished in short order. Amelia cooked a big supper for all of them, and
her father was in a rare good mood, laughing and joking
with everyone. For a little while, he was the kindly
father of her youth, and she relaxed as she hadn't been
able to since their move to El Paso. It would be different
here, she thought. It would!

The rest of the week went without incident. Her father was civil and courteous, and the headaches had
actually seemed to stop. But they were replaced by a
period of violent illness that came on suddenly and
lasted several days.

Amelia nursed him, feeding him broth and sitting
with him until the spell passed and he was back to
himself again. By Friday evening, he was able to sit
up. But he seemed not quite as alert as before, and
when Amelia insisted on calling for a doctor, he
couldn't argue about it. The doctor who attended him,
Dr. Vasquez, took Amelia out into the hall after his
examination.

"It is not like any condition I have treated," he told
Amelia bluntly. "His pupils indicate a light stroke, but
he has none of the paralysis one would expect from this.
Señorita, he must be closely watched. I fear there is
much more to this condition than simple vapors."

"I will take care of him."

"He has violent episodes?" he queried suddenly.

"Why . . . sometimes," she faltered.

He put his bag down on the hall table. "Describe
them to me."

She did, leaving out the most damning evidence, because she was ashamed to tell this intelligent, cultured man that her father had taken a leather strap to her and very nearly killed her with it. She did describe her father's violent behavior toward animals.

The doctor said nothing, but he looked even more worried. "If you should need me, even in the dead of night, send someone to fetch me, and I will come. In the meanwhile, I wish you to give these to your father at bedtime each night. It is only a sedative, *señorita*," he added hastily when he placed the medicine bottle in her hand. "It will not harm him. In fact, it may bring a small improvement, if only temporarily."

"You think that it is more than bad temper that drives him," she guessed. "Might it have something to do with his headaches?"

"Yes," he replied. "Springing from the accident he endured some years ago. Are you strong, *señorita*?" he asked suddenly. "Can you withstand unsettling news without hysterics?"

"I can," she said without blinking.

He glanced toward the closed door of her father's bedroom. "I suspect a tumor of the brain," he said quietly.

She leaned back against the wall. "What?"

"A tumor. It is in keeping with his symptoms, which perhaps the accident worsened. If it is a slow tumor, which must be the case, the pressure on the brain would grow steadily worse. It would account for these moods and violent tempers, and the headaches. If this is the case," he added slowly, "I regret to tell you that nothing can be done to save his life. Inevitably, he will die of it. And judging by the severity of the symptoms, it

will not take much longer. I shudder to think of the
pain he must be suffering.''

She closed her eyes and shivered. No wonder he'd
changed so!

''Is there nothing that can be done?'' she asked
plaintively.

''Medical science, alas, has not progressed so far.''
He patted her shoulder awkwardly. ''I can arrange for
a nurse when it is finally necessary. You will not have
to bear it alone. Have you family, *señorita*?''

''My . . . my brother, only.''

''He must be told,'' he added. ''It is only a matter
of time. Not too much time, either, I fear. This attack
has brought on a fever which may have caused even
more damage. You should not be alone with him,'' he
added. ''Men inflicted with this sort of thing are often
violent. He could kill you.''

She shivered. ''Yes, I know.''

''So, it has already happened, has it not?'' he persisted.

She hesitated. Then she nodded. ''I tried to run away
a year ago in Atlanta. No one would believe that he
would hurt me; he was such a kind man, before. When
I went back home, he beat me very badly. He was sorry
for a few minutes, and then he raged that I deserved it.
He has been like that ever since the buggy accident.''
It was so good to talk of it, so good! She felt tears
rolling down her cheeks. ''I have never been able to tell
anyone,'' she whispered. ''I was ashamed of him, and
of myself for allowing him to mistreat me. But I was
afraid. . . .''

''With good reason,'' he replied solemnly. ''It is a
fact that you risk your life by disagreeing with him.

Señorita, there is an asylum in which he could be placed.''

"And have everyone know?" Her face was tragic. "He could not bear the shame!"

"Alas, the world we live in is a prison, is it not?" the good doctor said grimly. "Public opinion dictates our every action. A man can be ruined, or a woman, by only the slightest gossip. I pray that this will change one day."

"As do I."

"Can you have a relative come to stay with you, then?" he persisted. "Is there someone you trust?"

"My brother is a Texas Ranger," she said, "and he is rarely here. He lives in barracks. I would hate to put this burden on him."

"Nevertheless, you may have to consider it," he returned. "Your position is desperate, did you not realize? Your father will soon be unable to work, *señorita,*" he said flatly. "What will you do then?"

She felt her face go white. Unable to work! She had no way of employing herself. All of a sudden the enormity of her situation made her knees go weak. The doctor eased her into a chair and gave her some smelling salts.

"I'm sorry," she said. "I'm sorry. It's just that it's so sudden."

"I understand. I must go," he said regretfully. "Mrs. Sims is in labor. I was on my way to her when I stopped by. Please try not to worry so much. God looks out for us."

"Indeed He does," she replied with a tearful smile. "But I think that perhaps He is sleeping right now."

Chapter Nine

AMELIA DIDN'T SLEEP THAT NIGHT. HER FATHER seemed better, but he was very much changed from the man he had been only a day or so before.

"I don't think I should leave you," she said hesitantly, when it was time for Alan to come for her.

"You go ahead," he said huskily. He was hoarse and a little confused, too. "Go with Alan. I'll be all right. The pain isn't so bad now."

"I'm glad." She hesitated. He was so much like he had once been that she felt affection for him. "Shall I find someone to sit with you?"

"I don't need a damned bodyguard!" he yelled at her suddenly. His head turned, and his eyes were glazed, full of hatred and pain. "Get out! Get out, you stupid woman! Get out!"

Amelia felt frightened. He had started to get out of the chair where he was sitting, and she backed away.

She ran down the hall, grabbing her bag and parasol on the way, and darted out the front door as if all the hounds of hell were sharp on her heels. She was shivering, but she managed to get herself back together as Alan got down from the buggy, smiling, to fetch her.

"Hello, sweetie," he said, holding out his hand. The smile abruptly faded. "Amelia?"

She didn't realize that her face was white, her eyes like black coals. She was shaking.

"What is it?" he asked abruptly.

"My father," she began. "He's worse."

"I'm sorry. Shall I go in and speak to him?"

"No! No," she added more calmly. "He'll be fine. But I would like to stop by Dr. Vasquez's surgery and inquire if he'd look in on Father while we're away. I hate to leave him alone."

"We shall do that, of course. Has he been ill?"

"Yes," she said wearily. "Ill."

He stopped by the surgery, and she told Dr. Vasquez, out of Alan's hearing, what had happened.

"I will go by to see him, of course. I have a man who can sit with him a few hours, too."

"Thank you," she said fervently.

"You will be home before dark?"

"Certainly."

"Something must be done," the doctor added quietly. "This cannot be allowed to continue. You will be in constant danger."

"I know," she said heavily. "It's just that I don't know what to do! I do not wish to involve outsiders in what is a very private business!"

"It is an act of great courage to take the risk of staying with him, even for a member of one's family," he said quietly.

"He is my father," she replied. "Before the accident, he was a good and kind man who took wonderful care of his family. I love him. What else could I have done?"

He smiled at her. "You are a singular woman."

She flushed. "No. Only a weary one. Thank you for your help."

"It is my pleasure to do what I can for you. Good evening."

She nodded.

Alan put her back into the buggy and drove out of town. "Something's very wrong, isn't it?"

"Yes, Alan. But it's nothing I can tell you about. I'm sorry. I must handle it as I think best."

He frowned. "Aren't friends supposed to help each other?" he asked softly.

She sighed. "Alan, only God can help me now." She turned and forced a smile. "Tell me about this spot you've chosen for our picnic."

It was a lovely day. The rain of the past weekend, a brief storm with little substance, had not been repeated. There was a drought in the Rio Grande Valley, and talk of drilling more wells was on everyone's tongues. Alan was in good spirits, and the sun and crisp spring air made Amelia feel more relaxed and hopeful than she had in a long time.

She had worn a blue plaid cotton skirt and a lacy white blouse with a big, flower-covered hat for the picnic. Alan was in a neat gray suit that emphasized his good looks. What a pity, Amelia thought sadly, that she could not love him.

"I had Rosa's daughter pack the basket full for us. Rosa is . . . indisposed," he said, unwilling to mention that she was in labor in front of a lady like Amelia.

"It looks delicious, Alan," she said as she helped him unpack it and set the dishes out on the spotless white linen cloth that had also been provided. Crystal glasses were produced and a bottle of wine. Amelia exclaimed with delight when she saw it.

"It is a very light white wine," he assured her.

"Nothing which will threaten your senses. Do sit down, Amelia."

She did, wrapping her long skirt around her, taking off her hat to let the air touch her high-piled blond hair. Wisps of it teased her flushed cheeks.

"You look happy," he said, "but very tired. Can you not tell me what is wrong?"

"My father has been ill. I did tell you."

"Amelia . . ."

She reached over impulsively and put her hand over his where it lay on the cloth. "No more questions, I implore you," she said softly. "Let it rest."

"As you wish," he said heavily. "Here, dear, have some chicken."

They were just beginning to eat when the sound of a horse's hooves startled them. A lone rider was coming up the rise. He was long-legged and lean, with his hat tilted at a rakish angle across his right eye and his red and white bandana fluttering in the wind. Wide chaps with silver conchos lay over black boots in the stirrups. Amelia's heart jumped. Even at a distance, the arrogant way he sat that horse betrayed his identity.

"King," she said under her breath.

"I'd forgotten that he was working out here today," Alan said unconvincingly.

"He sits a horse like the centaur of mythology," she murmured, her eyes helplessly watching the approach of the horseman. "He is majestic, Alan," she added involuntarily. "How wonderfully he rides!"

"Quinn said that you used to ride. King didn't believe him, of course."

"I had a friend whose father owned a riding stable," Amelia said, smiling at the memory of the long afternoons she and Mary had spent in the saddle. "I rode

quite well, they said. Of course, when Mother died and
I had Father to care for, there was not much time for
it. Father was different in those days," she added quietly. "He drove me to the stables himself. It pleased
him that I had what Mary's mother called a natural seat
for riding. He was very proud of me."

"This change in him, when did it begin?"

"Only a handful of years ago," she said sadly. "He
is not the man he was, Alan."

He wanted to know more, but King was within hearing distance now.

The tall man swung out of the saddle with incredible
grace and threw the reins lazily over the horse's neck,
letting them trail the ground to keep him close. The
animal had been trained to stand when his reins were
dragging.

"Join us," Alan invited. "We have chicken and biscuits!"

"Coffee?"

"It is just brewing," the younger man said, nodding
to where he'd set the coffeepot boiling on the small fire
he'd made with fallen limbs.

King stretched out beside them, tossing his hat to one
side. His hair was sweaty, like his shirt. He looked
tired.

"Still branding new calves?" Alan asked.

King nodded. "It's hot and thirsty work." He glanced
at the crystal glasses. "Champagne?" he drawled
mockingly, with a silvery glance that Amelia avoided.

"Wine," Alan replied. "Lemonade was too much
work," he added with a chuckle.

"Fill a plate for me, Amelia," he instructed, and
leaned back against the tree trunk to watch her do it.
Her hands fumbled under his unblinking scrutiny. That

seemed to amuse him. A corner of his mouth pulled up, and his lids dropped over glittering eyes.

She handed it to him. He took it, his hand brushing hers deliberately as he took it.

She jerked her hand away and dived for a fork to give him. He did the same thing with that, making an excuse of it to caress her fingers with his. She met his eyes, and lightning seemed to jab through her body.

His eyelids narrowed, and the smile faded from his mouth. He sat holding the plate, holding her in thrall, while Alan handled the coffeepot, trying to get some of the steaming black liquid into a cup.

"Ah," Alan exclaimed, "there we go!"

King, his attention diverted, allowed Amelia to escape him. She went back to her own corner of the cloth and picked at her chicken and biscuit, her appetite routed by the shocking pleasure it gave her to be near King.

He ate heartily, while he and Alan talked about the state of the cattle and the far-reaching effects of the lack of rain.

"We'll have to buy hay to feed if we don't get some rain soon," King remarked, having finished his meal and returned the empty plate with its bones to the cloth. "Water is going to be the real headache. I've had the men start drilling a second well in the lower pasture."

"Good idea," Alan replied. He glanced at Amelia, who must surely feel left out of the conversation. "We have to make sure the cattle have enough water," he told her.

"I see."

King lounged back against the tree trunk again, taking his time about lighting a cigar. Thick smoke curled up from his lean fingers, and he stared at Amelia through it.

"How do you like your new home?" he asked her.

"It's very nice." She began to put the food away.

"Just . . . nice?"

"It is well-located, of course, in a good section of the city."

Alan looked from one to the other of them, secretly amused at the thick atmosphere of tension they were projecting.

King's eyes narrowed for a minute before he turned toward his brother. "Take my horse and ride down to the corral, will you? Ask Hank to move the next lot of calves in. I rode off to see who was up here without telling him."

Alan hesitated, just to seem reluctant. "Well, I suppose I could." He eyed the horse warily. "I don't like riding the 'iron horse' there."

"Kit won't hurt you," he was assured. "He's just strong-willed, that's all."

"Pretty dangerous, too, I'd say, but maybe he won't dump me off."

"He couldn't unseat you the one time he tried, could he?" King asked, smiling affectionately at his younger brother. "You can handle him."

"All right, then. I'll be right along, Amelia," he told her. "Save some of that coffee for me," he cautioned King before he swung into the saddle and rode off down the hill.

Amelia was unsettled at being left alone with King. They could see the corral, but were too far away to be seen, especially under the shade of the tree. She couldn't imagine why he'd sent Alan away unless he wanted to harass her again.

She turned toward him, ready to defend herself, and stopped dead at the look on his face. That wasn't mockery or sarcasm or a need to hurt. It was pure, helpless desire.

He put the cigar aside, crushing out the fiery coal at its tip. Then he turned his head back toward Amelia, his pale eyes blazing.

"Come here," he said quietly.

She hesitated, and his hand shot out, grasping her wrist. He jerked her down beside him and trapped her there, looming over her like a conqueror.

"King," she protested.

"Be quiet." He leaned closer, his chest pressing down on her breasts to prevent her from rising. Even as he moved, his head lowered and his mouth eased down over her startled lips.

She reacted helplessly to the taste and feel of him, even though she did try feebly at first to resist him. But his mouth was warm and coaxing, and she couldn't help her willing response to it. Her hands fell beside her head. She lay close in his embrace, feeding on the ardent tenderness of his hard mouth while the wind blew ceaselessly around them.

"Open your mouth," he whispered against her lips, and when she did, he deepened the kiss with deliberate passion. He felt her breathing change under him, felt her mouth tremble as she yielded.

A soft sound came against his body, and he knew that she was lost, completely his.

It went to his head. He groaned, and his hands found her head, cupping it, his thumbs exploring her cheeks, the corners of her mouth, while the hard, hungry kiss went on and on.

She sobbed something against his mouth, and he

lifted it just a fraction, his breath jerking out against her lips. "What?" he whispered, half-dazed by the sweetness of her in his arms after weeks of being haunted by the memory of her kisses.

"King . . . Alan . . . will come back soon," she choked.

"Kiss me," he said roughly, bending to her mouth again.

She did, but her hands came up to his chest and started to press against it.

"Not there," he whispered. "Here, Amelia. Here, little one, here . . . !"

He fought the buttons apart and drew her hand against his bare, hair-roughened muscles. She moaned at the sensations it gave her to touch him so intimately. Her lower body began to throb sweetly, and her nails dug into the thicket of hair, tugging rhythmically.

"Amelia," he groaned harshly, aroused beyond bearing. His body eased closer to hers, shockingly close.

She came to her senses at once when she felt his long, powerful leg sliding against hers. "King, no," she choked, dragging her mouth away, "oh, you mustn't!"

His head was spinning. He lifted it to look at her, seeing her swollen lips and big, dark eyes and flushed face. She wanted him. It was in every line of her body, in her eyes. He wanted her with such a fever that it took precious seconds for his mind to register that she was trying to make him stop.

"Alan . . . will be back any minute!" she exclaimed shakily.

"Alan." Alan. His brother. Amelia's suitor. His silver eyes flashed down at her angrily. "Do you let him kiss you this way?"

"No!"

It had popped out before she could stop it. She gaped at him, shocked by her abrupt answer.

King was placated. The anger left his eyes, his face, and he studied her in a trembling silence. His lean hand brushed against her cheek, her swollen lips. He looked at her as if he couldn't drag his eyes away, oblivious to everything except the soft womanly scent of her body and the beauty of her face beneath his. Slowly, boldly, he let his eyes slide down to the lacy bodice. It betrayed nothing except the quick beat of her heart and her rapid breathing. He wondered what she looked like under it and if her skin was as soft there as it was on her face and mouth. He wondered what her breasts were like. . . .

"Please," she whispered frantically, as the distant sound of a horse's hooves registered.

He heard it, too. His body lifted away from hers. Down the slope, Alan was just starting back up. Appalled at what he'd done, King's face went hard and cold. He got to his feet in one fluid motion and turned to watch his brother ride up.

"That is one fast horse," Alan chuckled, flushed with the pleasure of riding the beautiful animal.

"Get down from there," King said tersely.

Surprised, Alan dismounted. He was barely clear of the horse when King flung himself into the saddle and wheeled the horse. Without a word, without a backward glance, he rode off.

Amelia had managed to compose herself by the time Alan turned, puzzled, back to her. But her mouth was still swollen, her cheeks flushed, from the ardor of King's lovemaking.

"What happened?" Alan asked curiously. "Did you argue with him?"

"One is never permitted to argue with your brother," she said stiffly. "He simply says what he feels and goes away."

Remembering a dozen similar arguments, with King flailing him verbally and storming off, Alan could sympathize. But privately he thought that Amelia looked not as much argued with as kissed. And if King's expression was anything to go by, the older man was as upset as she was by the experience. Seeing King shaken was enough to amuse him, but he was careful not to let Amelia know that he suspected anything.

"Here," he said. "Do have some more wine, Amelia. We're in no hurry to leave, are we?"

She settled back on the cloth, keeping her eyes down. "Of course not," she said, and reached for the wine bottle and Alan's glass. If only her hands hadn't shaken so badly, she might have managed to convince him that she was quite calm.

Alan wanted to take her back to Latigo to spend the rest of the day and have supper, but she refused in a panic. He didn't press her. It didn't take a genius to realize how unsettling she found King, and the older man apparently had no more resistance to her than she had to him.

He stopped the buggy in front of Amelia's house and got out to tie the horse before he helped her down and escorted her to her door.

"I enjoyed this afternoon," he told her gently. "I only wish that it had not ended so soon." He held both her hands in his. They were cold, and there were new lines in her face. "If only you could talk to me," he added on a heavy breath.

"I will be all right," she assured him with much more certainty than she felt.

"It was because of King that you insisted on coming home, was it not?" he asked shrewdly.

Her face tautened. "Yes. Your brother does not like me. You must know it."

"I know more than you realize. If you need me, for any reason, will you promise to send for me?" he added solemnly.

She nodded. Her hands pressed his. "Thank you, Alan. You are a good friend."

"Don't you realize that King would be, also, if you were ever really in need?" he added suddenly. "All his imagined grievances would be immediately forgotten if you asked him to help you."

She laughed bitterly. "Do you think so? For I do not. If I were drowning he would toss me an anchor."

"That is a delusion. Very well, if I cannot convince you. . . ." He smiled at her gently. "Sleep well, Amelia. Will you come to dinner tomorrow? King will be lunching with the Valverdes," he promised her quickly.

"If I do not have to see him," she said hesitantly, "I will come. If my father is well enough to leave. I cannot ask strangers to sit with him, regardless of their kindness. He is my responsibility."

"I will come for you after church, in that case, and return you within two hours if it is necessary. Good evening."

"Thank you. I, too, enjoyed the picnic."

He smiled and waited for her to go inside before he left.

Her father was in the bedroom sound asleep. The man who had been sitting with him had left a note for Amelia, telling her that her father had been quite congenial for most of the afternoon and had wanted to take a nap about lunchtime.

That meant that he had been asleep for most of the day, Amelia thought gratefully. Perhaps he would sleep through the night as well.

She stood at the foot of his bed, contemplating his pale face and labored breathing. He was dying. The doctor had said as much. Now she was fiercely glad that she had realized her father was ill instead of brutal and that she had stayed with him.

Her father was going to die, that much was certain. But when, and how, she didn't know. She hoped that he wouldn't become too violent toward the end and that she would be able to cope. She could hardly leave him.

There was another very big worry to go along with that of his condition. If he kept deteriorating at this rate he soon would be unable to work. There would be no money coming in. Amelia felt a surge of panic. Quinn would not let her starve, but she would not be able to keep the house. She would have to have a job and rooms. Hysterically, she wondered if Miss Valverde needed a maid.

Of course, she could marry Alan, she reminded herself again. He had hinted in the past that he wasn't quite ready yet but would probably be agreeable to the idea now. But it would cheat him, because she could never feel for him what she felt for King. Her eyes closed on a wave of remembered delight. He had wanted her, as surely as day was separate from night. His arms had trembled, and his mouth had demanded for that sweet, sweet space of minutes. Amelia had never felt such love for any human being as she felt for him. But King only wanted her and took pains to make sure she knew it. He was not making promises he could not keep. Nor would he countenance any continuation of her relationship with Alan that might end in marriage. He would stop her if she even tried to marry his brother. Not that she would. Poor Alan could never be to her what King was.

She tiptoed out of her father's room and gently closed the door. She went to tidy the sitting room, wondering what was to become of her and how much worse it would get before her father was finally released from his torment, and she from hers.

Chapter Ten

KING HAD RAGED AT HIS MEN UNTIL ONE OF THEM threw a punch at him and got knocked into the dirt for his pains. That was what brought him to his senses and made him realize that he was losing his balance because of Amelia.

He rode back home that evening in a vicious temper, made worse by Alan's constant praising of the woman and his announcement that she was coming to the noon meal the next day.

"She's not for you," King told Alan harshly, his silver eyes flashing as he confronted his brother in the parlor. "I've already told you that I will countenance no alliance between the two of you!"

"You're my brother, not my keeper," Alan replied congenially. "I shall continue to see Amelia, and you can do your worst."

King's face actually went ruddy over his high cheekbones. He glared at his brother with something like hatred.

"And if we decide to marry, we'll live in town," Alan continued, pushing the knife in deeper. "You will hardly ever have to see her."

"Damn you!"

Alan's eyebrows lifted in twin arches. He couldn't

remember ever seeing his older brother so livid, so shockingly out of control. "Why do you hate her so?"

King's hands clenched at his side. He didn't answer. He couldn't.

"Besides, you had planned to have dinner with Darcy and her parents tomorrow, had you not?"

King turned on his heel and strode furiously out of the room, almost colliding with his father on the way. Brant stepped to one side, mildly surprised that King hadn't even bothered to speak to him.

"What ails him?" Brant asked Alan, jerking his thumb toward the hard slam of the front door.

Alan lifted the brandy snifter to his smiling mouth. "I won't stop seeing Amelia Howard."

Brant frowned. "You don't love Amelia."

"Nor does she love me."

"Then why . . ." He saw the twinkle in the younger man's eyes and let out a slow breath. "I see. You're tempting fate, in more ways than you know. It is unwise to prod King."

"You've seen how they are together," Alan defended his actions. "The air fairly trembles with emotion, but King has a low opinion of her and is perhaps afraid that fate will kick him down again. I'm merely helping him to see things as they are."

"You may be prompting tragedy for both of them," Brant said firmly. "It never pays to play God."

"What harm can it do to give them a helping hand? King is certainly smitten with her. And you must admit that marrying Darcy would be the worst mistake of his life."

"That much is certain," Brant said wearily. He lit his pipe and sat down. "I find Miss Howard delightful, and so does your mother. She, too, thinks that King is enamored of Amelia. However,'' he added, staring at his son with the same gray eyes that King had inherited, "from now on, leave things between the two of them alone. You could do severe damage.''

"I don't see how,'' Alan replied with a smile. "You must admit, it could hardly get worse.''

Brant adjusted the pipe between his teeth. "I wonder,'' he said, his voice deep and quiet and thoughtful.

Amelia's father was able to get out of bed the next day and acted as if he'd never felt better.

"It is amazing,'' he told her. "I feel my old self again.'' He smiled, although his eyes were strange. "I shall go to work.''

She hesitated to question him, fearful of inciting him to violence even now.

He turned to look at her. "You should buy some fabric and sew yourself a new frock, Amelia,'' he said unexpectedly. "My word, you look dowdy!''

She cleared her throat. "I . . . there is not sufficient money for luxuries, Father.''

"Nonsense,'' he scoffed. "Have them put it on the account at the dry goods store.''

She wondered if miracles did still happen, because his improvement made her heart lift. "Alan has asked me to eat with his family today,'' she said.

"Then, go, by all means! You know that I approve wholeheartedly of Alan.''

"Thank you. I shall.''

He picked up his hat and cane and gloves, pausing at the doorway. For a moment he was a little unsteady on his feet. "Odd, my head feels light.'' He laughed. "It must be the medicine Dr. Vasquez gave me, you know. It has helped.''

"I am glad."

He turned and looked back at her. He scowled. "I struck you."

Her eyes widened. "Well, yes . . ."

"We must talk, Amelia," he said slowly. "I deeply regret this bad behavior. I am aware that I have not been quite myself, but I begin to feel a substantial improvement."

"I'm glad, Father," she said, and smiled.

He smiled back. "I will see you this evening."

She danced around the parlor when he left, so happy that she could barely stand it. He was better! He realized that he had behaved badly, and he was sorry. Things would change. Life took on new beauty, and she felt radiant. The doctor must have misdiagnosed her father's condition! A man with a deadly tumor wouldn't change back to his old self like this without warning. She felt a sad loss of faith in Dr. Vasquez and at the same time a joy that she could scarcely contain.

Alan noticed her mood immediately and was delighted to see her smile.

"We shall have a lovely day," he informed her. "All the better for the lack of King in it," he added darkly. "He will be visiting the Valverdes."

"You sound as if you're glad."

"Indeed I am," he replied. "He has been . . . difficult lately."

"Because of me," she guessed sadly, and sighed. "Oh, Alan, why does he hate me so? I've never done or said one thing to antagonize him. Well, perhaps just one. I did call him an animal in French."

"You what?" he asked on a shocked laugh.

"I called him an animal. Indeed, there are times when he behaves like one."

"Not King."

"You may think him perfect, but I do not. He's arrogant and rude and unmanageable. Not to mention impatient, irritating . . ."

"Have we time for this diatribe?"

She laughed softly. In her blue suit and white blouse, she looked neat and very elegant. The pert wide-brimmed hat with its blue satin and black veil matched the black frogs that held her jacket together.

"You look very lovely today," he remarked.

"Thank you. My father was much better. He went to work. I feel that the doctor must have been mistaken," she added and then stopped, having given away more than she meant to.

"What did the doctor say?"

"Oh, that it would take much time for Father to improve enough to work," she said quickly. "Alan, are you certain that your parents don't mind my coming out here today?"

"Absolutely. They have to go to a reception for some friends this afternoon, but they will be home long enough to eat with us. They look forward to seeing you."

"You have wonderful parents."

"Not a wonderful brother, though?"

"I met Callaway only once, but I found him nice enough in a very abrasive sort of way," she said, alluding to the middle brother. "He is more like King than you."

"I was talking about my brother King, as you well know."

"I do not like King."

"You seem to find him fascinating enough," he teased. "You can hardly stop looking at him."

She cleared her throat. "It is with the fascination of someone watching a snake to make sure they can move aside fast enough when it strikes."

He burst out laughing. "What a comparison! I shall have to tell King."

"You dare, and I will never speak to you again!" she raged.

"He isn't the monster you make him out to be," he said in a more subdued tone. "In many ways, he's a lonely and sad man. You only know him from a distance. He's much more complex than he appears."

"I do not wish to know him, thank you."

She'd stiffened on the seat beside him. He gave up his efforts in King's behalf and began to talk of the drought and the latest news of the bandit Rodriguez, who had been seen reportedly heading for Juarez with his two brothers and several of his murderous companions.

"Is Rodriguez such a bad man?" Amelia asked seriously. "I've heard rumors that the booty from his raids is given to people in the pueblos, that he keeps nothing for himself."

"I've heard the same rumors. But he has killed men," he added. "In fact, King has reason to want him dead."

"King does?" she asked, curious.

"An old grudge. And in addition to the robberies, Rodriguez is still wanted for several murders which occurred almost ten years ago, including a charge that he killed a man on the outskirts of town and stole his children, spiriting them across the border. One of the children was a young girl. No one knows what happened to her. Some say he killed her."

"One wonders how it is possible to know the truth

about anyone. Gossip and rumor add so many lies to
it."

"This is true."

He drove the buggy down the long road that led to
Latigo, through the fence and up to the front steps.
There were three people standing there. One of them
was King.

"You said . . . !" she began, unnerved.

"He told me he would not be here," Alan said firmly.
"I promise you, he did."

King came forward with his parents. He was wearing
working jeans, without the familiar batwing chaps, and
a blue-checked shirt that made his silver eyes look almost blue. It clung to the muscles of his broad chest,
emphasizing the strength of his arms. His hair was clean
and neatly combed. He was so handsome that Amelia's
heart tried to climb into her throat just at the sight of
him. To disguise her nervousness, she spoke to his parents as Alan escorted her onto the porch and ended by
greeting King without really looking at him.

"I've just put everything on the table. Come along,
Amelia," Enid said with a warm smile.

She moved into the room beside Alan, deeply aware
of King at her back, watching her without saying a
word, his turbulent eyes at odds with his impassive
expression. He seated her, and she found herself much
too close to King, who ended up beside her with Alan
across the table from her.

"How is your father?" Brant asked from the head of
the table.

"He's so much better that I rejoice," Amelia said
with a smile. "He went to work this morning."

"I'm glad for you," Brant said. "You look very nice,
Amelia. Blue suits you."

"It suits King, too," Enid murmured, glancing at her son. "I always think it is one of his best colors."

Her remark drew everyone's attention to the fact that, in colors, Amelia and King matched perfectly. Amelia flushed at the unexpected realization.

"Say grace, Brant," Enid said guiltily, noticing Amelia's discomfort.

Brant led in prayer, and then Enid started the platters and bowls of food around the table. Amelia felt King's powerful thigh against her leg as he moved to take the big ceramic bowl of mashed potatoes from his mother just as she reached for it.

"This is too heavy for you," he said quietly. "I'll hold it while you fill your plate."

She fumbled with the silver spoon and almost dropped it twice before she finished. She looked up into quiet, intense silver eyes that made her breath catch. She dragged her gaze down to her plate with a murmur of thanks.

There was little conversation while they ate. But all the while, Amelia felt the heat from King's body, the strength and vivid presence beside her. He made her heart race whenever he looked at her, and she could hardly hide the feelings he aroused. It was not fair, she thought frantically, that he should do this to her. He must know that she was vulnerable. He was unsettling her deliberately, in another attempt to save Alan from her. If he only knew how little she cared for Alan!

After they ate, the elder Culhanes excused themselves to leave for their social obligation while Rosa worked to clear away the dishes and wash them.

Alan and King went into the parlor with Amelia, but quite suddenly Alan was called away by an urgent question from one of the well-drillers.

"Can't you go?" Alan asked King.

"What do I know about well equipment? You're the drilling expert," he reminded the other man, who had studied engineering.

Alan glanced at Amelia and read the panic in her face. "You can come with me, Amelia."

"Don't be absurd, it's much too hot out there and too rough for a lady," King returned with a lazy smile. "I'll entertain Miss Howard in your absence."

"You were supposed to be lunching with the Valverdes," Alan recalled.

"Darcy has a cold and is unwell, so I decided to stay home." He stuck both hands in his pockets, staring his brother down. "She'll be quite safe," he added firmly.

Alan didn't think so, but he allowed himself to be convinced. After all, he'd secretly gone to the driller early in the morning and asked to be persuaded out to the site. It was all part of his scheme to make King admit his feelings for Amelia. But now that he'd accomplished his end, he was worried. King looked odd. In fact, he looked as if he were plotting something himself. Alan didn't want him to hurt Amelia, and he might in his attempt to prevent what he thought was going to become an engagement between Amelia and his brother. King had a sharp tongue and no scruples to make him pull his punches when he thought he was in the right. He could verbally take the skin off Amelia if he wanted to, and Alan's conscience began to twinge. Of course, he told himself, Rosa was back in the house. Yes. Rosa would be within earshot, and even King would stop short at giving the help something to gossip about.

"It will take an hour or so to ride out there and get back," Alan told Amelia. "You don't mind?"

She shouldn't be such a fool, she told herself. She had nothing to fear from King. Rosa was in the kitchen, rattling pans. "I don't mind, if your brother doesn't."

King only smiled, but his eyes didn't.

Alan remembered that after he changed clothes and mounted his horse to ride out with the driller.

"Mind telling me why I had to invent an emergency for you to handle?" the driller asked Alan pleasantly.

"It's all in the interests of my brother's happiness," Alan returned with a grin. "Never mind my motives. Let's ride."

Amelia fidgeted with her small bag while King lounged idly against the door facing and stood just watching her in a stiff silence. The tension was almost at breaking point when Rosa came into the hall, wrapping her shawl around her thin shoulders. She spoke in Spanish to King, who replied in the same rapid-fire language, and quite fluently.

Amelia's head jerked around at what he'd told Rosa. She was fluent in Spanish herself.

The front door closed, and Amelia got to her feet. "How could you tell her that I wished to be alone with you, to leave us unchaperoned?" she asked nervously. "The impropriety will lead to gossip . . . !"

King turned toward her and moved forward. His silver eyes were intent on her flushed face, and what she read in them made her take a step backward.

"You speak Spanish?" he asked, surprised.

"Yes, I speak Spanish. What are you doing?!"

He took her small bag and tossed it into the chair. Then, with a faint sigh, he pulled her into his arms.

"Do you need to ask, little one?" he murmured quietly. His eyes fell to her mouth, and he bent without hesitation to kiss her startled lips.

It was like flying, Amelia thought dizzily as the kisses grew from tiny nibbles to open-mouthed teasing and then to passionate, hard fervor in the space of a few breathless minutes. She had neither the experience nor the will to resist him. After the weeks of excited infatuation and the growing hunger, it was like a dream come true to be in his arms at last, being kissed as if he could never get enough of her mouth.

When he touched her breasts, she panicked and started to pull away. But he gentled her, teasing her mouth with his, while his fingers lazily explored and tempted her body into relaxing and accepting his caresses. They made her feel funny. Weak-kneed and boneless. Her nipples grew very hard and began to ache for more than his cursory teasing. Her body began to tremble.

When it was that he lifted her and carried her down the hall, she didn't quite know. She was lost in him, aching for more than the feel of his mouth. He took her into a room and kicked the door shut behind them. She knew in the back of her mind that this was wrong, that she should not allow it. But he was very strong, and his kisses were masterful, expert. She was alive only while he held her, while he kissed her. Drowsily, she whispered his name, his given name, against his tender mouth.

"Jeremiah," she moaned.

The bed was under her back, and his powerful body was above her, against her. He kissed her again. His fingers worked at hooks and buttons, and she helped him, because even the light touch of her clothes against her burning skin was unbearable. She wanted the cool air on her breasts. She wanted him to see them.

He lifted his head and held her eyes while he eased

off the jacket and blouse and then the light cotton chemise that was the last covering. His silver eyes glanced down, finding the creamy perfection of her in a silence that was broken only by the faint sounds of birds and wind outside the window.

King touched her breasts then, his fingers lightly exploring, his eyes darkening with passion. "Your skin is very soft," he said quietly. "And your breasts have the silkiness of gardenias."

She gasped at the realization of what she was doing, and her arm started to come up, to cover herself.

He caught her wrist and brought it to his mouth, savoring the faint perfume there. "Do you think I mean to let Alan have you?" he asked roughly, his eyes blazing down into hers. "When I want you so desperately for my own?"

She stared at him blindly. Did he mean, could he mean, that he loved her? Her heart raced madly.

While she was trying to think, his dark head bent and his mouth hovered over a firm, pretty breast, his warm breath teasing it.

"I want you, Amelia," he said. His breath made tiny ripples along her nerves, and she ached suddenly for him to move down, to touch her there. "I want you for myself."

She could bear the torment no longer. In thrall to her senses, she reached up suddenly with trembling hands and tugged at his nape.

"Do you want my mouth on you?" he whispered softly.

"Yes. Oh, yes, please, King, please, King . . . !"

Her frantic little sobs made his body clench with pleasure. He opened his mouth and brushed it very lightly over her, just barely touching her hot skin. She pulled at his head convulsively, but he held back, deliberately tormenting her until she was moaning in anguish. Then, only then, did he allow her to draw him closer, and his warm, moist lips closed slowly over the throbbing tip of her breast and began to work on her flesh.

She cried out and shivered, her nails biting into his nape as she experienced the first sensual touch of her entire life.

King was shocked by her response. His only plan had been to bring her in here and make a little love to her, make her realize that she couldn't marry Alan when she was this attracted to him.

But the feverish response she gave him pushed him over the edge. It had been months since he'd had a woman. His body was starved for fulfillment, and here was Amelia, warm and soft and obviously ready for a lover.

Why should he hold anything back? his body asked his brain. She was playing Alan for a fool, because she didn't love him. She only wanted to marry Alan because he was wealthy and would help her escape from her father's overbearing presence. It would be for Alan's sake, he thought blindly. It would be to save Alan from what King had endured, from the humiliation of loving a woman who only wanted his bank account. It was no more than Amelia deserved, after all.

He gave in to all the rationalizations, realizing as he began to undress her with expert seduction that it all boiled down to the fact that he would die to have her. Protecting Alan didn't matter. Nothing did, except that Amelia's silky warm body was in his arms and trembling with pleasure as he touched it.

"Oh, no, you must . . . not," she wept, but he kept on.

His mouth fed on her softly swollen breasts while his hands eased away the covering under her skirt and touched her silky thighs in an agony of soft sensuality. He touched her where she was a woman, and she wept at the shock and embarrassment and then at the pleasure that made her body tighten all over and tremble.

Her legs parted for him without any coaxing. She held him and sobbed, because her need was as great as his own. She felt him move and even with her eyes closed became aware of the sound of clothing being moved aside. She couldn't look. She didn't want to move, to do anything that might stop the shameful pleasure he was making her feel.

His hair-roughened chest was suddenly against her bare breasts, moving abrasively, making her clutch at him. His mouth settled over hers insistently then, and she felt his powerfully muscled bare, hair-feathered legs between her own. Her eyes flew open, because she realized now what her foolishness had led to, only now, when it was too late.

He was breathing roughly, and the eyes that met hers were silver fires. "That's it," he whispered hoarsely. "Look at me. Look into my eyes . . . as it happens!"

His lean hand caught her thigh in a bruising grip to stay her sudden jerk as he pushed into her with a violent downward motion of his hips.

Her eyes dilated. Her mouth opened. There was burning, tearing pain, and she cried out piteously and tried to get away, but he held her mercilessly with that steely hand and the pressure of his body over hers.

"King, please, no!" she wept.

His teeth were clenched, and his face had gone ruddy.

His eyes blazed as he moved on her in a rough, fierce rhythm. "My God, Amelia," he choked. His eyes closed, and he began to shudder. "Oh . . . sweet . . . Jesus!"

It was reverence, more than profanity, that last startled exclamation. His powerful torso seemed to hang above her as he arched there, his voice breaking, his whole body suddenly convulsed in a rigor like that of a dying man.

Somewhere outside himself he saw his own helpless abandon, the death throes of ecstasy as he spilled himself in her body and suddenly collapsed, suffocating as he continued to shiver from the violence of his fulfillment.

Amelia felt him with shame and degradation. Her eyes closed to shut out the sight of it. Her body felt torn and used, and she wanted nothing more in that moment than to die. The tears slid hotly down her cheeks in silence, while the man lying so still against her slowly began to stop trembling and breathe normally again.

So that was what it felt like, she thought. All the soft words and long, hungry glances and tender kisses, they were nothing but a lie. Here, as in every other way, a man was an animal, a brutal, unfeeling animal who took his pleasure and repaid a woman with pain and debasement. Hadn't she heard her cousin cry and moan in just such a way through the wall at her home? How could she have forgotten!

King couldn't believe what he'd just done. His fall from grace had been sudden and unintentional, but she wasn't going to believe that. All the excuses and apologies in the world wouldn't undo what he'd done. He'd robbed her of her virginity, disgraced her. And now she'd expect marriage, he thought bitterly. Of course she would, because of the risk. He'd been a fool!

He pulled away from her without a word and turned to rearrange his clothing.

She did the same, quickly, with shaking hands, her face wet and her humiliation just beginning.

She got up from the bed on shaky legs. She felt the blood on the inside of her thighs and was only grateful that her outer clothing had been left in place, so that there were no stains on the bed linen to advertise her disgrace.

Moving away from him, her eyes lowered in unbearable shame, she went to the door and started to open it. His big hand slammed down beside hers, preventing her.

"I will not marry you," he said bluntly. "If this bit of seduction was planned toward that end, it has failed miserably. Nor will I allow Alan to marry you. If you attempt to lure him to a minister, I'll tell him what you permitted me to do to you in sordid, glorious detail. Is that understood?"

"Yes," she said in a strangled tone.

He forced himself not to remember how it had happened, that it had been himself, not her, who initiated it, who insisted. He had all but forced her, but he couldn't admit it to himself. He couldn't admit his weakness. It was part of his plan, he told his conscience. He had prevented her from marrying Alan, had that not been his intention all along? If his body had benefited by ending the whip of his hunger for her by satisfying it, then that was only part of his scheme. He had won. Why did he feel so guilty? Was she not a dishonest, dishonorable woman, as all her sex were? And was she not also a spineless woman of pitiful intellect who had the endurance of a hothouse orchid?

"May I leave, please?" she asked in a choked tone.

He hesitated for just an instant before he jerked erect and permitted her to open the door.

She went straight out onto the front porch, too shaken to even remember her bag lying on the sofa. "If you would . . . ask someone to drive me home, please," she whispered wildly. "I would rather not wait for Alan to return, or your . . . your parents."

"As you wish." Her back was as straight as a poker. He turned away before the sight of her stricken face made him feel worse than he already did.

He went down to the stable and spoke to one of the men. He didn't go back up with him when the buggy was ready. He didn't look at Amelia or speak to her. He turned his back and went into the barn to pitch hay to the animals.

She didn't look in his direction. Her body was sore and hurting, and she felt like a lady of the evening. Hysterically, she thought that if her father became very ill, she was now suited for a profession that many women before her had practiced. King had taken her innocence, and no decent man would ever want her now. She was ruined. Disgraced.

"Are you all right, ma'am?" the young cowboy who had been dispatched to drive her asked with concern. She was white and shivering.

"I am very well, thank you," she said. "It is only that I feel a little sick. I must have overeaten."

"Yes, ma'am."

She dried her tears and put a stoic face on it. When she was back in her own house, she quickly threw off her clothes, leaving them on the floor of her room, and went to soak in the bathtub. She stayed there a long time, thinking of what lay ahead. King might very well decide to brag about the experience to his brother or his friends or even his men, she thought hysterically, and laugh at how easily she had given in to him. He might think nothing of adding to her disgrace. He might even tell her father!

Things had been going so well. How could she bear her life now? She had been stupid, stupid!

The water was cold when she finally climbed out of the bathtub and put on her robe. There was a noise out in the hall and then in her room, followed by her father yelling for her.

She wrapped the thick robe closer and opened the door. Her father was standing just inside her room, his face livid. He was staring down at the upended slip and dress she'd worn out to the Culhane ranch. The stains were unmistakable.

But he wasn't looking at them. He was shaking with fury. He looked at Amelia with fury in his whole expression and jerked off his belt. The glazed eyes and white face told their own story. His arm came up and caught her just as she tried to run.

"You slut!" he raged, lifting the belt. "Did you think I would not find out? King Culhane himself came to see me, to tell me that you blatantly offered yourself to him! Do you think any man will marry what he can have for the asking? Alan will never want you now! You have disgraced me! You have disgraced us all!"

Amelia had stopped hearing him when he said that King had gone to him. She didn't care after that what he did. She was numb with shame and anguish. So that was what King thought of her. He hated her enough to do this. . . .

Her father jerked her robe down from the nape of her neck, baring her back, and violently brought the doubled leather belt down on her soft skin with killing force.

Chapter Eleven

A<small>LAN CAME HOME TO FIND</small> K<small>ING JUST UNSADDLING</small> his horse in the barn and Amelia gone. Judging by the look on his elder brother's face, everything had gone wrong. He didn't ask any questions. He left his horse with the cowboy outside the barn and went quickly about his own business without further ado.

The elder Culhanes came home in time for the evening meal, which King barely touched. He sat stiff-faced and brooding throughout, hardly hearing what anyone said. Later, the men went into the parlor to smoke, and Brant reached down into the chair and picked up Amelia's purse.

"Amelia left her purse," Brant murmured, glancing curiously at his sons. "Didn't either of you think to give it to her?"

"King should have. I wasn't here," Alan confessed reluctantly. "I had an emergency at the drilling site. King took her home."

"He did not," Enid said from the doorway, her eyes flashing. "Rosa was sent home, and young Billy Edwards drove Amelia, in tears, back to her house. I want to know what happened here. I want to know, especially, why you did something almost guaranteed to ruin Amelia's good name, King."

"Alan had plans to marry her," he said, staring

coldly at his brother. "I have said repeatedly how I feel about having that featherbrained little coward in my family."

"I shall marry her if I please," Alan said curtly, playing his part to the hilt. King was obviously jealous. It seemed that something had happened while he was away.

But just as he was congratulating himself for making King realize his feelings for Amelia, the smile on King's face grew suddenly triumphant and cruel. "Will you marry her? Even if she was willing to give herself to another man? Which she was, in your absence," King added brutally. "She confessed that she would do anything I asked of her. I sent her home," he said, stopping just short of confessing all that had happened, "and then I went by the bank and had a long talk with her father. There will be no more attempts on his part to throw Amelia into your arms as a prospective wife, I have seen to that. She will not marry you now. Nor will her father dare to speak of marriage after what I said to him."

Alan's conscience exploded, along with his temper. He threw a punch that caught King off guard and actually knocked him down. His parents, horrified at King's behavior, stood quietly by, not saying a word.

"You fool!" Alan raged at him. "You arrogant fool, don't you realize what you've done? Her father is a madman! He will kill her!"

King sat up, fingering his jaw. "You exaggerate," he scoffed, surprised by his brother's fury. "He was upset, certainly, but not murderous."

"I never thought to say this to a son of mine," Brant said angrily, "but I'm deeply ashamed of you, King. You have disgraced us."

"The shame you have caused Amelia is unforgivable," his mother added coldly.

"Indeed," Brant added icily.

"She has no loyalty. She professes to care for Alan, but she offered herself to me!" King said roughly as he got to his feet.

"You have no idea what a victim she really is," Alan told him. He ran a worried hand over his hair. He took her purse from his father's hand. "This will give me an excuse, if I require one. I must get to town!"

"He would not hurt her," Brant began slowly, alarmed by Alan's attitude. "Surely, he would not."

"I had a chance to speak with Dr. Vasquez. Didn't you suspect that her father had already beaten her once, and that he was violent enough to kill in one of his rages?" Alan asked. "And you have driven him to murderous fury. . . . This is my fault. My fault! I am so ashamed!"

He was out the front door running. King stood stockstill, his face white as paper. He recalled Amelia's face when her father was nearby, her irrational fear of the man. Now it all made sense, when it was too late. And he had gone to that brute with his tale of Amelia's weak character. . . .

A minute later, he had his hat in his hand and was rushing out the door after Alan.

It took precious minutes to get into El Paso, and the streets were crowded. Alan reached Amelia's house seconds before King, neither of them sparing their mounts on the way. They didn't even take time to leave the horses at the stable but threw the reins the minute they arrived and ran to the front door.

Alan knocked and knocked again, but there was no

answer. "Oh, God," he groaned, because it was past time for the elder Howard to be home from work, and Amelia would surely be there, in any case.

With a muffled curse, King went around to the side of the house and began looking in through the slitted curtains, room by room. Suddenly he stopped. The sight that met his eyes made him sick.

He ran back around the house. "Get the police!" he yelled to Alan as he made a run at the front door. Pray God he could break it in, because Amelia had been covered with blood. He didn't dare let himself think about her condition beyond that. He knew he couldn't live with himself if she died because of his stupidity. Why hadn't he known?

Alan hadn't argued. He'd gone at once, at a dead run, when King had called to him. Now King went about breaking the lock. It was a heavy door but not bolted, thank God. He gave it one last furious kick, his fear for Amelia spurring him on, and felt it give.

He ran down the hall to the room he'd seen from the outside. The door was open. Her father was shaking from his exertion, slumped over a chair.

"Damn you!" King cursed roundly as he went past the man to kneel beside Amelia. She barely seemed to be breathing at all. Her poor back was covered with blood. It had soaked into her white robe and into the floor rug beneath her, onto the floor. King thought that he'd never seen so much blood in his life. Her face was as white as flour paste, and she was obviously, mercifully, unconscious.

Running footsteps impinged on his anguish. His head turned as Dr. Vasquez and a policeman dressed in a suit and Stetson hat came into the room. The situation took no guesswork at all, because Amelia's father had the belt still clutched in his hand. But he wasn't moving, and his eyes were wide open and unseeing as he laid with his head back against the chair.

Dr. Vasquez went to him first, despite King's demand that he look at Amelia. He listened to Hartwell Howard's chest with his stethoscope, felt the pulse at his neck and, with a heavy sigh, got up to strip a blanket off the bed. He covered the man with it, face and all.

Then he went to Amelia, while the others were reacting to the shock of knowing that Amelia's father had died in the act of his brutality to her.

"A tumor of the brain," Dr. Vasquez murmured as he gently examined Amelia. "You knew, of course?" he asked the two men.

"I suspected," Alan said thinly.

"He grew steadily worse. Dangerously violent, especially to a man with blood pressure which is already very high. I tried to entreat her to go to her relatives or stay elsewhere, but she would not. A very brave young lady, impossibly loyal. And see what it has cost her. He could have killed her or brought on a fatal heart attack for himself at any time, and she knew it, because I made certain she did. Foolish, foolish girl."

"Will she live?" King asked through his teeth.

"She has lost a great deal of blood, and there is the shock of it as well. I want to move her to my surgery, but covertly, you understand." He glanced at the men. "There must be no gossip. She will have to bear the brunt of this if word gets out. Constable, can you think of a way to remove her father without undue attention?"

"I think so," he said. "We'll wait until dark. It is almost that, now. In the morning we'll give a notice to the paper that he passed away peacefully, in his sleep.

We can say that the young lady was exhausted and in shock from the trauma of seeing her father die.''

"Yes," Vasquez nodded. "An eminently practical solution. But she will have to be moved now. Bring me some towels and water in a basin, if you will, and we will see how much damage he has done. I expect there will be scars beneath this latest wounding as well.''

King went for the things the doctor requested, so that he would have a little time to himself. He had never meant this to happen. The pleasure Amelia had given him made him crazy with jealousy over his brother, determined to prevent any marriage between them. He hadn't thought it through, he'd only reacted, and in an unnatural way. Amelia had paid for his stupidity. She might yet pay with her life. He didn't know how he was going to survive the next few days. And if she did live, she would hate him. That was the most damning thought of all.

He took the basin and cloths he'd found back into the bedroom. The doctor made the other men leave while he did what was necessary. He cleaned the deep lacerations and put salve and bandages on them, exchanging Amelia's soiled robe for another that he found hanging in her chifforobe. She would have to be watched all night, he thought. It would be better to have someone care for her here, at home, than to try to keep her in his surgery, where questions about her condition might be prompted. She was still unconscious, too. Apparently her father had struck her hard enough to send her flying headfirst into the bedpost. There was a bruise high up on her temple, and the fact that she was unconscious presented the possibility of concussion. That state was always dangerous. There was something much more damaging to her reputation than this, as well.

When he finished ministering to her wounds, he gathered up her stained, discarded clothing, and parceled it up with the bloodstained robe. At least he could spare her that humiliation.

He called Alan and King back in when he finished. Amelia lay facedown on the bed. Her eyes were still closed, and her breathing looked labored. The smell of blood filled the room.

"There is washing that needs to be done, and any washerwoman is going to carry tales if she sees this," Dr. Vasquez said solemnly. "These things need to be put into a bag, taken out, and burned."

"I'll see to that," Alan said grimly. "And Amelia?"

"She is concussed," the doctor added. "I do not want to take the risk of moving her. She needs to be watched until she regains consciousness, and even then she will need to be under constant supervision for several days. Concussions can be fatal. You must already be aware of this."

"One of my men died of it," King said, feeling hollow and nauseated deep inside.

"As could this lady, I will be frank."

"I'll stay with her," King said quietly.

"And if she wakes up and finds you here, she'll scream the house down, I don't doubt," Alan said venomously.

"I will not leave her," the older man said firmly, his silver eyes flashing. "We can make other plans when we have to."

"Can you be trusted not to do anything further to make her suffer?" Alan demanded icily.

King averted his eyes to the still figure on the bed. He winced. "Yes."

Alan saw the look on his brother's face then and relented. "I'll take care of everything else. It might be as well if I brought Mother here."

"I agree," King said dully. He was barely able to think. Amelia looked so fragile, like a broken doll.

"Let us remove Mr. Howard first," the constable suggested. "It might be more than she can bear, to have to see it all at once."

"I will take my time about getting home," Alan promised.

The doctor left, promising to come back as soon as he'd finished his rounds, because he might be needed. The constable called in the undertaker, who brought two men with a stretcher. They transported Hartwell Howard's still form, under the concealing blanket, out of the house under cover of darkness and over to the mortuary.

The house was quiet then. King had opened the windows to air the room and let the smell out. The floor rug had been rolled up and taken away, too stained and smelly to leave in place. Amelia's stained clothing had been removed by the doctor while he was tending the woman, discreetly added to the bundle of things Alan had removed. But King knew why the garments had been left on the floor, instead of being neatly put away for washing. Amelia had planned to throw them away, to remove them from sight. She hated him for what he had done and wanted no memory of it.

He sat down on the edge of the bed, his hand reaching out to touch the disheveled fall of blond hair that lay unruly on her pale cheek.

"Forgive me, Amelia," he said into the silence. His silver eyes mirrored his guilt and horror. "I did not know."

But she didn't answer. She remained still and silent,

and while he sat with her the spectre of her gentle smile haunted him unendurably. She had been so tender, so giving. Her body, this same broken thing that was so unmoving under the covers, had been all his. Her mouth had pleaded for his, her arms had held him and cradled him. She had been everything he'd ever wanted a woman to be, and he had repaid that loving generosity with treason. Betrayal. His eyes closed. In his mind, he could see that double belt in Hartwell's hand being brought down mercilessly on Amelia's soft, bare back. How could he do that to her? How could he!

All King had wanted was for Hartwell to know that Amelia couldn't marry Alan, and why. He should never have done it. He should have behaved like a gentleman. But when he thought of Amelia married to Alan, he could not contain himself. He simply went crazy with fear. Amelia in his house, married to his brother. It would have been impossible.

He paced the room, trying to fight the images. Amelia in his arms. Amelia begging for his kisses. Amelia, tears on her cheeks as he shamed her. Amelia, cowering under the whip of her father's belt while the blood flowed from her . . . !

He cried out, his hands gripping the windowsill until the knuckles went white. He couldn't live with it, he couldn't!

Vaguely he was aware of the front door opening and footsteps coming up the stairs. He turned just as the bedroom door opened and his mother came in with Alan and Brant.

Alan was subdued, too, all the venom gone out of him. It was like a funeral parlor, King thought absently. Everyone was so quiet, afraid to move too much or speak too loudly.

"Has she come to herself at all?" Enid asked.

King shook his head. His face was heavily lined, his hair mussed where his fingers had run through it time and time again. He looked so unlike his usual vital self that Enid didn't say the words that had been sitting on her tongue all the way into town.

"Tricky things, concussions," Brant said quietly.

"She's got spunk," Alan replied, his eyes on her. "She'll come through it."

King wasn't inclined to agree. She had more courage than he'd dreamed, but he'd given her too much reason to want to die. He'd shamed and disgraced her, and such a woman would have a hard time living with the way she'd yielded to him. At least he hadn't told anyone the truth of how far it had gone. He had given only the impression that Amelia had been prepared to sport with him, not that she in fact had. But even that insinuation was enough to ruin her.

Amelia would know and remember every detail. She'd think of herself as a fallen woman, and she might not want to live.

His face clenched with the thought. Could someone will herself to die? Was it possible? What if she did?

A soft hand shook him. "That won't help," Enid said firmly. "Go and make some coffee."

He hesitated, his silver eyes anguished on Amelia's face.

"Please," his mother emphasized.

"Very well."

He left, reluctantly, and started a fire in the stove. It was like a wake, he thought. A damned wake!

Brant came in while he was filling the coffeepot and sat down at the small kitchen table. "Enid was looking for some clothing in her chifforobe," he remarked quietly. "She found a bundle of books, hidden there probably to keep her father from knowing she had them."

"Dime novels?" King asked without malice.

"Plato, in the original Greek," his father replied, shocking him. "French poetry. Latin hymns. Apparently Quinn has been teaching her. They were imprinted with his name. But there were notations in the columns, not in Quinn's handwriting. She seems to be quite well read."

King pulled two mugs from the china cabinet and put them on the table. His very posture was defeated. "She told me nothing," he said.

"She was probably afraid to," Brant replied. "She wouldn't have trusted you not to tell her father. I can understand now why she found Alan such good company. He was the exact antithesis of her father."

"Yes." That had occurred to King, too. A lot of things had occurred to him.

"Since Quinn lives in barracks, she will have no place to go. Your mother and I want to take her back to Latigo."

"Have you sent for Quinn?" King asked suddenly.

"We sent word to the Ranger post at Alpine, yes." His eyes narrowed worriedly. "You are good friends, but he will not be able to justify the shame that you have caused Amelia, to say nothing of inciting her father to violence against her."

"Do you think I can justify it to myself?" King asked quietly. He moved the boiling coffee to another part of the stove.

"Why?" Brant asked fiercely.

"I was saving my brother from her," he replied. He lifted the coffeepot with a cloth and poured the black liquid into two mugs on the table. "I wanted someone more learned and spirited for Alan."

"Alan has no need of a spirited woman," Brant said, his voice very low. "He is a gentle man. A gentle woman would suit him very well." His dark eyes narrowed. "You wanted her for yourself."

King's hand was momentarily unsteady. He finished filling the mugs and replaced the coffeepot on the stove with slow deliberation. "That does not change the fact that she is ill suited to life on a ranch." He turned, his face pale but composed. "I have chosen a wife with my mind, not my heart. I will marry Darcy, when I marry."

He was totally discounting the fact that he might have made Amelia pregnant during that feverish interlude in his bed. He didn't dare speak of it, even to his father. Better to ignore the fact and hope, pray, that when Amelia recovered, there were no unwanted consequences of his folly. He would be honor-bound to marry her in such a case, and it was the last thing he wanted. He was already vulnerable to her physically. He wanted no more weaknesses to battle. She would recover, and he would find a way to help her go back East to live.

"You must live your life as you see fit," Brant said wearily. "But I would not have Darcy were she the last marriageable woman in Texas."

"As you said, it is my affair."

"Yes."

Brant took a cup of coffee to Enid and Alan and then came back for his own. King didn't go back into the bedroom. He went outside to smoke a cigar.

Alan joined him shortly afterward.

"She's regained consciousness," Alan said quietly.

"Did she speak?" King asked, turning his head toward his brother to listen intently.

"Only to groan. Her wounds are painful."

"Dr. Vasquez promised to return soon. Once he does, Mother can mix some of the sedative that Dr. Vasquez left for her, and perhaps she will go back to sleep," King replied.

Alan nodded. He leaned back against one of the posts, his face solemn. "Despite all these precautions, it is inevitable that there will be gossip. It is as well that we are taking her to Latigo to recover."

King didn't reply. He was thinking about how he was going to bear having the evidence of his cruelty exposed to him day after day.

"I intend to marry her," Alan said suddenly.

King whirled and started to speak, but his brother held up a hand and dared him to.

"I shall marry her," the younger man said again, with some of King's own spirit. "You have disgraced her and the rest of us. I will not allow you to drive her to suicide."

"Suicide . . . !"

"King," Alan said heavily, "did you not notice the lack of evidence that she even tried to defend herself? There are no marks at all on her forearms or her hands, as there would be if she had attempted to shield herself from the blows."

King felt sick all over. He took a deep draw from the cigar, almost smothering himself.

"She knew that her father would not spare her. Perhaps she even hoped that he might inflict enough damage to kill her."

King groaned out loud. The possibilities were tearing at his conscience like knives.

"The gossip will only bring it back. Despite the relative innocence of the situation between you and she,"

Alan added in blissful ignorance of the true circumstances, "the sordid things that people will say will
make her life here hell. At least I can offer her the
protection of my name."

"She does not love you," King said harshly.

"Do you think she loves you?" came the short reply,
and a coldly mocking smile from Alan's lips to accompany it. "Even if she had loved you before, and I think
this possible, she will hate you now."

King was very still. "What do you mean, you think
she loved me?"

"You were blind, were you not?" He folded his arms
across his chest. "She confessed to Quinn once that she
would swoon if you ever smiled at her, as you smiled
so easily at every other woman. She dressed to attract
your attention, but you never looked at her. And just
lately, whenever she was at Latigo, she would shake as
if with a fever when you came close. Her eyes were
always on you. It hurts her to see you with Darcy, and
Darcy knew and made it worse. She taunted Amelia for
her feelings, which were all too evident to everyone
except you."

Of all the revelations that had come out of the terrible
day, this had surely to be the worst. King had refused
to entertain any thoughts about Amelia's reasons for
giving in to him, for allowing him to possess her.

Now, he was faced with the only true reason she could
have had: that she loved him. It was a sobering, sick-
ening thought to have treated her as he had when she
cared for him. It had been novelty enough to have a
woman want him even physically. He was too aware of
his lack of conventional male looks, defensive about his
being wanted only for his wealth. Amelia had wanted
him because she loved him, and he hadn't allowed him-

self to admit it. Now, as Alan said, it was a moot point. Because whatever Amelia had felt for him before, she would certainly hate him now.

He threw the cigar down into the dust and stared at the glowing orange tip with eyes that hardly saw.

"You couldn't help your lack of feelings for her," Alan said to placate him. "I didn't mean to taunt you with something you can't help. But you must realize that Amelia is dear to me. I care for her, as I would a beloved sister."

"That will not be enough," King said through his teeth.

"It will be. She and I have many things in common. We will have a pleasant life together, and, eventually, children will bond us even closer."

King wanted to tell his brother the truth then: that a child was already possible even if not probable. But he couldn't bring himself to make that damning confession on the heels of what he'd already done to Amelia. Besides, he thought, a child was really a very distant possibility. It had been quick and not at all pleasurable on her part at the last, did that not guarantee that there would be no issue from the coupling? He sighed. He wished that he knew more about the mechanics of reproduction. He had to believe that Amelia would be spared that terrible consequence. But to let Alan marry her and not know. . . .

"Alan," he began slowly, reluctantly.

"Alan! King! She's awakening!" Enid called softly from the doorway.

The two men followed their mother upstairs, one with hope, the other with anguish.

Brant was standing by the bed, looking oddly perturbed and preoccupied. He glanced at his sons as if to warn them of something.

King reached her side first. He had to know. If she hated him, he had to see it in her eyes, to take his medicine like a man.

"Amelia?" he said softly, wincing at the pain in that soft, gentle face, in those huge, soulful brown eyes.

She blinked once. Twice. "My back is very sore," she said with some confusion. "It is bandaged. Why?"

"You have . . . had a mishap," King began. "Amelia . . ."

She stared at him with apprehension and curiosity. He stirred something in her that was frightening. But her eyes were very soft, and his knees went weak at the lack of hatred in her face. He felt like dancing around the room, all his fears and misgivings routed in the wonder of her reaction to him. She couldn't hate him and look at him like that, even if there was a little apprehension in her face. His breath caught in his chest, and he was astonished by the surge of joy he felt. It was like nothing he'd ever experienced in his life, all because Amelia wasn't hating him. She was so beautiful, he thought dizzily.

"May I ask a question?" she ventured.

"Of course," he said huskily. "Anything!"

She hesitated. "Who are you?" she asked softly.

Chapter Twelve

QUINN HAD MADE A CAMP MIDWAY BETWEEN DEL Rio and Juarez, beside a small stream in a canyon. The girl was quiet and unresponsive, and he wondered if she was brooding about what he'd shared with her or about the man who'd put her in such a circumstance.

"You're very quiet," he remarked as he worked the tin opener on cans of beans and peaches. The beans he poured into the small black frying pan he carried. The peaches he left until the beans were hot. There was a little hardtack as well. He turned that into the pan with the beans to flavor them. "Are you hungry?"

"*Sí*, I think so," she replied. She pulled the serape he'd given her closer around her slender body. "I was thinking about Manolito and what my papa will do to him when he knows what has happened. I think he will slit Manolito's throat!"

"What does your papa do?" he asked. "Is he a *campesino* or a *haciendado*?"

She laughed. "He is a *bandido*," she said.

He started, and she laughed even more. "Ah, that shocks you, *señor*," she said, nodding. "He will not harm you. In fact, he will be most grateful to you for rescuing me from that foul place. Although," she added worriedly, "you must never tell him what we did together. He would . . . it would hurt him."

"I know. It hurts me," he said heavily. "I have never been with an unwilling woman. I had no idea that you weren't what you seemed to be, or that you had been drugged. I deeply regret it."

"And I," she said. "But all the wishes in the world will not undo it. The Blessed Virgin will forgive us, *señor*. It was Manolito's treachery which will be punished." She crossed herself.

He ran a hand through his thick blond hair and studied her quietly. "Tell me about your papa, Rodriguez?" he asked, deliberately careless.

"He is a good man, *señor*," she said solemnly. "It is not true, many of the things people say of him. He takes care of our people. He feeds and clothes the poor and provides medicines for the sick and milk for the babies. The government lets us starve, and the *haciendados* have no love for us. If it were not for Papa and his brothers, our pueblo would be a place of the dead already."

He stirred the beans. In his pocket, the five-pointed star was uncomfortable. "How did you come to be his daughter?"

"My real father died when I was ten years old," she said, wrapping the serape closer. "I had three little brothers, and my mama was alone. She married again, because there was no money and she had a farm that she could not manage by herself. But the man she married was an animal," she said coldly. "He made my brothers and me into slaves, to do the chores and work on the farm from dawn until dusk. He starved us and beat us, and my littlest brother died. My mama cried, but she did not send him away. And he noticed me." She looked up. "You understand? He . . . noticed me in a way that was not proper."

"I understand," he said gruffly, because he could imagine what she meant, very well.

She flushed. "He had only just sold some livestock and had a little money. He got drunk in the town and bragged of it before he came home. There were some very bad men in the town. They decided to raid the farm and take the money." Her eyes were wistful. "The barn was set alight by these men, and my mama and my oldest brother were killed." She took a deep breath. "These men decided that I would be as much a treasure as the horses they took from my stepfather. They threw me onto a horse and took me away. They took my little brother, also.

"But Rodriguez heard of what these men were doing and knew that he would be blamed for it, because the burning of the barn was his, how do you say, his trademark. So he set out on their trail and caught up with them when they tried to make the safety of the mountains. He hunted them down and killed them."

"Them, and not you," Quinn remarked.

"Not me. I was crying for my mama and worried about my little brother and what would become of him. This big, stocky Mexican man in a wide-brimmed sombrero came over to me, his spurs jingling in the night with the camp fire behind him making him into a giant. He needed a shave, and his face was heavy, and he had this enormous mustache." She smiled. "But he had the kindest eyes I had ever seen, *señor*. He sat down beside me and held my hand and began talking to me in the Spanish language. I understood not one word—*ninguna una palabra*—of what he said. But he sounded so kind. And when I began to cry again, he cradled me in his arms and I wept, there in that warm prison which smelled of horse and smoke. Later, when I was calm,

he brought a man to me who could speak a little English. He explained that I was not to be harmed and
that they were going to take me home with them and
take care of me, and my little brother, also. I did really
cry then, *señor*, because of what I thought would happen to me when they did.''

"Did you tell them what your stepfather was like?"
he asked.

She nodded. "It was embarrassing for me, but I told
them everything. Rodriguez's eyes—I have never seen
eyes burn like that! He turned to his men and said
something, I have only been able to guess at what. Then
he had the man tell me that I would be taken to Malasuerte, in Sonora, and that I would become his daughter
and that no hurt would ever be done to me again. I tried
to tell him about my small brother. He patted my hand
and told me to go to sleep, that all would be well.''

She moved closer to the fire. "I did sleep. When I
awoke, my brother was curled up beside me.'' She
laughed softly. "It was like a miracle! I could not believe my good fortune. I was in the company of bandits,
and I had never been so safe, nor had my little brother.''
She paused. "There is not much more to tell. My stepfather was found dead, along with my mother. I never
asked what circumstances led to this, and I do not want
to know. I mourned my mother, you understand. But
from that day, Rodriguez was my father. He has taken
care of my brother and me, and although we have been
very poor, we have been loved and wanted and
needed.'' She looked at him across the camp fire, her
face soft with love. "Rodriguez is Papa, not only to us,
but to everyone. That is what we call him. *Papa Viejo.*''

"He is old?" Quinn asked slowly.

"Sí," she said. *"Muy viejo.* But he can ride with the

best of the young men, and his aim is straight and true.
He is the world to us. To me, especially. I would do
anything for my papa.'' Her eyes narrowed. ''He will
kill Manolito. I hope he does!''

Quinn grimaced. So it had been the girl's brother he
had taken into Juarez, to the *barrio*. Fate had dealt him
a strange hand. It was a good thing he hadn't told the
boy his real mission in Mexico. And now he couldn't
tell her, either, that he was sworn to bring in Rodriguez
and see him hanged in Texas for his crimes.

''You are troubled,'' she said perceptively. ''Please.
It is not your fault. When you found me in that terrible
place, apparently of my own free will, it was not unexpected what . . . what you must have thought. I do
not blame you for what happened.''

''I blame myself,'' he said shortly. He poured beans
and peaches into a tin plate and handed her that and a
fork.

''It would have been someone else, if not you,'' she
continued, gingerly tasting the hot beans and smiling,
because they were good. ''Perhaps someone less gentle
and concerned for my welfare.''

Quinn felt his cheeks go hot. ''Nevertheless, it should
not have happened.''

''Just the same I will not let Rodriguez harm you,''
she said doggedly. ''These beans are very good, señor.''

''Thanks.'' He made a mental note to hide that star
in his boot before they went any further. It seemed that
he was going to make the acquaintance of the wily Rodriguez. That he would inevitably have to betray this
girl's trust was something he refused to consider.

''What is your name?'' he asked suddenly.

"I was christened Mary, but I am now called Maria," she said softly. "And yours?"

"Quinn," he replied.

"Quinn." Her voice gave it a soft accent. "I like it very much. May I have some more beans?"

He lifted the pan and ladled a spoonful onto her plate. Her face was grimy and lined, and there were dark circles under her eyes. But he thought he'd never seen anyone quite as lovely. He wondered what Amelia would think of her.

King wasn't certain that he'd heard properly. He leaned closer to Amelia. "What did you say?" he asked, aware of the stares of the others behind him in the soft glow of the gaslights.

"I asked who you were," Amelia replied a little drowsily. "My head hurts."

"You don't know me?" he persisted.

She lifted her eyes again and stared straight into his. He had eyes like old silver in candlelight, she thought. He wasn't handsome. He was very tall and fit, though, and she liked the flat-nailed, long-fingered hand that was absently holding one of hers in its dark grasp. He was deeply tanned. Despite the suit he was wearing, he didn't look like a city man. "Are you a cowboy?" she asked.

"In a manner of speaking." His voice sounded odd. "Do you know any of us?" he asked.

She looked past him. There was a handsome blond man with a mustache and dark eyes. There was an older man, also dark-eyed and a little heavier than the younger ones. There was a woman, too, with silver-sprinkled dark hair and dark eyes. The woman looked as worried as the men.

"I'm so sorry," Amelia said gently. "Are you relatives of mine?" She knew that the silver-eyed man wasn't related to her, but she didn't know how she knew it. He made her feel very uncertain and uncomfortable, as if they were linked in some unpleasant way. Funny, to feel like that about a total stranger.

"No, my dear, we aren't relatives," Enid said. She moved forward, displacing King. "How do you feel?"

"Well, I have a headache, and my back seems very sore." She touched the disheveled blond hair around her face. "I feel a bit sick, too." Her hand touched her forehead, and she winced. There was an enormous bump there. "Have I hit my head?" she asked.

"Apparently," Enid said. "Oh, my dear," she groaned.

"Get the doctor," King said to Alan, his face drawn and very nearly white.

"He'll be at Mrs. Sims'. She was delivered of a son this afternoon, one of the ladies at the dry goods store said," Enid offered.

Alan didn't stop to argue. He left, his heart beating madly as he went quickly down the street. As luck would have it, he met the doctor halfway.

"Has she regained consciousness?" Vasquez asked.

"Yes," Alan offered quickly, "but she doesn't know any of us!"

The little man shook his head. "After so many shocks, is it any wonder? The blow to her brain must have damaged her memory."

"Will it come back?" Alan asked.

"*¿Quien sabe, señor?* Who knows? That is up to God, not to any of us."

He and Alan went back to the house and up the stairs. The three people standing near Amelia were quiet and subdued. The doctor ran them all out and began to examine her.

"I'm all right," she insisted. "I seem to be a little addled, but . . ." She stopped, frowning up at him. "My . . . father," she said slowly as her mind tugged at a vague memory. "He was hitting me." She caught her breath. "He was hitting me!"

Dr. Vasquez took her hand and held it tightly. "Your father has died, my dear," he said sadly. "I regret to tell you."

"Died. He has died." She bit her lower lip hard and felt hot tears in her eyes. "Oh, my."

"He had a tumor of the brain," he told her. "I examined him just an hour ago, to be sure of it. It was a very large and malignant tumor," he added solemnly. "Had he lived, the pain would have been unbearable, and nothing would have spared him, or you, its agony. It is God's will, and a true mercy, *señorita*."

She felt the tears running down her cheeks. "I don't remember him. All I remember is that he was hitting me. Why was he hitting me?"

"I do not know." He didn't mention his suspicions. But perhaps he could trick her into telling him, if she remembered. "Had you been somewhere yesterday, *señorita*?" he asked. "With someone?"

She thought and thought. "I . . . I went on a picnic with . . . Alan," she forced her mind to work. "Yes! The blond man . . . that's Alan!" She smiled with relief. "That was Alan. And his mother and father." The smile faded, and she frowned. "The other man . . ." She felt a surge of panic. "I don't remember. I don't remember him. I won't remember him!" She put her hands to her head and squeezed.

The doctor began to understand. "Gently," he said.

"Gently, do not force it. The memory will return when you are ready to face it. Sometimes, the brain hides from us things which are too distressing, you understand? Let it be, *señorita*. Be at peace."

She began to breathe normally. There was a veil, a curtain, and behind it was terror. She didn't want to look. She didn't want to raise the curtain. Her wide, frightened eyes opened and looked into the doctor's. "I don't know him," she said firmly.

"Perhaps it is just as well," he agreed. "Now, I will give you something for the pain, to make you sleep. The Culhanes will take you out to Latigo, where you will be cared for."

"No!" She shivered. "No, I can't go there, I can't . . . !"

"Mrs. Culhane will care for you," he insisted, calming her. "You will be in no danger at all. None whatsoever. Your brother is being sent for. Do you remember your brother?"

"Brother. Quinn." Her mind pictured a tall, strong man with thick blond hair and dark eyes in a lean face. Her brother Quinn. She smiled. "Oh, yes!"

"I am sure they will find him quickly. It will do you good to have a member of your own family here."

"My father," she said hesitantly. "The funeral."

"It will be arranged, but you must not go," he told her firmly. "You are in no condition, *señorita*, *lo siento*. I will make certain that it is understood by all that the shock of your father's sudden death has caused a collapse."

She understood even through the fog in her brain. "God bless you, *señor*," she said gently.

"And you."

He stood up, fastening his bag. "I will check on you

in the morning before you are moved to Latigo. *Buenas noches.*"

"Thank you."

He smiled. *"De nada."*

He went out and closed the door, facing three anxious sets of eyes.

"She has partially regained her memory," he told them. "I have told her that she must not attend her father's funeral, and it will be in her best interests to remove her from this house at the earliest possible moment."

"We'll hire a carriage and take her out to Latigo first thing tomorrow," Brant said firmly. "You said that she's partially regained her memory. What does she remember?"

"Very little. Being hit by her father and his collapse. And she remembers her brother and the three of you."

"And me?" King asked, joining them with a brandy snifter in one lean hand, his face set in lines none of the others had seen there since Alice's tragic death. "Does she remember me?"

The doctor glanced worriedly from the others back to King. "No," he said. He suspected that Amelia did remember, but she was determined not to admit it. Her fear of this man was not a physical one, but that made it no less damaging to her recovery. If it helped her to pretend that she didn't know him, the doctor wasn't going to give her away.

King was silent. He took a sip of the brandy and stared into it with eyes that didn't see.

"Is it temporary, her loss of memory?" Enid persisted.

"I do not know," the doctor replied gently. "These head injuries, *señora*, can be very unpredictable. She has some nausea and a headache, and she must be carefully watched. You must send for me if there is any change. I have given her only a light sedative, but she must not be left alone."

"I'll sit with her," Enid said.

"So will I," Alan volunteered. "She won't be alone for a minute."

King was swirling the brandy in his glass, not looking at anyone, while the doctor quietly outlined the necessary care and his prognosis. King was now the only one who knew what had happened the day before in his bedroom. Amelia herself didn't know that she could be pregnant, and neither did anyone else. That burden was his alone, and he might have to bear it for life. If her memory didn't come back, what then? Could he allow her to marry his brother when she might be carrying his child without being aware of it?

The doctor was speaking to him, and he hadn't even heard. Nor had he realized that he was alone in the hall. His family had gone back into the room with Amelia.

"What?" he asked the little man dimly.

"Come with me, please."

The doctor went downstairs into the parlor, waiting for King, and closed the door behind him. The little man's dark eyes were vaguely accusing.

"You must answer a question for me which I cannot, dare not, ask in front of the others. She was not only beaten. On her underclothes was the unmistakable evidence that she had experienced sexual intercourse very recently. Did her father rape her?"

"Of all the sordid accusations . . . !" King exploded.

"Are you naïve enough not to believe it happens?" Vasquez asked quietly. "*Señor*, if you only knew the things I have seen. I must know about her condition. If she has been raped, there is the possibility of a child. I know of a way to terminate it. There are herbs I can give to her without her knowledge, you understand, to expel the baby, if this is the case.''

King was shocked. He stared at the doctor, feeling sick all over. Kill the baby. That was what he was proposing to do. He was proposing to give her an herb, like those used by women in the back streets of town who slept with men for money. Any madam knew how to get rid of an unwanted baby. But if Amelia became pregnant, it would be with his child. His own flesh and blood.

His white face spoke volumes. The doctor stared at him without speaking for a long moment. ''You have known her intimately,'' he said to King.

The younger man slowly nodded. He averted his eyes. ''It was not her fault,'' he said gruffly. ''I seduced her.''

''And she does not remember.''

King threw down a swallow of brandy and grimaced as it stung the back of his throat and then began to warm him all the way down. ''No. She does not remember.''

''What do you want me to do?''

King didn't know what he wanted to do. He took a deep breath. ''I do not want you to do anything.''

''And if there is a child?''

King looked up, his silver eyes stormy. ''It will be mine. And the responsibility for all of it. Just as the crime was mine.''

''You do not love her?''

''Of course I do not love her,'' King denied violently, averting his eyes with a cold laugh. ''She is everything I detest most in a woman.''

"But she loves you."

King turned around and went back to the brandy snifter. "She did," he said. "Not anymore." He filled the snifter and snapped the top back on the crystal decanter. He moved back to face the smaller man. "You know, don't you, Vasquez?" he drawled. "You've reasoned it out. I didn't want her to marry my brother. So I seduced her and told her father what she'd let me do, and he beat her nearly to death. The violence caused his own death. Well, I don't need you to recount my sins," he added fiercely. "I'm all too aware that I've tried to play God here. Ironic, isn't it, that the only other person who knows what really happened is Amelia, and she doesn't remember. I should be happy, because she can't accuse me of my crimes." His face hardened. "Perhaps that's to be my hell. I have to watch her and wonder if I've given her a child, while she walks around in blissful ignorance of it."

"What will you do if it happens?"

"I'll marry her, of course," King said. "I'm not totally without honor."

"If you do not love her, to marry her would be an act without honor."

King stared at him. That was all. He simply stared at him with steady silver eyes that were as dangerous as a pointed gun.

Vasquez shrugged. "I will keep a close watch on her," he said. "If she is in a delicate condition, I will know it."

"Don't . . . don't do anything," King said, lowering his voice.

"In good conscience, I could not, unless the child was conceived of incest." His face hardened. "In that one case, *señor*, I would act without conscience."

"Her father had a tumor, you say?"

"A malignant tumor. It is truly a kindness that he died. In the end, he would have killed Amelia. Her loyalty to him would have meant her death." He left King with a curt nod of his head.

King stayed in the parlor drinking brandy until his mind began to go numb. The doctor spoke of mercies, but a numb brain had to be the best one right now. He couldn't, didn't dare, think about what he'd done to Amelia. If he did, he'd go mad.

He sat down in her father's wing chair and drank until there wasn't one thought left in his head.

The snifter in his limp hand fell onto the floor rug and made a dull thud. King lay back with a heavy, relaxed sigh, his body boneless, like his mind.

A few minutes after midnight, Enid came downstairs to check the fire in the parlor. She saw her son sitting there and instantly connected his slumped posture with the empty brandy decanter and the equally empty glass beside his chair.

With a sad smile, she found a bearskin carriage blanket folded on a chair near the door. She draped it gently over him, watching his eyelids flicker.

He was taking it very badly. She knew that he felt something for Amelia, even if he wasn't quite sure what it was. The fact that she remembered everyone except him was, she was sure, the worst of it. He was tormented, and she was sorry for some of the things she'd said to him. Well, time would heal Amelia's memory and her wounds, and perhaps it would do the same for King's conscience.

Chapter Thirteen

AMELIA WAS TAKEN IN A CARRIAGE OUT TO LATIGO the next morning. Word had come that Quinn still hadn't been located, although he had been seen in Del Rio. Hartwell Howard lay in quiet repose in the mortuary. He would be buried tomorrow, whether or not Quinn was found, because they could not leave him lying in state indefinitely.

Although Amelia had wanted to see her father, the doctor and the Culhanes had not allowed it. She was weak and disoriented, and they felt that she had had enough shocks already. For the same reason they told her nothing about the funeral arrangements. Her head was giving her so much pain that she was hardly able to think at all.

King went back to Latigo alone, refusing to accompany the carriage. Amelia wouldn't even look at him now. They said that her memory of him hadn't returned, but he wasn't sure of it. The one time he'd caught her eyes, they had been evasive and wounded. He couldn't bear the hurt they dealt him, so he rode on alone. If Quinn wasn't found today, he decided, he'd go and look for him on his own. It would spare him Amelia's contempt, if nothing more.

Alan and his mother sat with Amelia in the back of the carriage while Brant drove. The dust was bad, and

194

she felt less than well. Her head was pounding by the time they reached Latigo. Amelia didn't remember exactly why it should disturb her so much to see the ranch house, but she was disquieted by just the look of it. She remembered coming here with Alan. She remembered the belt in her father's hand. Why couldn't she remember what had happened in between? And why did it upset her to look at King?

Alan helped her down from the carriage. He wanted to carry her inside, but she would have none of that.

"I'm quite fit, really," she assured him with a wan smile. "Just let me hold on to your arm, please, Alan." She hesitated at the front door, though, turning to Enid with big, worried eyes. "I'm imposing on you," she said. "And your other son doesn't want me here. He's very polite, but his eyes wish me far away every time he looks at me. I mustn't stay for long. . . ."

"My dear," Enid said worriedly. "King would never presume to say who we may have as our guests. But he isn't wishing you away. He's as concerned for your well-being as we are ourselves."

Amelia didn't believe that, but she didn't argue. She allowed herself to be shepherded down the long, wide hall to a guest room. It looked familiar, but it was another room they had passed that caused her some inner distress. She was careful to keep it hidden, because she had no idea why a room should upset her. So many things did, in very odd ways.

Enid and the pretty Mexican Rosa unpacked Amelia's sparsely occupied bags and filled two drawers and only a small part of the chifforobe with them. They didn't say anything to the girl in the four-poster, but they exchanged speaking glances over her pitiful few clothes.

King didn't come home that afternoon, and Alan

didn't feel right about sitting in Amelia's bedroom. Despite the circumstances, it was a bit unconventional, with Amelia in her nightclothes. Enid sat with her until she fell asleep, and then she went into the kitchen to cook supper.

She and Rosa were talking about Amelia's wardrobe when a weary, dusty King came in the back door.

"You were expected much sooner," Enid told him.

"I got tied up," he countered coolly. He hung up his hat and washed his hands in the sink at the hand-pump. He dried them on a cloth and turned to face his mother. "What was that about Amelia's clothes?"

"Rosa and I were merely remarking that she hardly has any," Enid said as she made biscuits. "And the few in her chifforobe were badly worn and patched. Yet her father had several new suits of clothing."

"He called her frivolous," King recalled, frowning.

"Indeed he did." Enid finished rolling the biscuits into the pan and washed her own hands at the sink. Flour turned the water in the wash pan white. "Hang the bread tray up for me, will you please, Rosa?" she asked the Mexican woman, nodding to it.

"How is she?" King asked after a minute.

"Her headache has not passed," she replied. "And she is not very pleased to be here." She looked up at her tall son. "She says that you make her feel unwelcome."

He stared at his mother impassively. "Do you expect me to pretend that I want her here?"

Enid took him by the arms and shook him. "This isn't like you," she said curtly. "When you were a boy, you were forever bringing me hurt animals to bandage or strays to be taken in. Yet here is Amelia, who has been beaten within an inch of her life, who has seen her father die in front of her very eyes, and you have no feeling for her whatsoever!''

He moved away from her, her face no softer than the table upon which the pan of biscuits was setting. ''I'm sorry for her, of course,'' he told his mother, vaguely ashamed as he realized that his attitude had made things even harder for Amelia.

''She won't be here for very long,'' Enid added quietly. ''She has mentioned a cousin and we intend to contact her. The house will have to be sold, and Quinn lives in barracks. He lacks the financial resources for a house.''

King felt his stomach contract with fear. If Amelia were sent away and found herself with child, how would he know? She might not regain her memory, in which case she would have no idea of the circumstances behind her pregnancy. She wouldn't dream of writing to him about it, because she wouldn't know that the child was his!

''Well, we needn't settle it tonight,'' Enid was saying, curious about the look on his face. ''I'll fix a tray for Amelia. She won't be well enough to join us at the table.''

King didn't reply. He joined the men in the parlor, preoccupied and withdrawn while they talked of business matters.

''Quinn has still not been found,'' Brant added after a few minutes. ''I have no idea how to inform him of his father's death. I had a wire from the post in Alpine that he was on the trail of the bandit Rodriguez down in Mexico, and they have been unable to locate him. We can hardly keep the body lying in state for the rest of the month. Hartwell must be given a Christian burial as soon as possible and his business affairs concluded.

Amelia is in no condition to deal with it, and I know almost nothing of Hartwell's business.''

''If Quinn hasn't been found by tomorrow afternoon, the funeral must be conducted without him,'' King said. ''I could ride down to Mexico and backtrack him from Del Rio. Perhaps I can find him.''

''Mexico is a big country,'' Alan remarked, ''and Rodriguez has been known to attack lone travelers near the border. We do not need another tragedy.''

King gave his brother a vicious look. ''I'm well aware of that,'' he said curtly.

''Enid thinks that Amelia will be better off back East, did she tell you?'' Brant asked directly.

''Yes. I disagree,'' King said, his deep voice short. ''She and her cousin aren't close. She has no business in a home where she is barely tolerated, especially in her present state.''

The other men gave him curious looks. ''You are the one barely tolerating her here, are you not?'' his father remarked gently.

''I may not find her company stimulating, but at least she won't be maltreated here.''

''Except by you,'' Alan said coldly.

King's teeth clenched, and his silver eyes began to glitter. ''I have not maltreated her.''

''Not in the past twenty-four hours,'' Alan agreed, ''but I remember how she came to be in her present situation. And I think she may be anxious to leave this place when she regains her memory and gets a good look at you!''

King took a step forward, which Brant quickly blocked, inserting himself between his two hotheaded sons. ''Stop it,'' he told King. ''This is neither the time nor place for more violence. Try to think of your mother. She has had a difficult time herself.''

Alan shifted and straightened his suit jacket. ''As you say,'' he replied. But he was still glaring at King.

Enid came to the doorway before the older son could speak, a tray in her hands. ''I have Amelia's supper,'' she announced. ''I'm taking it to her. The rest of you can sit down. I won't be long.''

The atmosphere relaxed a little. She was aware of the confrontation she had interrupted, and she worried about how much worse the situation would get. Alan blamed King for Amelia's condition. King probably blamed himself as well, which would explain why he was so defensive when her condition was mentioned. Enid felt sorry for him. Her eldest had never learned to bend at all.

She knocked perfunctorily on Amelia's door and walked in. The younger woman had just opened her eyes. She blinked, trying to focus on her visitor, and then she smiled drowsily.

''I have been asleep,'' she murmured.

''Indeed. Sleep is the best thing for you. Sit up, my dear, and try to eat a little something. I have soup and corn bread for you.''

''You're very kind to me,'' Amelia said. Her long, blond hair was down over her shoulders in braids, to keep it from tangling, and the white lace of her gown, worn as it was, made a beautiful frame for her pretty neck.

''It is easy to be kind to someone as gentle as you, Amelia,'' Enid said softly. ''Here.'' She helped Amelia prop up on pillows against the headboard and then slid the tray onto her lap. ''You look very pale. Shall I mix you another of the headache powders?''

"After I eat, yes, please," Amelia said. "My head throbs so."

"You have a dreadful bruise," Enid said sympathetically. She touched the swelling and winced. "Is it terribly painful?"

"Not at all," Amelia said. "It is just the headache which accompanies it. I shall be better tomorrow." She hesitated with the spoon in the soup and looked at Enid. "My . . . father. When is the funeral to be? And has my brother been told?"

"We have not been able to find Quinn, who is on assignment down in Mexico. The funeral will be tomorrow. And no," she said gently, "you must not try to go. You are simply not able. The doctor will have explained to those whose opinions matter why you cannot attend."

"What a horrible situation," Amelia said sadly. Her eyes closed, and she shivered weakly. "What must I have done to cause my father to react so violently that he would treat me thus?"

"Your father had a tumor of the brain," Enid said quickly. "It was nothing that you did."

Amelia's big, dark eyes were tragic. "But it must have been, do you not see? Why would he have struck me, unless I had committed some terrible sin? And why can I not remember what it was?" she added huskily. "I remember that I came here with Alan for a picnic. Then I remember my father striking me with the belt. But I can remember nothing, nothing, of what happened in between! Does Alan know?" she added hopefully. "Can he tell me?"

"Alan did not see you after you went home," Enid said evasively. "I am sorry. He knows nothing."

"Then it must have been something that happened

when I returned home but before my father was finished for the day at his job," she puzzled, frowning. "Perhaps my father said something to someone at the bank. I will ask when I am better."

"Yes, dear," Enid said slowly, "you may do that, certainly." Even as she said it, she was already thinking of ways to prevent Amelia from doing it. She must not connect her tragedy with King until she was better and able to cope with it. She was weak and sick and helpless now and needed time to get better.

"This soup is so good," Amelia said, as she sipped it from the spoon. "Oh, but you are good to me!"

"You eat that right up," the older woman said, moving away from the bed, "and I will be back to collect the tray."

She went back into the dining room, where the others were already seated. She took her place and kept her thoughts to herself while they ate.

"Is she eating?" Alan asked.

Enid smiled. "Yes. She likes the soup." She looked from Alan to the taciturn, silver-eyed man across the table from him. "She cannot remember what happened between the time she left here and her father beating her," she said suddenly. "Don't say anything that might jar her memory. She must not be worried with anything else on the heels of her father's death."

"I had no intention of saying anything to upset her," Alan said quietly. He glared at King. "My brother more than likely cannot say the same . . . !"

King's eyes stabbed at him. "That's quite enough," he said curtly.

"She might have died, damn you!" Alan said huskily.

King knew that and was tortured by it. He threw down

his napkin and got up, striding out of the room without a backward glance. He went out the front door, slamming it behind him.

"You must stop this," Enid told Alan, and her husband echoed the thought. "Alan, can't you see that King is cut up inside and hiding it in bad humor?"

Alan couldn't. But his mother's soft question brought him to his senses. "Perhaps I overreacted," he confessed. "But he has been so cruel to her."

"He knows it and will have to live with it," Brant said. "Let him be."

King mounted his horse and rode toward the Valverde estate, his hat cocked over one eye and a smoking cigar in his hand. He didn't take time to change clothes. He had to get away from the accusations, from the sight of Amelia in that bed, from the memories. He urged the horse into a trot and followed the long trail from the ranch without turning his head in either direction. Darcy would make him feel better, he told himself. Darcy would help him forget. She was going to be his wife. She might as well start being a comfort to him now.

But she was in a foul humor when he arrived at the Valverde ranch. The maid had ironed one of her best dresses and burned the lace. She struck the poor woman and screamed abuse at her, with King standing stoically in the doorway. He hadn't seen Darcy act this way before, and it startled him to find her so venomous. His mother had never struck a servant.

"Fool!" Darcy muttered, fingering the lace. She glanced at King, and her full lips pouted. "See what she did? It was my prettiest dress. I was going to wear it just for you, my dear." She moved close to him and peered up through her lashes with a teasing smile.

"Would you like to kiss me? Mama and Papa have gone visiting, and I am on my own. It is quite all right if you do. After all, we are very nearly engaged, are we not?"

Until he heard her say the words, he had tried to pretend that they were. But the thought of living the rest of his life with Darcy made him choke. He looked at her and for the first time saw her as she really was. She had eyes like a snake, he thought idly. She was selfish and cold, unless she could profit by being affectionate. She had no patience with what she considered incompetence, and she was vindictive. Her beauty was a poor match for her personality.

"No, we aren't engaged," he replied quietly.

Her eyebrows arched. "I beg your pardon?"

He was not himself. He could not reconcile his feelings, and Darcy was confusing him even more. "I can't talk about it now. We have a houseguest," he said wearily. "Amelia Howard's father died of a brain tumor last evening, and she's staying with us, because she has nowhere else to go. We can't find Quinn."

"Mr. Howard is dead? I am so sorry," Darcy said formally. "Amelia is doing poorly?"

"She collapsed from the shock of it," he lied. "He died in front of her eyes." That much, at least, was not a lie.

"Poor thing. I shall have to pay a call on her tomorrow. Is this why you came, to tell me about Mr. Howard?"

"Yes," he said abruptly.

"And to get away from Miss Howard, I expect, if she is in residence," she guessed coyly. "I am aware of your contempt for her."

King didn't reply. He was feeling not at all himself. He wondered why he'd ever come here. Comfort was the last thing he was going to get from Darcy, unless he paid for it. "I have to get back," he said.

"Please tell your mother to expect me tomorrow afternoon. I will only stay for a few minutes. You haven't forgotten that I invited you to a dinner party in town at the Sutton House at six?"

"I haven't forgotten."

"Senator Forbes will be present with his wife. The good offices of a superior politician are always of value," she reminded him.

King couldn't have cared less about being in the good graces of a politician. But this was something Darcy set great store by.

"I'll see you tomorrow, then," he replied. He bent to kiss her cheek with cool lips. "Good evening."

She frowned. He was acting totally unlike himself. The old King was more forceful, less reserved. Tonight he was preoccupied and out of humor, and when she had mentioned their upcoming engagement, he'd acted as if the subject had never been approached. She would have to play up to him more. For her family's sake, she couldn't afford to lose the Culhane fortune.

King rode back to Latigo slowly, his mind on Amelia and what to do about her. If her memory didn't return, things could become complicated indeed. And he didn't dare think of marrying Darcy when another woman could even now be carrying his child. Honor sometimes demanded much of a man. He could hardly deny that the entire terrible situation was his own fault. He had brought it on Amelia, and on himself. Now he had to cope as best he could. But pray God, let her not be pregnant, he thought. That would lock them both into a prison from which there would be no escape.

* * *

Across the border, Quinn was escorting his lovely companion into the small town of Malasuerte. It was, like most Mexican pueblos, very poor and without much more than a fountain and a mission. The people glanced at him from their dirt-floored huts with the thatched roofs, some smiling, some not. Gringos were viewed with suspicion here.

"My papa will be happy to see me and grateful to you for bringing me home," she said warmly, smiling at Quinn from her blue, blue eyes.

"Until he learns what I've done to you," he murmured ruefully.

"I will not tell him," Maria said firmly. "And neither will you. It is between us, as you said."

He only nodded. But inside, he was worried. Her papa was Rodriguez. Whatever his personal feelings, he had to bring the man in. It would be difficult to get Rodriguez extradited, too, because he had friends in government here. The best way, the only way, would be to tie him over a saddle and take him out by night over the Rio Grande. That, too, would be difficult. He was a Ranger. But he was also one man, and Rodriguez had many, many friends.

Besides, Maria appealed to him. She had courage, and she was beautiful. Quinn found himself drawn to her more and more. He didn't want to hurt her by arresting her father.

He stopped his horse in front of the small hut where the girl indicated she lived and helped her to the ground. She felt light and warm in his arms, and he smiled at the way she made him feel inside. She was very pretty. She made him feel like a man, in a way no other woman had.

"It will be all right," she whispered, smiling back at him. "You do not need to be afraid of my papa."

"That was the last thought in my mind."

"Then what, *señor*, was the first?"

"That I should like very much to kiss you," he replied. "You are very lovely."

She lowered her eyes shyly. "You must put me down. This is not a good way to meet my papa."

"So there you are," a deep, accented voice came from the doorway. "Praise the saints, you are all right!"

Quinn turned, and there was the man himself, the bandit Rodriguez.

══ Chapter Fourteen ══

KING WAS UP BEFORE THE REST OF THE FAMILY THE next morning. He stopped by Amelia's room, opening the door very slowly, so as to not awaken her.

She lay quietly under the covers, her pale cheek against the white pillowcase, her eyes closed. He stood by the bed, scowling down at her. This woman had aroused more violent emotions in him than any woman he'd ever known. He couldn't imagine why he despised her so, when the rest of his family seemed to adore her. It was a bad time indeed to remember how she felt without her clothing, the joy of her body in an intimate embrace, the yielding soft response of her mouth to his rough kisses.

She stirred unexpectedly, and her eyes opened. They were dark and soft as they sought out his face. She frowned as if trying to focus.

"How are you?" he asked stiffly.

She touched her head. She was still disoriented, confused. It disturbed her to be in here with him, to see him, even to hear his deep, slow voice. She pulled the covers closer.

"I am . . . very well, thank you," she said faintly. She frowned more, as turmoil grew inside her.

King understood, as she did not, the uneasiness that showed in her face.

"What do you remember?" he asked bluntly.

She gnawed unconsciously at her lower lip, trying to focus one of the wild thoughts whirling around in her mind. "I remember . . . the picnic. Alan took me on a picnic. And then my father . . . my father hit me."

His face lost all expression. Only his eyes were alive in it. "What else?" he persisted.

She touched her forehead and winced. "I don't know. . . . I can't remember . . . anything else. My head hurts!"

He wanted to pick her up and shake her, to make her remember what she had permitted him to do. It was she, not himself, who was to blame. Was that why she fought the memory?

She saw his eyes, and her whole body tensed under the covers. Fear grew in her soft face, in her eyes. "Please go away," she said stiffly.

"Fear," he scoffed. "You are full of it!"

Her nails bit into the cover. "Only when I see you!" Her dark eyes were accusing. "You have . . . hurt me . . . in some way! I do not remember how, or when, or even what, but I know that you are my enemy!"

Her eyes were huge, and he was almost overcome by sudden guilt.

"And you are mine," he said heavily. "They all feel sorry for you. My own family has turned against me, because of you!"

"Indeed?" she asked. "It is only because of me that they have found fault with you, Mr. Culhane? What a shocking person I must be, to bring out such sad qualities in you."

His eyebrows lifted in surprise at her tone. It was mocking, and what he'd mistaken for fear in those dark eyes was something much more astonishing. "I hardly think my faults are any of your business."

"That is so, thank goodness," she agreed readily, and with a cool smile. "Your mother has mentioned that you may see fit to marry the daughter of a neighbor, and I will certainly remember her in my prayers. Marrying you, she will have need of divine support!"

He didn't seem to move. When he finally realized what she'd said, his silver eyes went molten. "So will you, Miss Howard, if you continue to toss insults at me. I find it frankly surprising that a mealymouthed opportunist such as yourself . . . !"

He broke off, because she threw a carafe of water at him in midspate, her eyes flashing. He sidestepped in the nick of time, but the carafe splintered noisily against the wall just past his shoulder and crashed water and glass onto the floor at his feet.

"You get out of here!" she said fiercely, sitting up in bed to glare at him, despite her throbbing headache. "I had to put up with my poor father's tempers, because to provoke them might kill him, but you are not fatally infirm! Not yet, at least!" she added darkly, looking around for something else to throw.

King moved back to the doorway and stood there, astonished, as he registered the sudden change in their houseguest. Perhaps she was still concussed.

"Amelia? Are you all right?" Enid asked, ducking past King into the room as she glared at her son.

"Is she all right?" King exploded. "My God, she threw a pitcher of water at me! She could have knocked me out with the damned thing!"

"Stop cursing, please, and what did you say to her to warrant such a violent response?" his mother wanted to know.

King glowered at her and then at Amelia. "She's not herself."

"Oh, but I am," Amelia shot back, her dark eyes glittering at him. "You just didn't know me, dear man. Now will you please leave? Why don't you go and serenade your loved one with those invectives?"

"It can wait," he drawled. "In fact, she's coming here this afternoon to see you."

"I can hardly contain my impatience," Amelia said haughtily. "Does she arrive by carriage or broom handle?"

King stepped forward, but Enid put a hand on his chest and pushed. "Out," she said.

"I will not have . . ." he began hotly.

"Out!" Enid repeated. She pushed him through the door and shut it. Then she collapsed back against it in laughter.

Amelia shifted irritably against the headboard. "The arrogant, unfeeling, contemptuous *beast!*" she raised her voice, hoping King could hear her. "How dare he walk in here without my permission?"

There was a rough curse outside the door, followed by the sound of angry footsteps going back down the hall.

"My dear," Enid said, recovering, "how lovely to see you so . . . changed!"

"I am changed for the worse I fear." Amelia pushed back her hair and laid against the pillows with a long sigh. "I feel a little wobbly, but I shall improve. Your son said his fiancée was coming to see me. I do not wish to have company." She looked at Enid warily. "Do you mind?"

The older woman beamed. "Not at all," Enid murmured wickedly. "I shall convey your regrets to Miss Valverde."

King was on the porch with his father, apparently having given the older man a replay of what had happened, because King was glaring daggers at his father. Brant was doubled up with laughter.

Enid joined them, casting a mischievous glance at her son. "You will have to explain to your fiancée," she stressed the word, "that Miss Howard is indisposed and unable to receive guests."

"She'll be indisposed if she flings anything else at my head," he promised hotly.

"Did she really do that?" Brant asked, recovering. "I can't believe it!"

"Obviously, she knew of her father's condition and acted as she did only to placate and calm him," Enid told the men. "Quinn never mentioned Miss Howard being particularly docile, and I have heard of some of her exploits, especially when her younger brothers were still alive. Their deaths and her mother's, and her father's accident before his violent tendencies appeared— all of it must have been very difficult for her. I don't doubt that it made her docile, for a time." She glanced at King. "Not anymore, of course. If I were you, I should be more careful about how I addressed her in future. I have every intention of providing her with a replacement carafe."

She smiled at her husband and went back into the house.

Brant watched his son, correctly assessing the conflicting emotions on the younger man's dark, lean face.

"I didn't know she had it in her," King murmured

reflectively. He lit a cigar and glanced at his father with a rueful smile. "I suppose you think I deserved it."

"Indeed I do," came the instant reply.

King sighed. "Perhaps I did." His silver eyes twinkled. "What a temper!"

"A woman without one would be a poor choice for you." He saw the flicker in his son's eyes and nodded. "As you knew already, I gather?"

King moved away. "I have some chores to finish before Darcy arrives. She won't be happy about making an unnecessary trip."

Which was an understatement. When Darcy alighted from her buggy only to be told that Amelia had suffered a slight relapse and couldn't have company, she exploded.

"What nonsense, letting me come all this way for nothing!" she raged.

Brant and Alan had left the house to escape her tirade, but Enid was trapped with King while the young woman vented her spleen.

"I'm certain that Amelia didn't have a headache to spite you, Darcy," Enid said with faint malice. "And I hardly think your behavior is any credit to your parents. Please give them my regards. I'm sorry that you have to leave so quickly."

Enid got up before Darcy could backtrack over her behavior and left the room, but not before giving King a speaking look that conveyed her opinion of his intended.

"And now she's got her tail feathers in a tangle, hasn't she?" Darcy demanded petulantly as she stomped out to the porch. "Take me home!"

King took her arm and pulled her around, not too

gently. "My mother is not a hen. And your behavior leaves much to be desired, indeed!"

He went off to the barn to get her buggy and his horse, leaving her to steam on the porch and remember how badly she wanted to be Mrs. King Culhane. By the time he returned, she was in a better mood and playing up to him all over again.

Amelia heard the commotion as Darcy left. She was sorry for causing Enid any trouble, but she was delighted that she'd managed to throw King off balance.

Apparently he hadn't realized that she'd only been deferring to her father, not because she was that afraid of him but because she didn't want to make him any worse. She still didn't understand what had caused his last, fatal outburst, but at least he was at peace now, and she could go on with her life. She had no intention of going on with it as she'd had to for the past four years. No man was going to keep her subdued ever again, least of all *that* man!

Enid visited her several minutes later. "Darcy is gone. She had King go home with her, because the trip was so tiring, and she wasn't sure that she could make it home all by herself."

"How sad."

Enid chuckled. "That was only after she'd shown her true nature to all and sundry. And believe me, King wasn't any too pleased with her. Maybe this will open his eyes. Amelia, you don't even look the same. You are better, aren't you?"

"I would like to get up tomorrow," the girl replied. "I feel a fraud lying here, when I am almost well."

"Not quite, but you will be. As for getting up, well we'll see about that tomorrow."

Amelia smiled. "If you say so." She smoothed the
covers. "I'm sorry about throwing the carafe. It must
have been dear. . . ."

"It was old and not my best one. You should have
seen the expression on King's face," she added, chuckling. "My dear, it was worth losing the carafe to see
my son taken down a peg. Feel free to throw anything
you like at him. I think it may do him good."

"So long as you don't run out of glassware," Amelia
added wryly.

King was sitting quietly in the buggy with a miffed
Darcy. Her coy flirting hadn't produced any results at
all, so she'd gone back to grumbling about wasting a
whole afternoon visiting a woman who wasn't well
enough for company.

"You might have ridden over to tell me she was in
such a state," she told King. "It would have saved me
this trip."

King didn't reply. He was still getting over the after-
effects of having a carafe flung at him by his mother's
pet mouse. He'd discounted a lot of things Quinn had
said about Amelia because of her subdued presence
when her father was around. Now, he wondered how
much was true. It seemed that he hadn't known her at
all, if that bout of temper was any indication. Amelia
in a flaming temper was a totally different proposition
than Amelia bending her head to take any abuse offered
her. He actually felt disconcerted.

"You haven't said a word," Darcy muttered, glaring
at him.

"I've been listening," he said pleasantly.

"What was that you mentioned last night about Quinn
being missing?"

"He's down in Mexico, and we can't find him. The funeral is at four, tomorrow. I hope he can be contacted in time."

"Do you realize that it's almost two o'clock?" she replied. "I wasn't even offered a meal!"

"We had already eaten by the time you arrived," he said evasively. "How is your father's bad back? He mentioned the other day that it was bothering him."

Diverted, she began to talk about that, forgetting his sudden reluctance to talk.

Rodriguez embraced the girl and laughed as he swung her up against his ample girth and spun her around. "*Niña mía, niñita mía*, I have been so worried!" he cried, and there were tears of joy in his dark eyes. "Oh, my Maria, Juliano has just been brought home by Aunt Inez and Uncle Lopez, crippled and upset. He has told me that Manolito left you alone in Del Rio. . . . I was even now getting together my men to come and find you."

"Manolito, *está aquí*?" she asked quickly.

"No more, *niña*," he replied. His face clouded. "Manolito is dead," he added coldly, and his eyes held death. "How did you get back? And who is this gringo?" he added belatedly, glancing at Quinn.

Quinn was glad he'd hidden his star. He stared at the bandit with a total innocence. "I'm from Texas, sir," he drawled, extending his hand. "I found this here young lady in bad straits down in Del Rio, and, well, I sort of rescued her."

"This is true," she said heavily. "Papa, that Manolito, he left me in a . . . a *casa de putas*."

Rodriguez's face seemed to blow up like a red balloon. "A what!?"

She shook her head. "No, no, it is all right. *Señor* Quinn, he saved me! He protected me through the night from the attentions of other men, and at first light, he carried me out of that terrible place and put me on his horse and brought me back to you!" In her dialogue, she neglected to mention, of course, exactly how Quinn had "protected" her.

"You saved my little girl." Rodriguez caught Quinn in a bear hug, his big body heaving with sobs, tears running down his unshaven face as he stared up at the taller man. "The Blessed Virgin preserve you, my son, for this wonderful thing you have done! She is my life, *mi vida*. Without her, I have nothing!"

Quinn was embarrassed and uncomfortable. He felt as if he were flying a false flag. He didn't like doing dishonest things. On the other hand, this was a God-given opportunity to bring a notorious bandit to justice. He couldn't afford to turn his back on it. But the camp was full of heavily armed men, and he had to wait for the right opportunity to do what he had to do. Besides, he wondered how he was going to bear the look in her eyes when the girl discovered who he really was.

"Come. *Mi casa es su casa*, you know this saying?" Rodriguez was saying, clapping Quinn on the back as he led him into the small, bare-floored hut. "It is not much of a house, I agree, but you will always be welcome here, *todo tu vida. Aqúi estás siempre bienvenídas.*"

Rodriguez was already addressing him in the familiar tense, the one used only with close friends and relatives. It made Quinn feel worse than he already did.

They sat around the small fire where Rodriguez's woman cooked enchiladas and beans for them, drinking mescal while the girl told of her ordeal in the soft, elegant Spanish which she spoke so well. After a minute, with a shy smile at Quinn, she excused herself and went to bathe and find a change of clothing.

"Ah, *pobrecita*, what a life she has had," Rodriguez told Quinn after she was out of earshot. "Did she tell you about her home, her old home, *señor*?"

"Just that her stepfather was cruel to her and her brothers."

"He was a madman," Rodriguez said coldly. "He tried to rape her, many times. She tell you this?"

Quinn lowered his eyes to the camp fire. No, she hadn't told him it was that bad. So it had been fear, not just innocence, that had made her fight. Afterward, he'd registered the ease with which her body accepted him. Now he felt worse than ever. She'd been emotionally scarred, and he hadn't known. What if he'd made things worse?

"What happened to her stepfather, after you got her to safety?" Quinn asked Rodriguez.

The man drew his forefinger slowly over his raspy throat. "It took a long time," he added quietly. "And I felt no pity for him. If you had seen the little boys, *señor*." He closed his eyes and sighed heavily. "He did to them what he had done to her, and more. Men can be animals. I had not realized how savage a man could be until I found her cowering in the bushes. She was ten years old. She stood up when she saw me and closed her eyes. She stood there very quietly, waiting for me to kill her." The bandit's voice choked up. He had to stop and take a sip of mescal before he could continue. "She pleaded with me to save her. She meant with a bullet, but I could not kill a child so beautiful. I took her up in the saddle with me, and her last living brother was also found by my men. We brought them here, and

they have been with me ever since. I cannot have children of my own,'' he said with faint embarrassment.
''I have a . . . how you say . . . *accidente*. But I have
these two *niños* now, and they are my own, you know,
even if I did not know their mother. I have loved them
like my own. I think they like me a little also,'' he
added, chuckling, and his eyes twinkled as he remarked, ''because they never try to run away.''

As if an abused child would run from love, Quinn
thought. He remembered his childhood, when his father
had been a kind, happy man and his mother a delightful
companion. Those days were so far away now, and his
father had become a virtual madman. Amelia was
trapped there, and Quinn could not make her leave. She
felt sorry for their father. She was convinced that something was wrong with him. Perhaps there was, but
Quinn was afraid that Hartwell would lose control one
day and hurt her badly. He had to do something to help
her, he told himself. He must find a way out.

''You are silent, *señor*,'' Rodriguez prompted.

''Sorry,'' Quinn said. He sipped the mescal, feeling
warmth slip into his very bones. ''I was thinking of my
sister. She has had a very hard time of it with our father. He is not kind to her, yet he once was a good
man.''

''*Ay de mi*, how the world changes,'' the Mexican
said sadly. ''I have watched men become animals, because they cannot give their little children enough food
to eat or even a pair of sandals to wear or a blanket to
keep them warm at night. They live like dogs while the
rich gringos come into our country and live like kings
on our silver and gold. It has been the way of things
since the days of the *conquistadores*, but I tell you, it
must change. It must!''

Quinn frowned. "*Señor*, you sound like a revolutionary."

"A man should be when his people go hungry for the basic necessities of life," came the quiet reply. "You are not a rich man, *señor*?"

"I own my horse and my gun, and not much more," Quinn had to admit, smiling ruefully.

"Then surely you know what it is like to be without the things you most need. You know the gnawing emptiness of a stomach which craves food when there is none. You know the cold of a desert night when there is no wood to burn, no blanket to cover with."

"I have known these things," he had to admit.

"I have watched a baby starve to death," Rodriguez said, the horror still in his eyes. "It was my own little baby sister, and there was not enough food for both of us, so my mama gave the milk in her breasts to me. It is why I am alive, that sacrifice." Tears poured down his cheeks again. "Do you know why she did it, *señor*?" he asked, lifting his red eyes to Quinn's. "Because I was male, and when I grew up I would be better able to provide for her and *mi familia* than a daughter could. She had to choose between us. The little girl was new, but she had had me for three years, and I was precious to her. It was sacrifice one or both, and she could not let me die." He took another long swallow of mescal. "When I am tempted to stop robbing those rich gringos across the border, when I am tempted to come home and raise my goats and plant my fields, I go to the cemetery to that little grave of my sister, who died for me. And as I pray for her soul, I think of our beloved Virgin Mother whose only son was sacrificed to save us all. It makes me more determined than ever to keep on, *señor*. To keep fighting, so that no more little babies will have to starve because the gringos have all the money and all the land and all the power in this country!''

Quinn hadn't interrupted once. He stared at this terrible outlaw who was wanted by so many people for his lawless acts—and he hated the star in his saddlebags for bringing him to this. If Rodriguez was a bad man, where was a good one?

"I am wrong, you think, no?" Rodriguez asked, staring at the other man with eyes that did not waver or fall. "I shoot up the towns and kill the gringos and steal money and cattle, and for that I must be arrested and tried and hanged in Texas''—he pronounced it in the Spanish way, *tehas*—"for my crimes."

"I think that you have a long way to go before you can qualify as a criminal in the true sense of the word,'' Quinn said evasively. "Your people would die for you."

"*Sí*, that is true."

Quinn looked around at the Spartan little hut. Rodriguez had very few possessions, most of which were very old. There was a set of spurs and a nickle-plated, ivory-handled Colt .45 which Rodriguez was wearing, and they might have some intrinsic value. But there was nothing here that spoke of ill-gotten gains.

"Are you looking for the great wealth I am supposed to possess?" Rodriguez asked pleasantly. "Let me show it to you."

Quinn expected him to pull out a strongbox and open it, displaying coins and jewels. But the bandit got to his feet and motioned Quinn along with him.

They went through the pueblo then, and Rodriguez began to point to various new additions. There were good oak buckets for the central fountain from which the people got their water. There were carts and good harnesses to hitch, and mules to hitch them to, so the farmers could transport their goods from the fields. There were horses and cattle and pigs, shared between all the families. And most of all, there was a chapel with a gold cross at the altar and stained glass windows.

"Is it not beautiful?" Rodriguez asked as they stood inside the small chapel, with its long wood pews. "My people made these things. We did not steal them," he added carefully. "We did, I am sad to say, steal the artisan who makes the windows," he murmured, and crossed himself, "but it was in a good cause. We gave to him our prettiest young single woman, Lolita, whom he married. He now has five children, and he is one of us, and his windows are a glory to God and our people. So perhaps it was not such a very bad thing to steal him, huh?"

Quinn threw back his head and laughed heartily. "Perhaps it was not," he agreed.

Maria came back while they were walking in the pueblo, scrubbed, with her long black hair brushed clean. She looked very pretty in her white peasant dress and black mantilla and small sandaled feet. She walked beside Quinn, gently grasping his hand in hers.

"I see that you, too, may someday become a resident of our pueblo, *señor*," Rodriguez murmured dryly, glancing at the small hand curled trustingly into his big one. He pursed his lips in obvious calculation and eyed the taller man insistently. "So, tell me, what skills do *you* possess that will benefit our poor village?"

═══ Chapter Fifteen ═══

AMELIA WAS TIRED OF BEING BEDRIDDEN. SHE hated staring at four walls and feeling so weak and helpless. Her headache was better, although she was drowsy from the medication. But she felt different already. She had been released from the prison her father's illness had made for her, and life even with its uncertainties had taken on a new brightness. She might not even have a place to live when she was recovered, but she could face that. She could work as a seamstress or a nanny or even a governess. It would mean leaving Latigo. But there was no choice about that. King wanted nothing to do with her.

King had avoided her for the two days she'd been in residence. She had one glimpse of him, dressed in his nice dark suit the day before, as he joined the others for her father's funeral. Rosa sat with Amelia, who cried a little for the father whose memory was just beginning to return to her. But it was the old memories that made her sad, not the most recent one. She prayed for her father and hoped that he would be untormented in the realm he'd advanced to. The man who had beaten her was not her father; he was a product of the killing tumor, and she could not find it in her heart to hate a sick man.

It was time to think of getting back on her feet, though.

"May I get dressed and come to the table for supper, do you think?" she asked Enid later.

The older woman pursed her lips. "If you feel like it, certainly. It should prove interesting."

"Your oldest son is avoiding me," she said bluntly. Her eyes twinkled. "Do I frighten him?"

Enid chuckled. "I wonder," she said unexpectedly. "He talks to himself lately."

"A sure sign of insensibility," Amelia said. She got up and put on her robe, steadying herself by holding on to the bedpost. She tied the ribbons in front. "I can't stay much longer, you know," she said unexpectedly, meeting the old woman's eyes.

"Alan would very much like to marry you," Enid began.

"I'm very fond of Alan, but I will not marry him," came the quiet reply. "I have a cousin in Jacksonville, Florida. I can cable her and see if she will have me to stay." The words hurt when she said them, as if she were considering tearing out her heart. To leave King would be like that. She hadn't remembered much, but she had remembered how she felt about him, and that her feelings weren't reciprocated.

"Oh, Amelia," Enid said worriedly. "It is so far from us and from Quinn. He will be devastated!"

Amelia smoothed her hands over the silky wood of the bedpost. She was trying to think and failing miserably. "I know he will, but I have very few alternatives."

Loud footsteps caught their attention. King paused in the doorway, scowling at the picture Amelia made in her lacy night things with her blond hair loose around her shoulders.

"Peeping Tom," she said icily, her eyes flashing at him.

His eyebrows lifted. "If you will stand half-naked in front of an open door, what do you expect?"

"Courtesy, sir, and I get little enough of that commodity from you."

He leaned insolently against the doorway, half a smile on his lean face. "You might get more if you stop flinging glass objects at my head," he pointed out.

"What? And give up the only pleasure I have left?"

King chuckled. "I came to ask about your health. It seems there was little need for it." He shouldered away from the door and walked on down the hall.

Amelia's cheeks went rosy from the encounter, which rather embarrassed her. "I do beg your pardon," she told an amused Enid, "but he seems to bring out unfamiliar qualities in me."

"I don't think he minds, Amelia. Let me close the door, and you can get dressed. I was just about to put the food on the table."

It was a spirited meal. Amelia's appetite was still small, and she was struggling against the effects of her travails of the past few days. But she was more animated than any of the Culhanes had seen her. Alan was watching her with curiosity and faint misgivings.

"Are you certain that you're better?" Alan persisted. "You don't seem at all like yourself."

"I haven't been myself for four years, Alan, not since my little brothers died and my father began to have violent spells," she said quietly. "I learned how to keep him calm, at first for Mama's sake, and then for my own.''

"Weren't you afraid?" Alan asked.

"Of course," she said. "He lost control completely in those moods, but he was my father, and I had loved him very much when he was still in his right mind. One does not desert loved ones, Alan, even when it entails some measure of risk. What would Quinn have thought of me if I had saved myself at my father's expense?''

King was listening, and watching, without adding to the conversation.

"We have still not been able to find Quinn. I'm sure he's all right," Brant added quickly, when Amelia began to look worried. "But he's in a part of Mexico that's far away from a telegraph office. I'm afraid it will come as a shock to him, if he knew nothing of your father's condition.''

"I made certain that he didn't," Amelia said. "He had his own concerns, and I was quite capable of tending Father.''

"My God, a paragon of all the virtues," King said flatly. "Had you no thoughts of self-preservation at all?''

She stared at him. "Mr. Culhane, in my position, exactly what would you have done?" she challenged.

He shrugged. "What you did, of course." He glowered at her. "But you might have told us how serious the situation was. It was stupid of you not to tell us the truth about your father.''

"What King means," Alan said, starting to smooth it over.

Amelia held up a hand. "What King means," she said for him, "is that I behaved stupidly, which I did. You have no need to gloss over his stinging remarks,

Alan, I have no fear of either Mr. Culhane or his nasty temper!''

Alan flushed and turned his attention back to his food. He didn't look at her again, and Amelia realized that he was intimidated by her. She gaped at him, disbelieving.

"Have some more potatoes, dear," Enid said quickly. She understood the whole situation, as did Brant. King eyed Amelia with twinkling eyes, animated and relaxed. He enjoyed her spirited repartee. Alan did not. Just as well, Enid thought, that things had happened as they did. Alan would have been miserable when he discovered that his sweet little sparrow was, in fact, a feisty little wren.

Amelia and King went from one subject to another, debating, fencing over issues as disparate as politics and the Boer War. She found their discussions uplifting, challenging. King lost some points, won others, but she'd never seen him quite as open. She was sorry when the meal was over and it was time for her to lie down again. But she was tired. Being out of bed had weakened her, and she was ready for her pillow.

"You debate well," King remarked as they passed in the hall. "Who taught you?"

"Quinn. He enjoys political discussions, and he knows a lot about what goes on," she said. She smiled. "So do I."

"As I noticed." His pale eyes swept over her wan face quietly. "You have overtaxed. Get some sleep."

"Do you think Alan would take me to see Papa's grave tomorrow?" she asked without looking up. "I should . . . like to see where he is resting."

"I'll take you," he replied.

She lifted her troubled eyes. "But . . ."

He searched her eyes. His were narrow and dark with pain. "There are things that I must tell you," he said slowly, reluctant to break the accord between them. "Things you must hear, that no one else knows."

She knew, then, that her memory was covering up something very unpleasant. "Do you know why my father beat me?"

"Yes," he said heavily. "God help me, I know."

She wanted to press him, but there were other people within earshot, and she knew instinctively that she wouldn't want to share what he told her. "You will tell me tomorrow?"

He nodded. He shoved his hands into his jean pockets and stared down at her without speaking for a long moment. "You did play Indians in the backyard with your little brothers, didn't you?" he asked unexpectedly.

She laughed, surprised. "Oh, yes, and climbed trees and went hunting for spring lizards in the streams," she said sadly. "Those days are long gone. I will always mourn the boys."

"As long as we remember those we lose, they don't die. Not really," he said. He reached out and touched her cheek, very gently. "Sleep well, Amelia."

"You do the same." She moved down the hall, a little unsteady on her feet, not daring to look back. He stood and watched her all the way into her room. His eyes darkened as he realized that she was going to hate him when she knew the truth, and he had no option but to tell it to her. Life was sometimes very harsh.

Quinn was still trying to find some way out of his own predicament. Maria's young brother, Juliano, had also latched onto him, and the village people treated him as if he were already part of their families.

He was here falsely, but he couldn't, didn't dare, tell them who and what he was. Many Mexicans were afraid of the Rangers, understandably in view of the turbulent past when plenty of them had been killed by the Texas lawmen. Maria would be devastated. And as for his own position, he would be fortunate indeed if he made it to a horse before these loyal men of Rodriguez's cut him to pieces with those horse pistols they were packing.

Rodriguez clapped him on the back heartily and laughed. "It was a joke, *señor*," he said. "I do not measure every man who comes here for a profession. It is simply that our poor village needs so much, you see. If I do not bring talented craftsmen here, how will we become a thriving city instead of a sad little pueblo?"

"There's a lot to be said for a small village," Quinn felt obliged to point out.

"*Sí*, that is so." Rodriguez looked around him with loving eyes, as if every person in the pueblo, every building, every rock and blade of grass was part of him. "We are very lucky, *señor*. We share, each with the other, whatever we have."

Quinn turned to the older man, his eyes steady on the other's face. "You steal to feed these people, don't you?"

Rodriguez shrugged. "A starving man begs or steals bread, *señor*." His dark eyes flickered. "I would rather die than beg."

There was a cold sort of logic in the answer, but Quinn understood what he meant. A man's pride was not lightly cast into the dirt.

"You think it is wrong. Perhaps it is," Rodriguez agreed quietly. "But there is a drought. We cannot grow our own food, and we have eaten what little was set aside last fall. Some will starve, in spite of what I do. *Madre de Dios*, the children," he groaned, and tears welled in his eyes. "*Señor*, I tell you, it is unbearable to watch a child cry for food and have nothing to hand it except promises of a better day." He wiped the tears away angrily with his sleeve. "I swear by our Blessed Virgin, I will not stand by and let these *niños* go without food, and if it is wrong, someday they hang me, and I don't care."

Quinn cursed under his breath. How did you argue morality when people were dying? "Still," he said heavily, "there must be some other way!"

"There is," the Mexican agreed angrily. "We could sit on the streets in El Paso or Juarez and beg."

Quinn blew out a breath. "Well, even in your situation, I could not do that."

Rodriguez chuckled. "Pride is Satan's best weapon, no? We have too much. Yet, *señor*, the wealthy also have too much and will not share with those less fortunate."

"That isn't always the case."

"Then why are so many people hungry?"

"Now that, I can't tell you. It's a crazy world."

"Fortunately, it contains enough banks to feed my *niños* and provide a few animals with which to farm, when the rains come again. And they will," he added with certainty, "because we have prayed to the Blessed Virgin each day to intervene for us. She will answer our prayers, *señor*. She hears the cries of the children. Always."

It wasn't easy for Quinn to understand that kind of

faith, but he didn't argue. He'd seen a miracle or two in his life.

He'd meant to leave the village immediately. It was impossible. Maria's big blue eyes pleaded, and he stayed. One day turned into two, then three, and finally into a week. All the while, he learned about the people of the pueblo and got to know them, was accepted by them, and by Rodriguez.

His conscience had twinges, because he felt he was betraying these people already. He was sworn to take Rodriguez in, but he couldn't. The man wasn't all bad. He had a wonderful, generous nature, and he cared about his people. Besides, he was Maria's adopted father, her whole world.

Of course, Maria was rapidly becoming Quinn's whole world. She was with him from morning until night, and he craved her as a thirsty man craved water. But he would not give in to the temptation to take her to bed. Not when he knew the anguish she'd suffered at the hands of other men. He was gentle and caring and tenderly affectionate. But the time finally came when he had to leave the pueblo, and Maria. It was very hard. Because he was in love, for the first time in his life.

"Will you not stay with us?" Rodriguez asked, sadness claiming his round face when Quinn stated his intention to leave.

Quinn ground his teeth together. "I wish I could," he said huskily, staring at a stricken Maria. "I would give anything if I could. But I have . . . business back in Texas. I'll come back when I can," he added.

Maria's sad face lightened.

"You will be welcome," Rodriguez said. "Bless you, *señor*, for saving my girl."

"She was worth saving," Quinn said, and in his dark eyes were love and anguish at having to leave her.

Maria went forward and took his hands in hers. "I will wait for you," she said gently, tears in her big blue eyes. "No matter how long it takes!"

He looked, and felt, torn apart. "I'll come back," he swore. "I'll come back for you!"

She caught her breath and impulsively hugged him with all her might. Then, before he could speak, she pulled away and ran toward her hut.

"Women," Rodriguez said with lazy affection. "So emotional." He extended his hand, and Quinn shook it. *"Vaya con Díos,"* he added.

"And you."

Quinn reluctantly mounted his horse. He did have business in Texas, involving figuring a way to bring this pleasant Mexican to the gallows. He didn't look back as he rode away. He didn't know how he was going to live with himself, either.

When he crossed the border into El Paso, he was dog tired, but he went by the telegraph office to send a wire to his post in Alpine. But he found a message waiting for him, and the fatigue was submerged in an anguish of grief. His father, the cable read, had died suddenly. His sister was at Latigo.

He forgot to send the telegram to his post in his haste to reach the boardinghouse where his father had lived.

"But your father wasn't living here," the landlady told Quinn. "He bought a house for himself and Miss Amelia, just down the street." She walked out onto the sidewalk and pointed toward it. "Buried him just yesterday. Not many people came, but he was new in town. Your sister wasn't able to come. She was with him when he died, they say. He treated her like dirt," she added, staring up at him. "Sweet girl, always doing her best to please him. He made her cry all the time. I'm sorry he died, being your father and all, but I was sorrier for your sister. All over town, about her and that rancher at Latigo, King Culhane. Said her father really laid into her when he found out. Pity, it was. Nice girl like that, who'd think she'd be a loose-liver?"

Quinn was shocked. He started to take her up on that slander and then thought better of it. He needed to find out what had happened before he started verbally flaying people. He thanked her stiffly and went to the house. It was locked. Presumably Amelia would have the key. He traded horses at the livery stable and rode out for Latigo. His grief at losing his father was equaled by his fear for Amelia's reputation and her sanity. She was a gentle, sweet girl. How would she handle the grief? And what in God's name did King have to do with Amelia that could cause gossip all over El Paso? For heaven's sake, King hated her!

King drove Amelia to the cemetery outside town, where her father had been buried. There was an oblong mound of dirt and a placard stuck into the ground with his name, age, place of birth, and date of death on it.

Until she saw it, Amelia hadn't been able to believe that he was actually dead. Now it hit her all at once, and she began to cry.

King pulled her into his arms and held her while the tears came, rocking her gently while the wind blew around them. The horse grazed on the thin vegetation, carelessly tossing his mane while he chewed and bugs bit him. It was green here. There were two mesquite trees putting out leaves, their long fronds flowing like green beards in the breeze. King found himself thinking that he wouldn't mind spending eternity here, in this quiet, peaceful place.

Finally the tears dwindled, and Amelia stood quiet in his arms, her lacy handkerchief pressed to her mouth and red nose. She sniffed. "King?"

"Hmmm?"

"Tell me why he hit me."

He didn't speak for a long moment. He couldn't find the right words to say. He didn't know how to tell her.

"It's something terrible, isn't it?" she asked quietly. "It's all right. I'm strong. I've had to be. Whatever it is, I can take it."

But could she? He drew away from her. "Come and sit in the buggy, then."

He led her to the vehicle and helped her inside, sliding in beside her. The horse continued to graze after a cursory, careless appraisal of the people behind him.

King fingered the reins in his lean, dark hands, staring straight ahead. "You and Alan were becoming close. I didn't like it. I wanted someone else for Alan, someone stronger and more intelligent."

"You thought that . . ."

"That you were the uneducated coward you seemed to be when you were with your father," he said bluntly. He glanced at her. "You said you could take it."

"I can." She lifted her chin. "But that isn't all."

He grimaced. "No. There's . . . something more." He looked down at the reins. "I seduced you."

She didn't think she'd heard him right. She couldn't have. "I . . . I beg your pardon?" she stammered.

He turned and looked into her startled dark eyes. "I seduced you in cold blood," he said flatly. "Then I threatened to tell Alan if you kept seeing him. But that wasn't all. I couldn't leave it there. I went to town and told your father that you'd offered yourself to me and that I wouldn't allow anyone that immoral to marry my brother.''

She didn't breathe. Her eyes stared into his, and only when he saw her losing color did he realize how shocked she was.

''That's why your father beat you. Probably why he died,'' he said, his eyes narrowed and glittering with self-contempt. ''I was playing God, Amelia. It was my mistake, but you paid for it.''

She scrambled in her mind for one solid thought, but they all escaped her. She looked out to the horizon, trying to understand what he'd said.

''Did you hate me so much?'' she asked on a cold laugh.

''I wanted you,'' he corrected. ''So I thought I might be able to kill two birds with one stone: spare Alan and . . .'' He broke off suddenly. ''No. Hell, no, it wasn't that. It wasn't that at all! I wanted you, and I made an excuse to trample all over my ideals and your innocence and have you. That's it in a nutshell, and all my rationalizing won't make it into anything prettier.'' He looked down at her with anguish. ''Everything that's happened to you is my fault, including your father's death.''

''Oh, my.'' She was staring at her hands, working them back and forth. She was disgraced. Ruined. He must have gone to see her father at the bank, and other people might have overheard.

She closed her eyes. As the thought probed her mind, she began to see shocking pictures of herself with King, in his bed . . . !

She put her face in her hands with a small, wounded

cry as unwanted memories of her own abandon suddenly flooded her thoughts.

"Don't . . . do that! No one knows all of it," he
said, trying to comfort her. "I told them only that you
offered, not that you . . . that we . . ." He cursed under his breath and wrapped the reins around his fingers
tightly. "Amelia, I guess you'd better marry me."

She shivered. It was worse than she'd thought, than
she'd dreamed. She was ruined. And she could be carrying his child. That was the most terrifying thought of
all. She must run, hide!

What had he said, something about marriage? She
lifted her face and looked at him as if she thought him
mad. "What did you say?"

"I said I guess you'd better marry me," he repeated
belligerently. "Unless you can think of some better way
to cope with it. Or didn't you realize that you could be
carrying my child?"

Her hands pressed involuntarily to her flat stomach.
She stared into his silver eyes and felt a shock of emotion so charged that it made her uncomfortable. His
child. A baby. A little human being who would look
like one or both of them. A continuation of their families for another generation.

She dragged her eyes away. No, a baby wouldn't be
something he craved. It would be an unwanted burden
that would prevent him from marrying Darcy Valverde.
And he would hardly want it. Or her. But if she didn't
marry him, what would she do? If there was a child, it
had to be a legitimate one. The disgrace would affect
not only her, but Quinn and even Enid.

"Well?" he muttered.

She didn't speak. She was staring at her skirts. "It is
not . . . certain."

"Not yet. You should know in a few weeks."

She flushed, uncomfortable to be discussing such an intimate topic with a man.

"I breed cattle," he reminded her. "I know more than you might think about how little things get born."

The blush grew worse. She twisted her skirt in her hands. "I don't know what to say," she said finally. "Marriage is the only way, but you are engaged to Miss Valverde."

"I am not," he said. "I have never been engaged to Miss Valverde. I considered it once or twice, that's all."

She glanced at him. His face was totally unreadable. "You would not be happy with me. The past would always be there, between us."

"Nothing matters except that your honor be spared any blemish due to my actions. And that our child, if there is one, be legitimate," he added. His eyes slid down to her flat stomach and rested there with the beginnings of hunger. "It might not be so bad to have a child, Amelia," he said thoughtfully.

"You should not speak of such things!" she said indignantly.

"The more I think of the idea, the more I like it," he continued quietly. "You are young and strong and hardly the coward I thought you. You have qualities that I admire, in fact."

"I'm honored," she said with exaggerated courtesy. "But your admiration is unsolicited. And you may consider me suitable material for a wife, but I do not consider you suitable material for anyone's husband, much less mine!"

His eyebrows lifted. "I'm very wealthy."

"Am I supposed to be impressed that you have material advantages over other men? What does that say of your intelligence, your courage, your kindness? You seem to feel that you will be doing me an honor to become my husband.''

"Hardly that,'' he returned curtly. He glanced at her. "However, there have been plenty of women who were more than willing to marry me.''

"Happily, I am not one of them,'' she said coolly. "You may take me home, now, please.''

His eyes glittered. "Willing or not, you will marry me, Miss Howard.''

"Not unless I want to,'' she shot back. "And right now, Mr. Culhane, there is not one man on earth I want less than you!''

He reached for her just as the sound of horse's hooves in the distance broke the silence.

King's hand stilled on her arm as a lone rider came closer and closer.

Amelia put up her free hand to shade her eyes against the sun, and the way the man sat the horse was so familiar that she wanted to cry.

"It's my brother!'' she exclaimed, tears stinging into her eyes. "It's Quinn!''

=== Chapter Sixteen ===

QUINN SPOTTED THE BUGGY AND URGED HIS MOUNT forward. He'd been all the way out to Latigo, only to be told that Amelia had gone with King to see her father's grave. He followed the road back to the cemetery, and sure enough, there they both were.

He rode up beside them and dismounted. Amelia was out of the buggy in a flash, caught close in his arms.

"Oh, Quinn, he's dead, he's dead," she sobbed.

He smoothed her hair, whispering gently to her. He looked over her shoulder. "Hello, King," he said.

King nodded. Quinn looked as if he knew a lot more than he'd said so far, and it might be the end of their long friendship when he knew all of it. He dreaded losing the younger man's respect.

"It was quick, at least," she said into Quinn's shoulder. "He won't suffer anymore. The doctor said that the pain would have been unbearable if he'd lived, with nothing that would ease it."

"Are you all right?" he asked, lifting his head and lightly touching the padding of bandage between her shoulder blades.

It embarrassed her that he knew how it had happened. "I will be all right," she said. She didn't look at King.

But Quinn did, with hot, angry eyes. "I know all of

it,'' he said flatly. "Or didn't you realize that El Paso isn't much more than a small town when it comes to gossip? Tell me all of it.''

King took a deep breath and jammed his hands into his pockets. "Okay. I went to see your father about Amelia and slandered her. What happened to her, and him, was my fault.''

"That was despicable.''

"Yes, it was,'' King admitted with quiet self-contempt. "If it's any consolation, my brother refuses to speak to me, and my parents find me beneath contempt.''

"And Amelia?'' Quinn prompted.

King took a deep breath and ground his teeth together. "Amelia refuses to marry me.''

"How could you blame her?'' Quinn burst out. "My God, man . . . !''

King held up a lean hand. "I don't blame her. But if there is a child, I can't allow her to bear it alone and in shame.''

Quinn's face drained of color. His hand dropped to the butt of his sidearm and quivered there.

King laughed coldly. "Go ahead,'' he invited, nodding toward the pistol. "It might be kinder than letting me live with what I've done.''

Amelia, broken out of her trance, moved between them and put her hand over Quinn's where it rested on the gun. "It is a complex situation,'' she began slowly.

"Complex, indeed,'' King replied. "And now you've become one of only three people who know the whole truth of it.''

"He . . . ?'' Quinn asked Amelia fiercely, daring her to confirm it as he glared angrily toward the other man.

Amelia grimaced and lowered her eyes. She nodded.

"You son of a . . . !" Quinn exploded, dark eyes blazing as he fought Amelia's restraining hand.

"No!" she cried angrily. "Don't you dare shoot him!"

King's eyebrows went up over startled silver eyes. Quinn gaped at her.

"Oh, I know he's a blackguard," she told her brother, "but at least he's offered to do the honorable thing."

"After the dark deed was accomplished, instead of before, when he should have!" Quinn glared at his friend. "And how is it that you were all but engaged to Darcy Valverde and now you're mixed up with my sister in a way no gentleman ever should be?"

King shrugged broad shoulders. "I was saving Alan from your sister," he said slowly, and looked down at Amelia with eyes gone suddenly soft. "She threw a carafe of water at me," he added with a faint smile.

"Sadly, I missed!" she shot back. "Next time, I'll lay your hard head open with a brick bat!"

In spite of himself Quinn's eyes began to twinkle at the byplay. With their father gone, Amelia was beginning to sound like her old self. Oh, yes, she would be more than a match for fiery King when she was back on her feet. He had a mind to feel sorry for the man.

"Darcy would never threaten me with a brick bat," King assured Quinn. "You can give her away. We'll have a church wedding with all the trimmings."

"We will not," Amelia said weakly, sick at the thought of going into a church when she'd broken a sacred law by anticipating marriage with King.

"What happened was hardly your fault," King reminded her gently. "Church is the very best place to be when we have smudges on our conscience."

She shifted restlessly. "I suppose so."

"Mother would be upset if you suggested a civil service," he persisted.

"I'm not suggesting a service of any sort. You're the one who's insisting that we get married," she reminded him hotly. "Which wouldn't have happened if you hadn't decided to start arranging everybody's lives for them!"

King grimaced and looked away, a ruddy flush on his high cheekbones.

"I agree," Quinn said coldly. "But the thing is, you have to make it right. This gossip can't be allowed to continue. It will ruin Amelia's good name."

"I contacted the minister this morning, before I drove Amelia out here," King said, shocking her. "We've arranged the ceremony for Sunday after church, pleading that her father's death leaves her in such dire need of housing that a quick marriage is a necessity to prevent her being homeless."

"She doesn't *have* to marry you," Quinn said angrily. "She can live with me."

King's eyebrows arched. "In the Ranger barracks with the men? I can see how this idea would stem gossip about your sister," he said with a mocking smile.

"Don't be absurd. I meant that I could get a house," he countered.

"On a Ranger's pay?" King moved forward, confronting the younger man. He looked just a little dangerous as he stared Quinn down with glittering silver eyes. "I'm not letting her out of my sight. Not when she could be carrying my heir. If that doesn't suit you, you know what you can do."

"Anytime," Quinn returned immediately.

Amelia sighed loudly, glaring at both of them. "Do you never think of anything except fighting?" she raged.

Her fists clenched at her side. "Physical violence will solve nothing."

"Then why did you throw that damned carafe at me?" King asked conversationally.

She bit back more furious words. Her face colored with high temper as she glared at him.

"The wedding will be Sunday," he told her firmly, and then looked back at Quinn. "If you object, we can settle it right here."

Quinn wanted to hit him more than he wanted to eat. He bristled with bad temper and vengeance. "My father would be alive but for you. . . ."

"I know that," King said quietly. "I'll have to bear the burden of it for the rest of my life."

"Quinn, he would have died anyway," Amelia said wearily. She looked at her brother with sad, wistful eyes. "He would have suffered more, and as the doctor said, he might actually have killed me."

"He almost did that because of what King told him!"

"I'm not defending what King did," she replied. "But you know that anything could have, and did, set Father off. He slapped me on the way home from Latigo after the hunting trip, because I protested a charge he made against me."

"You didn't tell me that," King said angrily.

"He had become more violent in the past few weeks." She unclenched her hands. "I mourn for the father I knew as a child." She stared at the lonely grave. "But I rejoice for the tortured man who died, because he was spared more pain."

"Which still doesn't solve the problem of Amelia," Quinn muttered.

"I told you," King returned, "that we're getting

married on Sunday. That will certainly solve her problem. My parents dote on her.''

"Well, you don't," Amelia said, her temper rising
all over again. "If I made a list of the insults you've
heaved at me since I came out here the first time, it
would stretch all the way to El Paso!''

"I didn't want you being tempted to marry Alan,"
he said easily. "He's afraid of her now, by the way,"
he added with a smile at Quinn. "When she loses her
temper, he runs for cover. It would never have worked.
She'd have him henpecked by the end of the first week
they were married.''

Amelia knew that, but she didn't like hearing it in
that smug drawl. "Perhaps I loved Alan, didn't you
think about that before you started spinning your vicious web?''

He smiled lazily. "If you had, you'd never have let
me touch you in the first place.''

"You . . . you . . . !'' She couldn't find one single
adjective that was adequate to describe him.

"Calm down," he murmured. "You're not recovered
enough for war, even verbal war." He bent and lifted
her gently off the ground in his arms. "Come on back
to Latigo with us," he told Quinn. "I expect you came
straight here when you got to town. You could probably
use a good meal. Do stop struggling, Amy, it's so un-
dignified.''

"Don't call me . . . Amy!'' She gasped, pushing at
him.

"Why not? It suits you." He turned and walked back
to the buggy with her, enjoying the soft warmth of her
in his arms.

She subsided, because she didn't want to be dropped
on the hard ground, she told herself. But when he put

her in the buggy and his dark, lean face came momentarily too close, she went breathless and boneless.

He looked straight into her eyes and sparks seemed to leap between them. The unexpected longing he felt prodded his temper. He moved away from her with undue haste, his face like stone.

She clenched her hands together. So now he couldn't bear to touch her. What had she expected? He was being forced by honor into a marriage he didn't want. He would make the most of it, but he certainly didn't love Amelia. He could offer her none of the feelings she had for him, which she would now have to keep carefully hidden. There must be some way out of this dreadful situation.

"I could go back East. . . ."

"You'll go nowhere, except to the church on Sunday," he said, his voice deep and cutting.

He moved around to the other side of the carriage, lighting a cigar as he went.

Quinn had mounted and rode up beside Amelia, who was smouldering quietly in the buggy.

"I do not wish to marry him. You must save me," she told her brother firmly.

He pulled his hat low over his eyes, commented that he thought it was King who needed saving, and rode on ahead of them.

Amelia took one last look at her father's sad, lonely grave, and turned her attention toward Latigo.

The announcement of King's marriage to Amelia had predictable results at Latigo.

"I couldn't be happier," Enid said with tender enthusiasm as she hugged Amelia. "I saw it coming, you know," she added teasingly, while the others eavesdropped. "All those long, slow looks that passed between you, the nervousness and shyness. Imagine, my King, shy!"

"You exaggerate," King said lazily.

"I thought he hated me," Amelia said.

"That could hardly be the case, since he has asked you to become his wife," a blissfully ignorant Brant noted.

Amelia didn't look at King. She glanced toward her brother. "Did you catch Rodriguez?" she asked suddenly.

Quinn looked uncomfortable. "I trailed him down into Sonora," he said.

"And . . . ?"

Quinn took a sip of his coffee. "And nothing. I lost his trail," he lied.

"That's too bad," King said curtly. "I hope to live long enough to see that cutthroat swing at the end of a short rope!"

"The Mexicans love him," Quinn pointed out. "To them, he's a saint."

"No saint cuts people up and leaves them for the vultures," King said bluntly. "Which is what he did to my fiancée."

Amelia started. She hadn't known about any fiancée, or that the woman had been killed. She stared at King without breathing, waiting for him to elaborate. So that was why he was cold-bloodedly thinking of marrying Darcy, because his only love had been lost. And now he was cold-bloodedly going to marry Amelia, because he might have made her pregnant. It made her heart ache to realize just what a hollow marriage it would be.

"He waylaid a carriage which contained my fiancée and a . . . friend of hers," he said. "He robbed them,

stripped them, and hacked them to pieces. Forgive me,"
he added when his mother went pale. "But it is the
truth. No one who saw them would hesitate to hang
Rodriguez on sight."

"Are they certain it *was* Rodriguez?" Quinn asked,
surprised by this latest admission, because he knew
King had been engaged but nothing more. He'd assumed the engagement had simply been broken.

"There was an eyewitness," King said. "A Mexican
named Manolito Lopez."

Quinn's heart jumped. He almost burst out what he
knew about Manolito, who had just been killed by Rodriguez for leaving a drugged Maria in a brothel. But he
couldn't defend Rodriguez without admitting he'd seen
him. Brant Culhane had friends among the Texas Rangers, and he, like most of the ranchers who'd had cattle
stolen, also hated Rodriguez.

Amelia saw the torment on King's face and had to
look away. There was little doubt that he still mourned
the woman he'd lost. She sighed, glancing at her
brother. Oddly, he looked worse than King. "Are you
troubled?" Amelia asked.

He forced a smile. "It is Father," he said, and partially it was. He grieved for the man. "I shall miss him.
As you said, Amelia, there were wonderful times when
we were younger. He was a caring and kind father,
then."

"Let us remember him as he was," she said softly.

King was staring down at his plate, quiet and brooding. Memories of Alice as he'd last seen her made him
ill. He could almost picture it, but now it was Amelia
he saw there, and his head jerked up. He looked at her
with faint terror, as he began to realize how he would
feel if it had been Amelia instead of Alice. It was only

then that he came to the true depths of his situation; now, when he knew that life without Amelia would be no life at all.

He didn't want to face that unpalatable fact, so he pushed it to the back of his mind and concentrated on his almost cold coffee.

"Can you stay the night, Quinn?" Enid asked.

He shook his head. "I'm very grateful for the sandwiches and coffee," he said, indicating the full tray that he'd all but emptied while they sat drinking coffee and talking in the front room. "But I have to report back. Then, I'll have to make arrangements about Father's things."

Amelia's face fell as he discussed that business. It was a sad thing to realize that the precious bits and pieces of her father's whole life had to be liquidated.

"I thought his pocket watch should go to you, as I have his pistol," Quinn told Amelia. He handed it over to her, watching her eyes water as she took it, opened the back of the gold case, and saw her father's initials there.

"There is so little of him left," she said quietly. "A sad collection of bits and pieces that contain a man's entire life."

"You will always have the memories of him," Enid said comfortingly. "The good memories, Amelia."

She smiled at her hostess. "Yes, I will have those."

Later, after Quinn rode back to town, Amelia sat on the porch step and looked at the stars. Far away, she heard the sounds of cattle and horses making soft noises. In the distance, a wolf howled. The dark silhouette of trees on the horizon made her think of happier times.

"It's too cool for you out here," came a stiff voice from behind her. "Come inside."

She had her arms wrapped around herself against the chill, but his cold concern made them unfold. She glared at his shadowy figure. "I shall sit outside if I please," she said formally.

There was faint laughter. "And I thought you were biddable."

"What do you want?"

He moved into the light, a smoking cigar in his hand. "I might ask you the same question. Are you regretting the fact that you didn't let Quinn shoot me? He wanted to."

"Killing you would hardly solve any problems. And you are friends," she added.

"Perhaps not as much as before," he replied. "He will not forget. Nor will I."

"Time heals many wounds." She got slowly to her feet. The night air was chilly.

"Wait."

His voice stopped her. He pulled her around to face him with his free hand gently but firmly, holding her upper arm. His knuckles were against the soft swell of her breast under her arm, and she felt an unwanted thrill of pleasure. She tugged against his hand.

He let her go at once, and she stepped back. His face was in the shadows, but his deep voice sounded strained. "You may withdraw from me all you like. I intend to marry you."

"I'm doing it only because I have no choice. I should sooner marry one of your cowboys!"

"Take care," he warned curtly. "A woman in your position should be grateful for an offer of marriage."

"A man in your position should be ashamed of himself!"

"I am," he said soberly. "Ashamed and disgusted. But all the regret in the world will not undo what has happened. We have to look to the future."

"Yes. You must tell Miss Valverde that your fortune will soon be out of her reach!"

"You have a stinging tongue," he accused. "Miss Valverde is my business, not yours."

"She will be, if you think to carouse with her while you are my husband!"

He stared at her curiously. "No such thought would ever occur to me. A vow is a solemn matter."

"Then make sure that Miss Valverde knows that, please."

His bold eyes slid up and down her lazily. They narrowed. "Then make sure that Alan knows it, as well."

"Alan is afraid of me, remember?" she chided.

"He does well to feel that way," he retorted. "He needs a house sparrow, not a vicious little ruffled wren."

"How dare you!"

She drew back her hand, but he caught it, jerking her against him, where he held her until she stopped struggling and stood panting for breath. His hand was steely from long hours of ranch work, his hold impossible to break. He didn't hurt her, but he held her securely.

"I am not vicious," she said through her teeth.

"Not to the others," he agreed. "Only to me. You fight me at every turn, Amelia. Why?"

"Because you hate me," she said unsteadily. "You've always hated me. Everything you've said and done since I've been in Texas has been to make me understand how much you hate me. Even . . . even what happened at

Latigo that day. You wanted nothing more than to shame
me, so that Alan wouldn't want me. I was afraid of
father, hopelessly alone . . . !''

He pulled her head against his chest and held her,
smoothing her hair, whispering soothing things against
her temple, her cheek, her nose, and then, her mouth.

The unexpected contact was so soft and brief that she
didn't feel threatened by it. She relaxed, until his mouth
began to part her lips in a prelude to the hard, insistent
passion she remembered from before. His arms swallowed her up, and his mouth became demanding. She
began to tremble as the need worked its way into her
body and made it throb with the desire that only he
could kindle. Her nails bit into his hard arms, and she
heard him groan against her lips.

The harsh sound penetrated her whirling mind. His
hands were on her hips now, pulling her closer. He was
aroused and not hiding it, and his mouth was fright-
eningly expert.

"No. No!" she began to fight and twisted harshly
out of his arms to back against a post and hang there,
her lips swollen and trembling, her body slumped with
the weakness he'd invoked.

He looked wild. His eyes were glittering in that hard,
dark face on which not one expression was discernable.
Only his eyes were alive in it.

"You want me," he said roughly.

"Want," she choked, fighting tears. "That's all you
know, all you understand. You hate me, but you want
to make love to me just the same. It's . . . disgusting!
It's degrading to make me feel like this and take advantage of it!''

His lips parted on a harsh breath. He glared at her.

"What do you expect our marriage to be, a union that allows hand-holding and nothing more?"

"That's exactly what I expect!" she raged. "I have no intention of sharing a room with you! Or do you think I could love my father's murderer?"

She hadn't meant to say that. She didn't think it. She'd been searching for a weapon, something to save her from him. But this weapon had cutting force. She saw his face go white, the light in his eyes go out. He ran a rough hand through his dark hair and took a hard breath.

"That's that, then," he said gruffly. "I'll relieve you of my presence."

He turned on his heel and stalked off down toward the barn. The cigar he'd discarded earlier lay in the dirt, its orange tip barely glowing in the darkness.

Amelia went back inside. She shouldn't have said that. She'd hurt him. She'd only wanted to keep him from discovering how she felt about him, to prevent him from having a weapon to use against her. Now she'd destroyed any small feeling there might have eventually been.

She went into her room and locked the door. Then she sat down and cried until she thought her heart would break. She heard a horse riding away into the night and wondered if she'd sent King back into the arms of Darcy Valverde. That would have been stupid, especially considering the circumstance in which they found themselves. They had to marry for the sake of her reputation, and his. But it could have been ever so much more pleasant if she'd just managed to be less abrasive to him.

It was knowing how he felt about her that drove her, she knew. She loved him. But he had no feelings to give her. How could she marry him when there was no love on his side to make the relationship work?

She brushed her long hair and put on her gown and robe, laying down and pulling the soft cover over her. He was going to hate her even more now, and she had no one to blame except herself.

If only she'd put her arms around him and kissed him back, who knew what might have come of it? But she'd missed her chance. The thought of his fiancée hurt her, because it was obvious from his face that afternoon that he'd loved Alice deeply. He might not be able to love anyone else ever again, but it was also obvious that he wanted Darcy even if he didn't love her.

Darcy wanted him for his wealth and position. Amelia wanted him only because she loved him. She closed her eyes and finally slept.

Chapter Seventeen

IT HAD BEEN A LONG TIME SINCE KING HAD GOTTEN drunk. He kept remembering Amelia's harsh words, though, and his conscience was already giving him hell. He went into El Paso and drank himself half insensible at the bar. Then, quietly, without even throwing a punch at anyone, he climbed on his horse and teetered back to Latigo in the wee hours.

He got angrier and more sober as the wind cut into his face and the sun began to rise. Amelia had no right to make him hate himself, he thought. No she hadn't, and he was damned well going to tell her so. Who did she think she was? He was marrying her to save her reputation, after all, not because he wanted her.

When he reached Latigo, he staggered off the horse and let it run free as he bumped and banged his way into the house and down the hall to Amelia's room. Her door was locked, but he carried a skeleton key, and it fit all the doors. He unlocked her room, after the third try, and let himself in.

He almost started a fire lighting the kerosene lamp, but he finally managed it. Light spilled out into the large, high-ceilinged bedroom, outlining Amelia's slender body under the cover, her long blond hair fanned out on the white pillow, her rosy cheeks vivid under closed eyes. Long, dark eyelashes rested against her soft skin, and her pretty pink mouth was slightly parted as she breathed.

"Amy," he called. "Amy, wake up!"

He shook her gently. Her eyes opened slowly, and then starkly, to find King standing by the bed, weaving a little.

"King?" she faltered.

He put the lamp down on the bedside table clumsily and sat down heavily on the bed beside her. She moved just in time to prevent him from sitting on her!

"Now, listen here, Amy," he began slowly, "I did not murder your father. I never meant for that to happen."

"Why, King, you've been drinking!" she exclaimed, because he smelled blatantly of whiskey.

"I only had a little, Amy," he persisted. He frowned. "Where was I? Oh, yes, about your father, I wanted to tell you that I never said you'd gone to bed with me. I said you probably would have if I asked you, only to make him stop pushing you at Alan. But I never thought he was going to hurt you." His face contorted. "The belt . . . had blood on it. You had blood all over your back. . . ." He closed his eyes, shivering. "I see it every time I close my eyes. All my fault."

And she'd thought it hadn't bothered him, that her accusations were just bouncing off him. She was shocked to see how deeply he did feel things. "Oh, King," she moaned.

He sat up, dragging in air. He ran his hands through his hair and lifted his face, as if trying to clear his head. "I don't know why I did it. It was just that I had to keep Alan from marrying you."

"You look very tired," she said, choosing her words carefully. "Why don't you get some sleep?"

"Sleep." He sighed heavily. "I don't sleep, Amy. I just lie in the bed and remember how you looked, lying on the floor."

He fascinated her. She saw through all the camouflage to the man underneath and was touched to find that he wasn't steel right through. "I'm all right now," she stressed softly.

His head turned. He looked at her through bloodshot eyes. "You don't want to get married."

She toyed with the cover, grimacing.

"Listen," he said wearily, "it comes down to this. I've dishonored you and, in turn, my family. Neither of us have much choice, I'm afraid. Even if you decide to go to Florida and stay with your cousin, Amy, you might get a baby from what happened. How would you live with that? Wouldn't your cousin be outraged?"

"Yes," she confessed, lowering her eyes. "I guess she would."

He sat staring at his dusty boots for a long time before he spoke again. "I like kids," he said suddenly. "It tickled me what Alan said that time, about seeing you out in the backyard playing cowboys and Indians with your little brothers. I didn't believe it, of course."

She smiled, reminiscing. "They were sweet boys. I was mostly responsible for them from the time they were born." The smile faded. "It was very hard losing them."

He looked at her quietly. "You haven't had it easy, have you?" he asked softly. "All that responsibility and then your father in a terminal condition with violence at every turn. I figured that was why Alan appealed to you, because he was gentle."

She nodded slowly. "I suppose you're right."

"What you haven't discovered," he added, "is that

Alan's temper is just like mine. Except it's worse, because he loses it so seldom. I get mad, and I'm over it. Alan gets mad and stays mad, sometimes for days.''

''Yes, I noticed he hasn't spoken to you since I came out here.''

''Neither he nor Quinn,'' he replied. He sighed heavily and gave her a rueful smile. ''They all hate me. You have plenty of company.''

''I don't hate you,'' she said.

''Shouldn't you?'' he replied.

Her slender shoulders rose and fell. ''Perhaps I should, but I don't. I suppose all of us have done impulsive things that we've regretted after a time. My father would have died anyway, King. He would have suffered much more, perhaps. I regret many things, myself.''

''Well, that's the worst of it for me,'' he said, catching her eyes. ''You see, I don't regret what happened earlier that day.''

She went scarlet, but she couldn't quite manage to look away from those glittery silver eyes.

''I still want you,'' he said deliberately. ''Even more, because now I know what it's like.'' He searched her eyes and nodded. ''You're shocked. You shouldn't be. I'm as much a slave to my passions as any other man.''

''Passion is . . . degrading,'' she choked.

''Unaccompanied by any finer feelings, it certainly is,'' he said. ''But you and I aren't indifferent to each other, mentally or physically. I daresay we'll find things that we have in common, now that I'm getting to know the real you, the one who's been in hiding for four years.''

''You might not like what you find.''

He laughed softly. ''I like spirit,'' he said. ''You're

welcome to throw anything you like at me. But," he added, his voice deep and thrilling, "next time, there will be consequences."

Her pulse raced at the look in his eyes. She didn't understand what was happening. It frightened her.

He put a big, lean hand over hers where it rested on her stomach over the covers.

"Most married people get off to a rocky start," he said. "We didn't have the beginning I'd have liked. But we'll put it all right in time."

"You don't want to marry me," she said sadly.

He brought her hand, palm up, to his lips and kissed it gently. "I don't want to marry anyone," he said honestly. "But I'm thirty. It's time I thought of settling down."

"I keep forgetting that you're older than Quinn, because you were at college together."

"I was the oldest in my graduating class. I got a late start, but I began to realize that education can make a difference in a man's fortunes." He smoothed her hand against his rough, lean cheek. "The future is going to require educated men. We have plenty of opportunity to grow out here, but it has to be planned growth, the right kind of growth. We've got to plan on more than cattle and crops to take us into the twentieth century."

"A prediction?"

"Of sorts." He kissed her palm again and laid her hand back down. "I'm drunk, Amy," he said on a roughly expelled breath.

"Yes, I think you are, a little," she replied smiling. "Do go to bed and get some rest."

His pale eyes searched over her face on the pillow, lingering on her soft pink mouth. "Darcy can't bear to have me touch her," he said. "This afternoon, when I held you, you pushed me away as if I disgusted you."

She stiffened under the covers. "I . . . do not like the way you make me feel when you touch me," she said evasively.

One dark eyebrow lifted. "Would you care to explain what you mean?"

"Not really," she replied, embarrassed.

But even in his intoxicated state, her meaning got through to him. He stared at her and began to smile. "Well."

"Don't let it go to your head," she said haughtily. "I'm certain that any man with your experience could produce the same effect."

"That's something you won't have time to find out," he assured her. "You'll be married before you know it. And there won't be even the hint of another man in your life."

"That sounds vaguely like a threat."

"You may take it as exactly that." His eyes were slow and bold on her figure, outlined by the heavy covers. "You are mine. I don't intend sharing you, ever."

"I am not property!"

He pursed his lips. "Indeed?"

Her eyes flashed. "And I don't intend to spend our married life being told every move to make by you!"

He leaned over her, resting his weight on the lean hands at either side of her head. "In some ways, you will," he threatened softly. "You know very little about how to please a man yet."

She gasped with outraged modesty, and he took the soft sound into his mouth in a kiss that was warm and slow and drugging. She lay helpless beneath the deli-

cate teasing of his lips as they touched and lifted, probed
and withdrew. It was like fencing, she thought dizzily
as the feeling grew to frightening depth. Her hand went
up to his chest, protesting weakly, only to spur memories of how he felt without the shirt covering it.

"We might have been made for each other, in this
way," he breathed into her parted mouth. "Each time
I kiss you, the feelings we share ignite me."

"You should not . . ."

"Try to sound more convincing, Amy," he teased,
and very quickly the teasing stopped as he brought his
mouth down with increasing insistence and hunger.

She reached up to hold him, drawing him down to
her, while his mouth made a mockery of her earlier
protest.

Neither of them heard the door open or a throat being
cleared very loudly. Enid gave up and slammed the
door. Hard.

They jumped, jerking apart. King looked shaken, and
Amelia's face blushed like a rose. She tugged the covers
up to her chin and sat up in bed, her eyes like saucers.

"How very guilty you both look," Enid murmured
wickedly. "I suppose there is a very reasonable explanation?"

"Of a certainty," King drawled. "May I have five
minutes to think up one?"

"Take ten," his mother said generously. "It will take
me that long to get the biscuits finished."

He groaned as he got up, putting a hand to his temple.

"You reek of whiskey," Enid complained, wrinkling
her nose. "I wonder that Amelia could endure you at
such close range."

Amelia flushed, because she hadn't even noticed the

taste of whiskey in his mouth, she'd been so hungry for him.

"I had a drink or two," King said.

"You had a bottle or two," his mother retorted. "Shame on you!"

"She drove me to it," he said, nodding toward Amelia. "She keeps refusing to marry me."

"Perhaps a reluctant proposal was not enough to win her," Enid replied.

He stared at Amelia and smiled slowly. "Then I must exert myself and mount a convincing campaign for her hand."

"A wise idea," his mother agreed.

"He is a reluctant bridegroom," Amelia protested. "It's hardly fair to land him with a wife he doesn't want!"

"Forgive me, Amelia, but from what I just saw it's very difficult to believe that."

"I agree," King nodded, enjoying Amelia's discomfort.

"You can be quiet," Amelia told King. "You did nothing but bad-mouth me from the day I arrived, and now you want to marry me?"

"But that was before you threw the carafe at me," he pointed out. His lips drew up in a slow, wicked smile. "I much prefer a ruffled wren to a tame house sparrow."

"Do go," Enid said, pushing her son toward the door. "All this is highly unconventional. You should not be in Amelia's bedroom with her in her nightclothes and no chaperone."

"How could I possibly kiss her with a chaperone in residence?" he asked reasonably.

Enid closed the door on him. She glanced at Amelia,

who looked more alive and radiant than Enid had ever seen her.

"I did not realize that he had a conscience," Amelia had to confess.

"Of course he does. But he is adept at hiding his deepest feelings. That has been true since his engagement to Alice."

Amelia got out of bed. "He must have loved her very much," she said miserably.

Enid glanced at her warily. "He thought he did."

"It . . . would have been tragic for him to lose her in such a violent way."

"Indeed it was. He went off on a hunting trip and stayed away for three weeks after it happened." Enid turned to the younger woman. "But she would not have made him happy, Amelia. She did not love him any more than Darcy does. King has become adept at choosing the wrong woman. Until now," she added quietly.

"But he didn't choose me," Amelia reminded her. "And he doesn't want me, except . . . well, perhaps in one way. It will not be a good marriage."

"You must make it one, then," the older woman said softly. "He is not a heartless man, and he is very much attracted to you. Do not give up on him now, Amelia."

Fortunately, Enid didn't know the reason they had to get married, and Amelia couldn't bring herself to admit it. She nodded, hoping that it would all come right, as King had said it would.

Quinn sat at his desk in the Ranger office, pondering the reward poster on Rodriguez that he was obliged to post. It was a good likeness of the bandit. Too good.

He'd tried to pretend that he didn't know where Rodriguez was, that he didn't have to tell anyone he'd seen him. But the badge was wearing a hole in his shirt. He had taken a solemn vow to uphold the law. Rodriguez had broken it. He had to do his job, no matter what the personal cost to himself. He would lose Maria before he even had her. But that was fate, perhaps.

He buckled on his gun belt. He could do it alone. He had to, because to involve other Rangers might endanger Maria and Juliano, not to mention the children in the camp. He could manage.

"Where are you off to?" his captain asked.

"Mexico. To bring in Rodriguez."

"You found him?" the short, older man asked.

He nodded. "But I didn't know it until this poster came in," he prevaricated. "When I was in Del Rio, I saw this man."

"Wait a minute, and I'll get some of the other men. . . ."

"I can do this on my own, Captain," Quinn said quietly. "There are some children with him. I don't want to put them at risk by taking a large contingent. Will you trust me to do it, my way?"

Quinn had been with the Rangers for almost two years, and Captain Baylor knew him very well. If Quinn gave his word, it was worth gold.

"All right. Be careful."

"I will, sir."

Quinn left with a leaden heart, on his way to Sonora to betray the one woman he could ever love. It was misting rain, and he thought that oddly fitting as he rode out of El Paso.

King joined the others for breakfast, still a little bleary-eyed, but sober.

"Where were you last night?" Brant asked him.

"Getting soaked in El Paso," came the dry reply.

"How much did it cost this time?" his father asked.

"I didn't break anything. I got drunk and came home."

"That's a first," Alan said, looking fully at his brother after a two-day sulk. "Did Amelia refuse you?"

King stared his younger brother down. "Not yet, she hasn't," he said after a minute.

Amelia glanced at him, irritable at being taken for granted. "The day is young," she said.

He cocked an eyebrow. "Would you really leave me in the lurch?" he chided softly. "Desert me in my hour of need?"

She blushed, because that should have been her own cry. She fumbled some eggs onto her plate, while Alan frowned with insatiable curiosity at the byplay.

"Have you told Miss Valverde?" she asked coolly.

He fingered his coffee cup. "Not yet. I have that chore to perform this morning."

"I don't envy you," Alan said. "She'll probably be audible in El Paso."

And she was, in fact. She screamed and cried; she accused King of leading her on; she accused him of ruining her good name. And all through it, he simply stood, arms folded, smoking his cigar like a man without a care in the world.

"You said you detested her," Darcy choked. "You're only marrying her because you've compromised her, and everyone knows it!" she raged. "In addition to her other failings, she is also a loose woman!"

King's face changed. His eyes became dangerous. "If

I ever hear that accusation from you or anyone else again, I will make you sorry.''

"Yes?'' She lifted her chin haughtily. "And what will you do?''

"Buy up your father's mortgage and dispossess you, if it takes that to bring you to your senses,'' he said without raising his voice.

Darcy went white in the face. All the raw temper seeped out of her, and she sought excuses for her outburst.

"It was the shock of losing you,'' she said quickly. "Only the shock. Of course I did not mean . . .''

King moved down the steps and back to his horse. He didn't say another word.

Later, as he mounted the steps at Latigo, he began to realize just how much harm he'd done to Amelia's reputation. If people were gossiping so much, the incident in the bank must have been greatly embroidered.

He found Amelia in the parlor, stitching up the hem of the dress she planned to be married in.

He knelt in front of her. "Can you go into church with me and overlook the gossiping, the scandal, I've created for you?'' he asked bluntly. "Or do you want to be married somewhere else? We could go back East, to Georgia if you like.''

She was breathless at the offer. He sounded concerned for her feelings, and that was a first. "Why . . . I am not afraid of wagging tongues,'' she stammered.

He searched her face, drinking in her beauty and grace. It occurred to him that he was a very lucky man, in more ways than one.

Amelia saw the affection in his eyes and responded to it with a warm smile. "I don't mind a few odd looks.''

"Nor do I. But I would have done anything necessary to spare you."

She put another stitch in. "How did Miss Valverde take it?"

He got up, dropping lightly into an armchair near her. "She took it with outrage. I suppose she was entitled. I had allowed her to believe my intentions were serious."

"Very . . . serious?" she fished.

He saw the blush and understood it. "One or two kisses hardly constitute a serious relationship," he said quietly. "It was my wealth that she wanted. Not me."

She finished her stitch and tied it off. "I would like to know about Alice."

His face closed up. It was a subject he hadn't discussed with anyone. He lit a cigar and pulled an ashtray close, all without speaking.

She looked across at him. "I shall have to know," she persisted. "If your heart is in the grave with her, I will not marry you, King."

His hand stilled, dropping the spent match in the ashtray. His eyes, curious, soft, searched her flushed face. "So you want more than my name, Amelia?" he asked quietly.

She clenched her teeth. "I will not share you with the living or the dead. It is the way I am made."

He leaned back, quietly smoking his cigar while his eyes sketched her soft face. "Very well. What do you wish to know?"

"Did you love her?"

"*Quien sabe?*" he asked heavily. "I thought I did. I thought she loved me. But when we were in danger of losing the ranch altogether, she took up with a tinker and started being seen, conspicuously, in his company.

It was during one of their drives that that Rodriguez's cutthroats attacked them.'' His face hardened as the memories came back to haunt him. ''I do not like remembering how we found them.''

''I'm sorry. It must have been very painful,'' she said helplessly.

''My father was in the cavalry back in the seventies,'' he said. ''He was with the company that found what was left of Custer and his men. What he described is pretty much what I saw after Rodriguez got through with Alice. I understand some Indians run with Rodriguez, so perhaps he turned them loose on the pair.''

''Savagery is hardly limited to Indians, or have you not read the daily reports on the Boer War?'' she queried.

''Indeed.'' He stared at the smoke drifting up to the high ceiling. ''We buried Alice and her companion and set out after Rodriguez, but he was too slippery to catch. He darted back over the border, and all our searching didn't produce him. Even the Rangers tried, but they couldn't catch him either. I gave up and went off into the mountains to try and get past what had happened. It took a long time.''

''Did she love you?''

His pale eyes met hers. ''She loved my money,'' he countered mockingly. ''Just as Darcy does. She could hardly bear my touch at all.'' His eyes narrowed. ''You are unique. You have no thirst for wealth, yet you unfold like a bud in bloom when I put my hands on you. It is . . . disquieting. Humbling.''

She moved her legs slightly under her long skirts and rearranged the fabric, avoiding his piercing scrutiny.

''As I have said, you are experienced. . . .''

''Experience is of no account where there is also revulsion," he pointed out. "But you love my kisses, Amelia. Not for all the world could you pretend such abandon."

She cleared her throat and fumbled with her needle. He was ferreting out all her secrets, making her nervous. "Perhaps I am only acting, too."

He smiled gently. "No."

She pricked her finger with the needle in her confusion and cried out, sucking it as blood welled at the tip. Over it she met his eyes.

"Do you ride, Amelia?" he asked.

"Yes."

"I will take you with me in the morning when I go to oversee the last of the branding. Unless branding makes you ill?" he added.

"I have found very little that turns my stomach," she confessed.

He got up, putting out his cigar. "I have some book work to do before I retire. Don't stay up too late, my dear."

The endearment, the first he'd ever used, made her flutter. She looked up at him when he passed. He bent and very slowly kissed her upturned mouth, his lips lingering until her own parted and offered him heaven.

His fingers slid up and down her throat, light as a breath, before he lifted his head and released her from the sensual spell of his touch.

"Sleep well."

She opened her lips to speak, and he bent and kissed them again. She reached up her hand to flatten it against his cheek, a soft moan escaping her throat.

He caught her hand and held it tight, tight, in his, glittery lights in his silver eyes as he watched her.

"I want that, too," he said roughly. "You in my

arms, your mouth abandoned to mine, the aching pleasure of feeling you against me completely. But if I hold
you, no power on earth will tear you from my arms
until morning. And that I will not have. The next time
you come to me will be honorable and lawful. God
forgive me, Amelia, I never thought to bring you such
shame and pain.'' He brought her palm to his mouth,
released it, and went quickly from the room.

Amelia held the hand he'd kissed to her breast and
tried to make sense of the confusing things he'd said.
He felt something for her besides guilt. But if he hadn't
really loved Alice, how would he be able to love
Amelia? And what sort of marriage could they have
without love on both sides?

═══ Chapter Eighteen ═══

I T WAS EARLY MORNING, WITH DEW STILL ON THE
grass, when King rode out to the cow camp with
Amelia riding beside him. She had, he'd told her, a
perfect seat in the saddle, and he watched her with pride
as she mounted and easily adjusted to the motion of the
animal.

Despite her fears of the night before, Amelia had
never felt more alive, more excited. It was as if they
were meeting for the first time, as if there was no dark
past behind them. King seemed younger, too, and light
of heart. She looked at him from under the brim of her
hat, feeling the rocking motion of the horse beneath her
as she studied the face that was becoming more beloved
to her by the day. The ghost of Alice had faded with
the dawn, and the invitation to ride out into the pastures
with King had made Amelia strangely shy and elated
all at once. He had become her world. She was resigned
to accepting whatever he had to offer her, even the left-
over love from his relationship with his late fiancée.
Without him, she had nothing.

He glanced toward her, intercepted that adoring
glance, and smiled without mockery.

She flushed. The way he smiled made her tingle all
the way to her toes, which amused her, and she laughed
secretively.

King laughed, too, lifting his face to the warm morning sun as the sounds of the wild place swirled around them.

"I'm learning things about you that please me very much," he remarked as they rode closer to the cow camp. "I never thought to see you on horseback."

"I love to ride," she remarked. "I love the country. It was torture having to live surrounded by buildings and hurrying people. This is heaven," she added on a sigh, drinking in the peace of the country.

King studied her longer than he meant to and turned his attention back to the trail. She was possessing him, day by day, taking him over. He found himself thinking of her all the time now, wanting to ease her path, protect her. It was new to feel these things with a woman. It was new to have a woman want his embraces with no thought of gain. He felt reborn.

"King," she began.

"What?"

"Did you notice a reserve about Quinn when you mentioned Rodriguez?" she asked suddenly.

He pulled his horse to a stop and sat forward in the saddle facing her. "Yes," he replied. "It puzzled me. His job, as you know, has become his life. I thought at first it might be because of your father or your own situation. But it was not. There is something about the way he looks when Rodriguez is mentioned." He shook his head. "I have no idea what it could be."

"It is not like Quinn to feel sympathy for criminals," she said, fingering her reins. "There must be more to this than we realize."

"I agree." He studied her, smiling. "Sunday is but two days away. Your dress is finished?"

She nodded. "Your mother helped me with the lace."

"She and my father find you a welcome addition to the family."

She started to speak, then hesitated. The reins in her hand felt suddenly cold. She wanted him to find her a welcome addition as well, but that was hardly likely to happen. She would always be a reminder to him of his loss of control, of his vulnerability. How could he want her in his life?

He rode forward, beside her, and one lean hand reached out to clasp hers where it lay on the pommel.

"This marriage might not been my idea originally," he said. "But I want you to know that I have no misgivings about it now."

He meant because of his sense of responsibility for what had happened, she knew. She forced a wan smile to her face. "Nor have I," she said.

"What is wrong?"

"It is only that you had no choice," she blurted out, and the eyes that lifted to his were turbulent.

"I had every choice," he said firmly. "Amelia . . . it is not seemly to speak of such things, perhaps, but did you not realize that I deliberately allowed it to go too far when we were together? It would have been possible for me to stop in time. I chose not to."

She flushed. "Because you wanted to stop me from seeing Alan," she agreed.

"No!" His hand on hers tightened. "Because I wanted you for myself, Amelia, on any terms I could get you. I was jealous of Alan, don't you see?"

Her eyes softened, darkened. "Jealous of me?"

He nodded. "What sane man would not be jealous of a woman who melted in his arms, yearned for his kisses, made him feel invincible when he was with her?"

She wanted to deny all that, but she couldn't. It was just as he said, she had no willpower when she was with him.

"I must have been very obvious," she murmured.

"Only when it was too late," he mused, smiling gently at her confusion. "What other motive could you have had for surrendering to me? You are neither mercenary nor casual in your morals. That being the case, it was not difficult to understand your feelings." The smile faded. "Forgive me for shaming you. I still find my own behavior inexplicable and disturbing."

She was embarrassed. She felt stripped of all her emotional armor. She fingered the reins too tightly, making the horse jump.

He reared and all but unseated her. King, alarmed, jumped down from his own mount and quickly controlled Amelia's with cold nerve. He threw his knee into the horse's chest and very nearly brought him down. Then, when the animal was stunned, he began to calm him, talking softly, soothing it with his hands.

Amelia shivered with reaction when her mount was standing calm again. King helped her down; he'd been so confident, so expert at handling the animal that she was shocked to find his face very pale, and a faint tremor in the hands that held her.

"You are all right?" he asked quickly.

His concern was almost her undoing. She managed a nervous laugh. "Yes. I'm sorry. It . . . it was my fault, I tugged too hard on the reins. The poor creature, I must have bruised his mouth."

"He could have thrown you!"

She was awed by the expression on his face, the barely contained fury in his eyes. Fascinated, she reached up and laid her hand against his cheek. "I'm all right," she said softly. "Truly, King."

He was quieting, but slowly. She could still feel the tension in him, the strength and temper barely held in check.

"You're certain?" he asked.

She smiled, nodding. "I wasn't frightened. You're very good with animals, you know. I never doubted that you'd quiet him."

He was breathing roughly. It had occurred to him somewhere in that brief struggle that Amelia could have been badly hurt. His reaction was no different than it had been when he'd seen her lying on the floor in her father's house. It shattered him to realize how much it had frightened him. He . . . cared.

She looked into his eyes and felt her heart run wild at the emotion that filled them. For that moment, he was incapable of hiding from her what he felt. It was all there, open in his face, naked to her gaze. The joy of it made her radiant, choked her.

"Oh, King, did it matter so much that I might be hurt?" she whispered brokenly.

With a harsh groan, he stepped forward, wrapping her up in warm, strong arms. "Amelia," he whispered roughly, and found her mouth with his own.

Long, lazy minutes slid by while they clung together in the shade of a mesquite tree while the horses grazed nearby. But eventually, as the heat of their passion began straining at the bonds they placed on it, King was forced to draw back.

"This must stop," he said unsteadily. He framed her face in his lean hands and sketched it with quick, loving eyes, from her radiant cheeks to her swollen soft mouth.

"We must not anticipate our vows a second time. But Sunday will not come soon enough for me."

"Or for me," she whispered. She lay her head against the heavy rise and fall of his chest and stood there until they both calmed. Across his shirt she could see the horizon, and she thought with a shock of happiness that she had a new future to look forward to now, one that was free from the terror of the past.

"I will let nothing hurt you ever again," he said huskily, brushing his lips over her forehead. "There will be no more pain."

"No more." She nuzzled her face against his chest, feeling the springy chest hair under the soft shirt. She smiled. "This time it will be very different, will it not? When we are . . . together, I mean."

His chest stilled under her ear and then began to rise and fall more quickly. "Very different, indeed," he whispered. "Because this time there will be tenderness and all the time in the world." His mouth traveled down her face and found, tenderly, her soft mouth. "Alan and my parents plan to leave after the wedding to see friends in Houston over the weekend. We will be alone for several days." He kissed her again, groaning faintly. "Amelia, how can I bear these next three days?" he moaned against her welcoming mouth.

"The time will pass very quickly," she whispered. "Very, very quickly."

"For the sake of my self-control and your virtue, I hope that is the case." He chuckled.

Quinn had ridden back to Malasuerte, feeling like a dog as he mentally prepared to betray Maria and her father. He had to keep reminding himself that he'd taken an oath to uphold the law and Rodriguez had broken it.

In the long run, that was the only thing that mattered. His duty didn't allow for a bleeding heart. Rodriguez's people were poor, certainly, but that didn't excuse the use of murder and thievery to feed and clothe them. He had to forget what the bandit chief had done for Maria and Juliano and concentrate on the deaths, including that of King's fiancée, that had been done by Rodriguez's hands.

But all the philosophizing didn't do his conscience any good as he rode across the dry wash and into the small pueblo. Things got worse when Maria spotted him and dropped the corn she was carrying in the dirt to run to him as if her life depended on reaching him.

The sight of her made him realize how alone and miserable he'd been since he left the pueblo. He was out of the saddle in a flash, just in time to meet her wild onrush. He lifted her clear off the ground and found her mouth with his, all in the same smooth motion. And for long, sweet minutes, she was his alone, she belonged to him totally.

Dimly, he was aware of the buzz of conversation and muted laughter. He lifted his head at last, to find the two of them half surrounded by the inhabitants of the small pueblo. Rodriguez was there, too, all smiles.

Quinn felt like a traitor. He wasn't going to be able to live with himself once he did this. Duty or not, he was always going to feel as if he'd betrayed everyone who loved him. With his father dead and King hell-bent on marrying Amelia, Maria was really the only person left who did love him, he thought miserably. But she wouldn't for long. When she found out why he'd come here, she was going to want to kill him.

It wouldn't hurt, surely, he told himself, to spend just a day or two in camp first. To spend time with Maria and catch what little happiness he could to last him for the rest of his miserable life.

"You have returned," Rodriguez said glowingly, offering his hand to be shaken and then hugging the younger man warmly. "My son, you are welcome among us. My poor Maria has been like the dead since your departure! It is good that you have come back to make her heart sing again!"

"My own heart didn't do much singing," he confessed, his eyes meeting Maria's with pure aching hunger. "My father has died," he said without meaning to.

"Oh, my dear." Maria went close to him and hugged him, giving him comfort and strength. "I am so sorry."

Quinn's arms slowly enfolded her. His heart ached clean through from this sweet comfort.

"*Lo siento, también,*" Rodriguez seconded. "It is never pleasant to lose a father. My own, he was a *haciendado*, you know," he added with a smile. "He was one of the Spanish grandees, but he married a mestiza woman, and eventually he lost everything he had because he drank too much." He spread his hands as if it didn't matter one bit. "Too much money is the ruin of a good man, *es verdad, señor?* Better to live like the birds, with the open sky and land for a home. *Ay de mi*, there is nothing more precious than freedom!" He eyed Quinn's closed face, and then Maria's. "Well, perhaps love is as important." He chuckled.

Quinn nodded. The dark eyes that looked down into Maria's blue ones were deeply troubled.

"You have come back to us with grief and some worrying problem to work out, *señor,*" Rodriguez said unexpectedly, clapping the younger man on the shoulder. "*Bueno.* You will stay with us, and these things will no longer make you look like a haunted man. Lopita, bring mescal and let us cheer up this weary traveler!''

Lopita, a heavyset, short woman with twinkling eyes and few teeth, grinned and produced a jug of mescal. Rodriguez took it, giving her a loud kiss on the cheek.

"She is my wife," he told Quinn. "And she may not be much to look at, *señor*, but she has a kind heart, and she makes the best enchiladas in the pueblo!''

"She has been *mamacita* to Juliano and to me," Maria added, grinning at Lopita as she scurried around the hut. "She is a good woman." Maria watched Quinn sit down near the small fire. "Your mother is not alive?''

He shook his head. "She died some years ago.''

"Your father, was he killed?''

"No. He had a tumor in his brain.''

Maria crossed herself. *"Que horrible para tu,"* she said softly. *"Lo siento."*

"It was much worse for my sister. He was . . . rather cruel to her at the end. It wasn't his fault, you know," he added, feeling the need to defend his father even now. "He didn't know what he was doing.''

"This tumor, it is a disease?" Rodriguez queried.

"It is a growth inside the head," Quinn told him.

"Ah. *Yo sé.* A growth. Very painful, no?''

"Very." Quinn took the mescal Rodriguez poured for him with a nod of thanks. He tasted it and found the hard bite of the liquor helped to ease his grief and shame.

"This sister, Amelia, is she like you?''

He smiled. "We could be twins. I'm much taller, of course. She is a courageous lady, but she, like your Lopita, has a kind heart.''

"Something which is worth rubies, I tell you, *señor*," Rodriguez said fervently. "It is good that you have come back," he added after a minute, and he looked thoughtful and worried. "I have a problem of my own which you might be able to help me solve."

"If I can," Quinn agreed.

Rodriguez stared at the mescal jug. "I am a hunted man, *señor*. The authorities in Texas want very much to lure me across the border and hang me. And now I hear that they are sending the Texas Rangers to look for me again." He looked up, surprising a strange look in Quinn's eyes. "I am not the man I was. I have not the wiles that kept me one step ahead. There is also my family and my people to consider." He took a slow breath. "I have been thinking that perhaps I should surrender myself, for the sake of my people."

"Papa, no!" Maria cried, anguished. She threw herself at Rodriguez, crying. "You must not, you *must* not, they would kill you! Oh, Papa, do not say such things!"

Rodriguez sighed heavily, patting the hysterical girl on the back. "Yes, I know, you love me. I love you, too, *niña*. But there is the danger that the Texas Rangers might come here. I heard rumors of this in El Paso. If this happens, many innocent people might die. These Rangers fight like demons out of hell, we know this. I do not want my people to suffer. It is better that I give myself up, rather than risk other lives."

Quinn was poleaxed. He didn't know what to say. Obviously, some people in El Paso had heard about his assignment to bring in Rodriguez and had embroidered it, as gossip did. But for once gossip might have aided him. Rodriguez was playing right into his hands. He could hardly believe his good fortune.

"What do you want of me, *señor*?" Quinn asked slowly.

"That you accompany me into Texas, *señor*, to hand myself over to the authorities in El Paso," Rodriguez said wearily. "My chances will be better of reaching them alive if I have a gringo companion."

"That is true," Quinn had to admit.

"Then . . . you will accompany me?"

Quinn hesitated, guilt-ridden, but Maria prodded him. "Please," she said softly. "Please, you must."

"Very well," he said reluctantly. "When do you want to go?"

"Tomorrow," Rodriguez said. "That will give me one last night at home to be with my family." He looked at Quinn levelly. "These charges that the Americanos have raised against me are not true, *señor*," he added surprisingly. "I have killed no gringos. I have robbed a bank or two, *sí*. But these crimes, these butcheries, of which they accuse me are false charges. I want to stand trial, to deny them. I am no butcher. I wish to be done with the past. I wish to start my life again, to . . . *como se dice* . . . turn the new leaf." He grinned at Quinn. "I wish to become a new man. So, you shall help me, no?"

Quinn was stunned and speechless. "Is this not rather sudden?"

"*Señor*, shall we be earnest? I am an old man. Inevitably the gringos will catch me, and I will be hanged. I do not wish this to happen before I have the chance to tell my story, to deny that I have cut up young women or killed in cold blood. I do not wish my children and my grandchildren to think that I was such a bad man, you understand?"

"Yes," Quinn said. "But if you expect a fair trial . . . !"

"Why should I not get one?" Rodriguez asked patiently. "I am not guilty."

"You are a Mexican," Quinn emphasized. "And there has been enough trouble on the border to prejudice people in El Paso against you already. It will be taking a terrible chance."

Rodriguez shrugged. "I have been taking terrible chances for many years. One more does not seem like so much."

"Then, if you feel that way about it, yes, I'll go with you," Quinn said.

Rodriguez smiled at him. "I know that you will take very good care of me, *señor*. I have no fear."

Quinn wished that he could say as much. Rodriguez would find out who he was the minute they hit El Paso, and his respect and the girl's adoration would cease to exist. Quinn would become the real bad guy, and despite his hopes, Rodriguez would be lynched to the nearest tree. He had never felt quite so helpless in all his life.

Maria, sensing his disquiet, snuggled up against his side and lay her head on his shoulder. "Do not worry so," she chided. "Papa is a fox. He will not let them hang him."

Quinn smoothed her long, black hair. All the while he was wondering how he would prevent that.

The night passed slowly. Quinn woke at dawn and got up, wandering around the small pueblo with curiosity. He was family, so no one thought anything about his restlessness. Rodriguez was in his own hut, sound asleep. Quinn paused outside it, wanting so badly to go in and confess everything.

Maria heard him and came out, wrapping a shawl around her shoulders to shield her from the chill of morning. *"Buenos dias,"* she murmured, lifting her smiling face to be kissed.

Quinn obliged her, but absentmindedly, because his mind was on Rodriguez and the long ride back to El Paso.

She saw his preoccupation. She took him by the hand and led him out of earshot of the hut.

"Tell me what bothers you so," she queried softly.

He grimaced as he met her blue eyes. "I'm not what you think I am," he said heavily.

"I know what you are going to say," she murmured, watching his face go blank. "You, too, are a *desperado,* and if you take my papa to El Paso, they may get you, too," she said misconstruing everything in sweet oblivion. "Papa will not go through with it." She laughed. "He takes these spells once in a while. He never gets past the outskirts of El Paso before he turns around and comes back home. It will be all right. Simply humor him. Shhhh!" she cautioned quickly when he started to protest, because Rodriguez was just coming out of the hut in search of him.

Quinn was forced not to argue, not to tell the truth. He gritted his teeth with the effort not to confess. They were going to hate him, he knew. But the die was cast.

He watched Rodriguez pack his saddlebags and say good-bye to his family and friends. That was hard enough, but when Maria began to cry, and Juliano, it was almost more than Quinn could bear. How could he have allowed himself to do this? Fate was working to his advantage, but he would be betraying not only Rodriguez but Maria as well. He looked down into her soft blue eyes and wondered how he would ever be able to live with his own conscience once the deed was done.

"Vaya con Díos," she said softly.

"I'll need to," he replied quietly.

Rodriguez smiled at her. *"Adíos, niña."*

"Hasta luego," she corrected. "You will be back very soon. I know it."

Rodriguez didn't reply. Neither did Quinn as they waved and rode slowly out of the village. He didn't know how to tell her the truth. It was the first time in memory that he'd deliberately avoided a confrontation. But it was also the first time he'd been in love.

The wedding was an important occasion. Every ranching family for miles came around to view the brief ceremony that took place at the small Methodist church. Afterward there was a parade of buggies and surreys out to Latigo for the reception. Every family brought something to add to the buffet table, and Rosa had made a majestic wedding cake.

Alan was a little sad as he congratulated his new sister-in-law, but he said or did nothing to spoil her happiness.

"He'd better be good to you," was all Alan said, and he smiled even then.

Remembering King's evident concern for her two days ago, when the horse had almost unseated her, made her smile. "He will," she said with certainty. King might not love her, but her welfare certainly mattered to him. Perhaps if she were careful, she might turn that concern into love. It was certainly a possibility.

King claimed her for the first dance, while the cowboy band played a waltz. She whirled in her pretty satin and lace wedding dress in the living room, cleared of furniture for the occasion. King's eyes were possessive and soft with affection. Amelia flushed a little at the look in them.

"My own sweet girl," he said quietly, smiling down at her. "I never dreamed that marriage would be such a welcome thing, or that I would find a woman I cared to spend the rest of my life with."

"You considered spending it with Miss Valverde," she commented.

"A man considers many women before he finds the right one."

"She isn't here today."

His face hardened. "Did you think I would insult you in such a way, by producing one of my old flames to dance at your wedding?"

"I'm sorry," she said. "I didn't mean to make it sound like an insult, but your parents are friends of the Valverdes. . . ."

"A friendship mainly of hopeful gain on their part," he said flatly. "Now that the chance of marriage into my family is passed, I think that we will see much less of them in the future."

Amelia didn't add that she hoped so, but she did.

Chapter Nineteen

RODRIGUEZ ALLOWED QUINN TO PRECEDE HIM INTO the sheriff's office in El Paso. He surrendered his gun without a protest, which only made Quinn feel worse.

"So you brought the greaser in," one of the men talking to the deputies said insolently. "Damned Mexican trash . . . !"

Quinn laid him out in the floor, right in front of the sheriff and his men. "You keep a civil tongue in your head, mister, or I'll pull your tongue out and thread it on my gun barrel!" Quinn said coldly.

He didn't raise his voice. He didn't have to. The man knew him all too well. He got up, favoring his jaw, and quickly exited the office.

"I want some guarantees from you about this prisoner," Quinn told the sheriff. "He's not what you think. And until he's given a trial—a fair trial—he's innocent."

The sheriff nodded. "I'll see to it that he isn't mistreated, Quinn. You have my word on it."

"I'll take him back for you." Quinn took the key and escorted Rodriguez down the row of cells to an empty one.

"These gringos respect you, *señor*," the Mexican remarked. "You are one of them, are you not?"

Quinn didn't look at him. "I'm a Texas Ranger."

Rodriguez gave him a searching look and slowly nodded. "I thought as much. You did not want to bring me here, yet it is your duty to arrest me. It is because of Maria, you hesitate, yes?"

"I love her," Quinn said heavily.

Rodriguez took off his hat and sat down on the bench inside the cell, smiling. "Then she and Juliano will be taken care of. I am glad."

"You won't be hanged," Quinn said stubbornly. "Don't give up now!"

"What I said, to Maria, was for the sake of the grandchildren I may have one day." He studied Quinn's hard face. "The charges are true, *señor*. All of them, except for the butchery. I have killed many gringos, stolen much gold from your banks, taken many head of cattle." He shrugged. "I am an old man. If they hang me, it will only end my suffering. You see, the faces, they have begun to haunt me," he added softly. A faint, bitter smile touched his dry lips. "I do not sleep so good these days. I am tired." He sighed wearily and leaned back against the cold wall. "Whatever they do to me does not matter. Now they will leave my poor people alone, and Maria will be free at last to live her own life and not have to live as a fugitive in mine."

"Rodriguez," Quinn began.

He held up his hand. "*Muchas grácias* for what you have done. But it is finished."

Quinn left, reluctantly. Caught between a rock and a hard place, the saying was, and that was how he felt.

He rode out to Latigo just in time for the end of the festivities as his sister married his best friend. He had hated the idea of this wedding, because he was certain that King had been forced into it for honor's sake, not for love of Amelia. But when he saw the two of them together, he began to rethink his objections. If ever a man was falling in love, it was King. He looked at Amelia with a frank adoration that dominated his lean, dark face.

"Welcome home, stranger!" an elated Amelia said, laughing, running to meet him with a fervent hug. "You made it after all!"

"Barely," Quinn said. "I've just brought in Rodriguez."

The minute he said it, he knew it was the wrong thing to voice. King's face changed. All the pleasure went out of it, and his posture became rigid.

"Where is he?" King asked in a dangerous tone.

"In the city jail. King, wait!"

King had whirled on his heel and was walking toward the stables. Quinn caught him by the arm, holding on relentlessly even when King tried to fling him off.

"Don't do this," Quinn pleaded with him. Beside King, Amelia's face had gone pale and unhappy. "My God, I shouldn't have come, I've spoiled everything for you! I'm sorry!"

"I'll kill him," King said coldly. "Do you think I can forget what he did to her?"

Amelia had thought King was falling in love with her. Now she knew the truth. It was all a lie. He'd been putting on an act, because he was trapped into marrying her. It was Alice he'd loved, still loved. The woman might have been cold in his arms, but that hadn't stopped King from loving her. Unrequited love was a fact of life.

"He'll be tried, fairly," Quinn said harshly. "If you try to go near him, I'll stop you. Don't make me lock you up on your wedding day!"

King seemed to vibrate. He stared at Quinn with furious eyes. "How can you defend him?" he asked harshly.

"He isn't what you think!" came the sharp reply. "He's not a monster. He had nothing to do with that butchery. The man who did it was named Manolito. He left Maria, Rodriguez's adopted daughter, in a brothel in Del Rio. I rescued her and took her home. But long before we reached the pueblo, Rodriguez knew that he'd deserted her in Del Rio and killed him for it. Manolito was a butcher; he killed the girl's family and stole her away. Rodriguez rescued her and her little brother and adopted them as his own. He's a good man, King. He didn't do that to Alice. It was Manolito, and he's dead!"

If Quinn had hoped to sway his friend, he was doomed to disappointment. King was too furious to listen. All he could see was Alice's poor body, cut to ribbons, mutilated.

He broke Quinn's hold and turned on him, as dangerous as his friend had ever seen him. "Get off Latigo land. And don't come back," he told Quinn in a cold, menacing tone.

He stared at the man with utter contempt and then went stalking off by himself while Amelia stood in the tatters of her dignity. Around them, friends and neighbors tried not to stare and failed miserably. Quinn turned and mounted his horse, deaf to Amelia's entreaties, to the Culhanes' apologies. He felt like a man carrying the weight of the world on his shoulders as he rode back toward town.

Enid and Brant had planned to go away for the weekend, to leave the newlyweds alone. As it turned out, a reluctant Alan went by himself. Enid couldn't leave the broken girl to face the house alone, because King had gotten on his horse and ridden away without another word to anyone. Apparently he wasn't speaking to Amelia because of Quinn and what he'd said about Rodriguez.

"It's the . . . the daughter of Rodriguez," Amelia had sobbed. "It must be. Quinn's in love with her. Did you see his face when he spoke of her? And he had to arrest her father. He'll be hanged, you know he will, even if they don't find him guilty of the murders, they'll hang him for bank robbery and rustling. He's probably sure she'll never forgive him."

"Poor Quinn," Enid said soothingly. "And poor you. King can be so inflexible sometimes."

"He still loves her, doesn't he?" Amelia asked, her tragic, tear-wet face looked to Enid for confirmation of what she already knew. "He hasn't stopped loving her at all. He wants vengeance for her death."

"He was very young," Enid said slowly.

"It's no use at all," Amelia replied, wiping her eyes. "He's given me what he meant to, the protection of his name to save mine. Now I can give him something in return. I can leave here and let him go on with his life. Later, perhaps, a divorce can be quietly obtained."

Enid was horrified. "Amelia, you must not leave!"

"How can I stay? King wants no part of me! If he had cared, he would never have let the capture of an outlaw destroy our wedding day like this. He did the right and honorable thing, I cannot expect him to pretend love where none exists." She wiped her eyes hurriedly. "I will stay the night. Tomorrow, I will go back to the boardinghouse, where I will stay until I can contact my cousin in Florida."

Enid didn't know what to say. She felt totally helpless. "Amelia, I am so sorry!"

"Yes. So am I. But at least I know the truth now. King cannot love me. His heart is buried with this Alice to whom he was engaged."

"She didn't love him!" Enid argued gently.

"But King loved her," came the wise reply. "Whether love is shared or not does not matter to one whose heart is stubbornly addicted."

"You love King," Enid stated.

Amelia nodded. "I will love him until I die. But it would never be enough for him." She reached out and kissed Enid's cheek. "Thank you for being so kind to me. I wish I could repay you."

"Amelia, King will be devastated if he finds you gone."

"No, he will not," she said simply. "I think you will find that he is only relieved. Now I must rest. I have so much to do tomorrow."

"Oh, brother Quinn! Why did he have to come today, of all days, with such news?" Enid moaned.

"Perhaps it is better to find the truth out while there is still time to save the situation, don't you think? Sleep well," Amelia said softly. She rose and went down the hall to her room, the one she would have shared with her new husband. She felt as if her heart were dead inside her poor body. All those glorious hopes that had risen in the past few days had been brought low forever.

King tied his horse in a thicket and stood watching the landscape until it was almost dark. In his mind he could see Alice's tortured body, feel the agony it had given him to know that she was dead and he had been unable to help her in her time of need. It had been worse, because the butcher Rodriguez could not be captured and punished. Now Rodriguez was within reach, and the best friend King had in the world was suddenly his ardent defender.

He broke a twig to pieces in his work-roughened hands while he fought to come to grips with his situation. If he tried to get to Rodriguez, Quinn would have him jailed. That would be an irony.

His mind was busy, wrangling with the problem, when something Quinn had said began to register. There had been a man, Manolito, who had been responsible for the murders. Rodriguez had killed him for leaving someone named Maria in a bordello.

His hands stilled. Maria was Rodriguez's adopted daughter, and Quinn was apparently in love with her. He'd had to arrest Rodriguez, and now Maria would surely hate him.

King let out a rush of held breath. He'd been so obsessed with the past that he hadn't seen his friend's anguish over the present. There was something else, too, wasn't there? Amelia!

He turned, striding back to his horse. He'd left Amelia almost at the altar, turned his back on her to go raving off after the murderer of a dead fiancée. Amelia would think he still loved Alice. She would be devastated.

He could have cursed himself for his shortsightedness. He reached for the horse's bridle just as the unmistakable sound of a rattlesnake sent him jumping back in the nick of time. The horse was spooked, however, and began to run madly away. King wasn't wearing his sidearm, so he had to walk wide around the damned snake instead of blowing his head off, as he would have liked. Here he was, miles from the ranch, with night approaching, horseless and gunless, feeling like a fool. He began to laugh. It was a poor start to a marriage, he thought ruefully. He hoped Amelia would be more

understanding than he had been. He started to walk
back to the path that led to Latigo.

Quinn wanted to ride back to Malasuerte and explain
himself to Maria. But he felt obliged to stay in town
and look after Rodriguez while he was imprisoned. He
felt terrible about his falling out with King and causing
Amelia grief on what should have been a happy day.
He had never been quite so miserable.

It was dark when he got to town, and he was too tired
to ride to Alpine to the barracks. He got a room in town
and went to bed. Perhaps, he told himself, things would
look better after a good night's sleep.

King, meanwhile, had decided that he'd do better to
sleep than try to walk on in the dark to the ranch,
through snake-invested brush and cactus. He made a
small camp fire, built himself a bed out of what vegetation he could find, and with an empty belly, settled
down for his wedding night. He wondered if anyone
had ever had a more uncomfortable one.

He would have known if he could have seen Amelia's
poor face when she got up before daylight and washed
it. Her eyes were swollen from crying, and she was
drawn and pale from her ordeal.

She packed her few things and begged a ride from
Brant back into town.

King's father muttered all the way to El Paso. Enid
had wept and tried to get Amelia to stay. But the girl
was determined. She'd had quite enough of King's behavior. The fact that he'd stayed out all night had surely
underlined his desire to be rid of her. He couldn't have
made his feelings more plain if he'd ordered her, along
with her brother, off the ranch.

"Idiot boy," Brant said audibly as they reached the city. "I'll have words with him about this. It's no way to treat a new bride, I'll tell you that!"

"I'm an unwanted bride, Mr. Culhane," she reminded him gently. "Perhaps it's for the best. He's spared my reputation, you know."

"It would hardly have been necessary to save it had he not ruined it in the first place. I tell you, Amelia, his behavior is incomprehensible to me. I never thought that a son of mine . . . !"

"Please," she said, stopping the flow of words with an uplifted hand. "It will all pass, like wind on the desert. He has made his choice, and I have been spared from having to live with a man who cannot love me. Yesterday certainly underlined the fact that he has never gotten over his feelings for Alice."

Brant couldn't argue with that. "I shall miss you," he said. "It has been very pleasant having a daughter in residence."

"I could not have wished for more congenial in-laws," she replied. "I shall write when I am settled, so that King will know where to contact me when . . ." She swallowed and started again, "when he is ready to proceed with a divorce or an annulment."

An annulment would require a lie from both of them, but only King would know that. Best to let everyone think there had been no real indiscretion. But Amelia was growing more certain by the day that she had conceived during that one intimacy. She was almost certainly pregnant. The child would be born without its father, never knowing him at all. She could hardly bear the thought.

"I must go," she said unsteadily.

Brant winced at her expression. He didn't know what

to say or do. He helped her down from the carriage at the hotel and carried her valise in for her. Just as they got in the door, Quinn came down the staircase and spotted his sister.

He strode toward her and, seeing her face, simply pulled her into his arms and held her comfortingly while she cried.

"I'm sorry, sister," he said miserably. "I've done a lot of damage with Rodriguez's arrest, haven't I? I've lost the woman I loved, cost myself a best friend and you a husband, and all in one day!"

"Oh, Quinn, don't," she said, now the one to comfort him.

Brant tried to offer his own condolences, but Quinn waved them away.

"It's done," he told his best friend's father. "Maybe King can forgive us both one day. For the time being, I'll see Amelia settled here. Then perhaps I can manage at least a boardinghouse for her. . . ."

"No," Amelia said firmly. "I shall go to Cousin Ettie in Florida."

"But if you stay here, King might relent," Quinn argued.

"It will not matter," she said, her face expressionless. "I shall go, and that is an end to it." She shook hands warmly with Brant. "Thank your wife and Alan, please, for their kindness. I shall never forget you."

"Nor we, you, my dear," Brant said miserably. He left them there, muttering all the way out the door.

Quinn saw his sister settled in a modest room in the hotel and went over to the jail to check on his prisoner. But when he reached the jail, a terrible commotion was in progress, men with guns drawn rushing around the building in a fever of industry.

Quinn immediately thought the worst. With his badge in place on his vest, he strode into the sheriff's office and stopped dead just inside the door. There, on the floor, lay Rodriguez. He had been placed on a stretcher. His expression was very quiet, peaceful, without strain or contortion. There wasn't a mark on him except for the small hole in his temple.

"Who?" Quinn asked the sheriff fiercely.

"That's what we're trying to find out. The pistol was lying on the floor of the cell, he was on top of it. . . ."

Quinn bent down to examine the wound and then examined Rodriguez's hands as a terrible thought began to occur to him. He examined the outlaw's left hand. It was the left temple where the bullet wound was located, and it was known that Rodriguez was left-handed. Quinn pulled out his white handkerchief and wiped the slightly grimy hand. Sure enough, there were faint powder marks on the fingertips. He laid Rodriguez's hand back on his chest and bent his head.

"You won't find an assassin," Quinn said very quietly. "He was left-handed. There are powder marks around the wound, which certainly means it was done at point-blank range." He looked up at the sheriff. "This was suicide."

The sheriff nodded. "That's what I thought, but they," he indicated the deputies outside, "swore it had to be someone who didn't want Rodriguez to stand trial. Accomplices, maybe, in his rustling confederation." He shook his head. "I've been in this business a long time. Never knew an outlaw to do this."

"He told me yesterday that his victims had come back to haunt him," Quinn said heavily. "I never thought he'd do this. He was a religious man, and Catholic. Suicide denies him an eternal rest."

The sheriff moved closer, his hand in his vest pocket. He frowned. "You really think so?" he asked philosophically. "Seems to me that suicide is the act of a desperate mind, so maybe God makes allowances."

"That could be."

The sheriff shrugged. "All the same, saves the city the cost of bed and board and the trial. Kind of him."

"He was a kind man," Quinn said. But he wasn't joking. He had to ride to Malasuerte and break the news to Maria. He dreaded it more than the thought of death.

He got up from the floor, took one last look at the tired old man on the stretcher, and went out the door.

King was picked up by one of his cowboys returning from the branding pens on a chuck wagon early the next morning as he walked down the dirt road a few miles from Latigo. He was in need of a shave, and he looked as tired as he felt.

"I'll kill that damned horse and make barbeque of him when we get back," he told the cowboy furiously.

"Don't blame you, sir," the man, an Irishman, said with a grin. "Don't blame you a'tall. Horses is the very devil."

"All because of a damned snake." King still couldn't believe his bad luck. He settled down on the seat, grateful for the lift, because his feet were killing him. All the same, it was like being batted in the rear with a board every time the buckboard hit a bump. He hated wagons.

When he got to the house, there was no one about. He left the Irishman at the barn and strode up on the porch. Amelia was going to be furious, and he deserved her wrath. He didn't even have a decent explanation for his outburst.

Amelia was not in her room, and it was with a cold sense of foreboding that he walked into the kitchen where his mother was cooking a late breakfast.

His father was sitting at the table, looking worn and angry.

"So there you are," he told King with cold eyes. "You're a little late. Your wife has left you."

King let out a slow breath. He felt suddenly hollow inside, faintly fearful. "Already?"

"She is now convinced that you have buried your heart in the grave with Alice and want no part of her," Enid added without looking at him. "She is doing the decent thing and letting you go without any recriminations."

"Did I ask to be let go?" he burst out furiously. "My God, I'm not pining for Alice!"

Enid glanced at him, disapproving of his dusty clothes and unshaven face. "You look terrible."

"I should look terrible!" he raged. "My damned horse got spooked by a rattlesnake and deserted me in the middle of nowhere! I had to bed down for the night in the desert and hitch a ride with the chuck wagon this . morning. I'm tired and cold and hungry and worn out, and now my wife's left me!"

"Which is no more than you deserve," his father said flatly.

King glared at him. "Quinn could have waited one more day for his disclosure about Rodriguez. He's ruined everything!"

"It seems to me that Quinn was just as upset over his own predicament," Enid said. "He was in love with Rodriguez's daughter. How do you think she will feel about him when she learns that her father is in jail because of Quinn?"

King sat down at the table and, reaching into his father's jacket for a cigar, also searching for a box of matches, lit it.

"I suppose Quinn must feel half as bad as I do," he admitted. "But it was poor timing. Where is Amelia?"

"Probably on her way to Florida," Brant said with cold pleasure.

King's fingers froze the cigar in midair. "What?"

"She is going to live with her cousin until you get a divorce or an annulment."

"An annulment?"

Brant glared at him. "Nonconsummation is certainly grounds for . . ." He saw the look in his son's eyes and stopped dead.

"There are no grounds for an annulment," King said icily, daring his parent to say another world. "Amelia is my wife. I do not intend letting her go to strangers when she may even now be carrying my child!"

He got up from the table and strode out the door.

Enid and Brant exchanged startled glances, but neither of them could manage to put their thoughts into words.

The trail to Malasuerte was longer than Quinn remembered it. He was tired and heartsick, but he had to go on. He had to confess it all to Maria, to tell her the truth, no matter how much it hurt. Then, if after knowing everything, she could forgive him, he would marry her. She wouldn't have to worry about Juliano, either, because he'd take care of him. He tried not to think about Rodriguez and what had happened. It hurt more than he'd imagined anything could. He'd grown fond of the old bandit. He regretted very much being the catalyst that had cost him his life.

He rode into Malasuerte late that afternoon. The pueblo was the same as always, except that when Quinn dismounted this time, people didn't gather around him. They hung back, looking at him with fear instead of affection. It took him a minute or two to realize what made the difference in their attitude. This time there was a silver star on his vest, denoting that the bearer was a Texas Ranger.

That wasn't the worst of it, though. Maria slowly came forward. She looked at him, and in her eyes was the worst kind of hatred and contempt.

"We have just received word that our papa has killed himself in the jail. He trusted you, but you betrayed him! You betrayed all of us. *¡Vaya!*" she spat, weeping. "Go away! You are not welcome here, Mr. Texas Ranger!"

He stood without moving, his reins in his hand, the horse neighing softly behind him while he felt the depths of despair well up in him.

"I love you, Maria," he said unsteadily.

She didn't answer. She turned and went back into the hut that had been Rodriguez's. The rest of the inhabitants of the small pueblo turned their backs on him and left him alone on the outskirts of the settlement. Quinn stayed there for a minute, but it was apparent that Maria was too hurt to come back. He mounted his horse and rode back toward Texas. He felt as if he no longer had any purpose in life. Everyone had deserted him. He didn't dare think about the loss of Maria, or he'd go mad. But the road ahead looked very lonely indeed.

══ Chapter Twenty ══

AMELIA WAS JUST SITTING DOWN TO DINNER IN THE
hotel's elegant dining room, all by herself, when
conversation stopped and heads turned toward the door.

A rough-looking, unshaven man in jeans and a
checked shirt and a disreputable hat and boots was
striding toward a nicely dressed young blond woman in
a white lacy dress and black shawl. She stared at him
from a face gone white, but he didn't appear to notice
her distress. He went to her table and, without a word,
pulled her chair out, lifted her high in his arms, and
strode out the door of the hotel toward a waiting buggy.
It would be a long time before the citizens of El Paso
forgot the sight of King Culhane carrying his escaped
bride back out to Latigo!

"How dare you embarrass me so!" Amelia raged as
he snapped the whip at the horse's rump to start him
off down the street. The straining sound of the leather
harness and the dusty thud of the horses' hooves on the
hard-packed dirt did nothing to muffle her angry voice.

"You shouldn't have run away," he said pleasantly.

"You left!" she accused furiously. "You rode off and
left me there with all our guests, after you ordered my
poor brother off the place! What did you expect me to
do, sit and simper while you went off to mourn your
late fiancée?"

"You're shouting, Amy."

"I am not. . . ." She cleared her throat. "I am not shouting. I am simply making a point. I do not wish to go to Latigo with you. I am making arrangements to live with my cousin Ettie in Jacksonville, Florida."

"Not without me, you aren't."

"I do not wish to live with you," she informed him haughtily. "You are rude, overbearing, domineering, mannerless, thoughtless, and cruel!"

He shrugged. "A man must have a few faults in order to be interesting." He glanced sideways at her, and his face softened magically, like the silver eyes that held hers. "You look very pretty in white."

"Flattery will not erase your past behavior from my mind."

"I have something much more physical planned."

"You will not touch me, sir!"

"Yes, I will." He glanced at her with slow, possessive eyes. "Until you make love with me, our marriage is not legal."

"You don't want it to be legal," she countered, face flaming.

"Indeed I do," he replied. "I find you congenial company. There is, of course," he added with a lingering appraisal of her, "the matter of your regrettable temper."

"I do not have a temper!"

"And you have a tendency to run away."

"I didn't run, you threw me out!"

"I threw your brother out," he corrected.

"There is no difference!"

"Between your brother and you? There most certainly is! I have no desire whatsoever to kiss your brother," he added with a slow smile.

She flushed, and her hands became nervous in her lap. She stared at them without looking up. Her anger was leaving her, and she was becoming vulnerable all over again. He was close beside her. She felt his warmth and strength and knew a slow-growing ache to be in his arms again, with a return to the affection that had been blossoming between them.

He pulled the buggy into the shade, where there were patches of grass for the horses to nibble. He looped the reins over the brake and rested his booted foot next to it while he turned to look at Amelia without humor.

"We got off to a bad start," he said bluntly. His silver eyes searched hers closely. "It was my fault. I lost sight of a lot of things in a burst of bad temper. That's something you'll have to get used to, because I can't change. I'm prone to outbursts and impulses, it's my nature. But you've a temper of your own, so you should be able to cope quite well."

"With your temper, yes. With the memory of Alice . . . no," she added weakly, averting her eyes.

He put a gentle hand to her face, turning it back to his. "Rodriguez has been a thorn in my side for a long time. It was being helpless, knowing that someone I cared for was murdered and I was unable to prevent it, to help her. Amelia, I would have felt just the same if one of my men had been butchered in such a manner."

"Oh."

He traced the hair at her cheeks, loosened it on the breeze. "I heard in town when I asked for you at the desk that Rodriguez was found dead in his cell today," he added. "The opinion is that he committed suicide rather than stand trial."

"Poor Quinn," Amelia said softly. "His Maria will not be quick to forgive him, I fear."

"Perhaps not. But I hope that you, and he, will be able to forgive me," he added quietly. "I said some unkind things in the heat of anger, Amy, things for which I am sorry."

She drew in a steadying breath and slowly relaxed, leaning toward the hand that was caressing her face. "You will be a very difficult husband," she said slowly.

He brightened, because she was no longer talking of leaving him. "Probably," he admitted. "But then, what challenge is there in a compliant one?"

She smiled, and all his fears began to vanish. He pulled her gently into his arms and turned her over his lap.

"I will not let you leave me," he said, breathing against her mouth as he took it slowly under his own. "Never in a thousand years!"

She reached up and held him, giving him back the long, slow kisses that left them both trembling with frustrated need. She finished with her face in his hot throat, clinging madly to his strength.

He held her until the feelings calmed somewhat, gently smoothing her hair.

"I will cherish you until I die," he said huskily. "All my life, Amy."

"And I, you." She shivered as she nuzzled closer. "Oh, King, I do love you . . . so!"

His arms contracted involuntarily, bruising. His mouth searched blindly for hers. "Say it again," he bit off against her lips.

"I love you . . . love you. . . ."

He whispered it back to her, parted her lips with his, found her soft body with his hands. She wept when he stopped abruptly and folded her protectively close but without passion.

"Don't stop," she whispered.

"I have to," he said hoarsely. "This is hardly the place," he added on a husky laugh.

"Your parents are still at the house."

"They are discreet," he replied gently. "They will find a way to absent themselves. For now," he added, clasping her hand in his, "it is enough that we're together."

A statement with which Amelia could hardly disagree. She had something very special to tell him. But it would keep, for a little while.

There was no one to greet Quinn when he rode back into town. Gossip was rife about Amelia and King, however, and he permitted himself a tiny smile when he realized that whatever King's qualms about the marriage had been, he knew what he wanted now. It looked as if King and Amelia were back together for good. He went upstairs early, carrying a bottle with him, and drank himself into quiet oblivion.

Brant and Enid were overjoyed when they saw King walk in with a radiant Amelia. They decided very quickly to go after Alan, and since their bags had already been packed, it was a simple matter to have one of the cowhands drive them in to the train station.

King and Amelia waved them good-bye from the porch and then went back inside, arms around each other, to begin their marriage.

He lifted his radiant bride and carried her down the hall to the bedroom, kicking the door shut behind them. He laughed softly at her flush as he carried her to the bed and put her down gently on the bedspread.

"Are you truly so nervous?" he chided. "This is not our first time together."

"I wish that it were," she said with faint sadness.

He sobered quickly. "I can understand why you might feel that way. I was wrong about you, Amelia. I made some terrible assumptions and acted on them. I wonder that you wanted to let our marriage continue at all."

Her dark eyes smiled up into his silver ones. "But I love you," she said simply. "What choice did I have? Although," she added with a soft sigh, "I do fear that I was right when I said you would be a difficult husband." Her arms circled his neck and gently pulled him toward her. She reached up to kiss him very softly. "You have a tendency to talk too much!"

He chuckled, all the sadness vanished, as he followed her down onto the bed. Not another word was spoken for quite some time.

She curled into his arms, shivering a little in the aftermath of the most tender loving she could ever have imagined. "Will it be . . . like this from now on?" she whispered, shaken.

"Always," he promised. He curled her closer into his body, cradling her while he sought to calm his violent heartbeat and erratic breathing. Her body had given his pleasure beyond belief, even surpassing their first time together. He had caused her no pain this time, making certain that he was slow enough with his caresses to bring her to an incredible level of need before he joined her body slowly to his. Even then, it was he who kept the lazy pace when she pleaded for him not to torment her. At last, when they fell through the stars together, she wept violently. Her sweet cries increased his own pleasure, so that it was an ecstasy that brought a brief loss of consciousness with it.

"What are you thinking?" she asked daringly.

"That I have never felt such pleasure," he said honestly. He looked down into her misty eyes and bent to brush his mouth over their tired lids. "Perhaps I dreamed you, Amelia," he whispered. "I could be forgiven for thinking so. I love you so much . . . !"

She clung to him, answering his hungry mouth, but too tired to do much more than that.

He laughed wickedly. "Have I exhausted you, my dear?" he asked gently.

"You, and our child," she whispered, watching his eyes as she said it and then smiling at the stunned reaction that stilled his expression.

He scowled. "Our . . . child."

She nodded. She took his lean hand and placed it over the faint swell of her stomach, no longer shy or inhibited with him, though neither of them were covered. "Will you mind, so soon in our marriage?"

"Oh, no," he said genuinely, and his eyes began to sparkle with feeling. "No, I will not mind." He began to smile and then to chuckle as his eyes boldly wandered over her. "I thought this very becoming radiance was my doing, but I can see now that it is not." He bent to kiss her, cherishing her mouth. But when he drew back, his eyes were troubled. "It was the first time, that we made this baby," he began slowly.

She put her fingers over his mouth. "I loved you even then," she said quietly. "Let us not speak of it again."

He brought her palm to his mouth and kissed it hungrily. "Forgive me!" he whispered roughly. "I wish that I could take back every hurtful thing I have ever said or done to you!"

"Time will erase it all," she promised. "And now we have not only our happiness together but a new life to look forward to. Oh, King, we are so, so lucky!"

He looked into her eyes and agreed with such fervor that she laughed and pulled him down to her again.

Three weeks later, King had to go into El Paso and rescue a very drunk Quinn from the county jail. He took his brother-in-law out to Latigo and established him in the guest room.

"It's that girl, Maria, Rodriguez's daughter, who haunts him, is it not?" Amelia asked King later, after she'd checked on her unconscious kin.

"I believe so," he replied. "He has resigned from the Rangers, they told me at the sheriff's office. I am certain that he would never have taken such a step unless he was not all himself."

"They have reorganized the Frontier battalion, and he was not happy with it," she reminded him. "Also, he has not been the same since Policeman Stewart was shot and killed by those army men from Ft. Bliss after the arrest of their disorderly comrade."

"A tragedy," he agreed, "but the perpetrators have been brought to justice."

"That does not bring back Mr. Stewart," she pointed out. "Quinn admired him."

"I know. So did many of us."

"What shall we do about him?"

King thought for a moment. "I believe there is only one solution," he said grimly.

"Which is?"

He brought her face up to his and kissed her warmly. "Don't wait supper for me."

He walked out while she was still trying to question him, got on his horse, and rode away.

* * *

Malasuerte was not hard to find. It took King a little
over three hours to get the information he needed from
the sheriff and proceed over the border.

He asked for the girl and was politely escorted to a
small hut in the pueblo which was, presumably, hers.

King took off his hat as he was admitted. The girl
was very pretty, he thought. She was slender and well-
made, with black hair and blue eyes. Those were very
sad eyes, though. Lonely eyes.

"What do you want, *señor*?" she asked dully. "My
papa is dead, you know. Rodriguez is not here anymore."

"I didn't come about Rodriguez." He twisted his hat
in his hands as he squatted down to talk to the girl, who
was making tortillas over a small fire. "I married
Quinn's sister, Amelia."

Her hands slipped, and one of the tortillas tipped off
the pan into the flames. She moved the pan off the fire
and stared, with tragic face and eyes, at King.

"Quinn!" she said miserably. "I sent him away. I
blamed him for Papa's death, for everything."

"Yes, I know," King said dryly. "He gave up his
Ranger badge and has apparently determined to become
an alcoholic. At least, he certainly gives that indication."

She gasped. "Quinn does not drink, *señor*. Well,
perhaps a drop or so of mescal . . ."

"He drinks to excess and has for the past few weeks
since Rodriguez killed himself," he informed her.
"Now there's only one way this can end. He'll keep on
going downhill until he ends up dead."

"No!"

His eyebrows arched. "Isn't that what you want?
That's what he told me."

"No, no, a thousand times no, I do not want him

dead!'' she cried, tears welling in her eyes. She went close to King, grasping him by the shoulders. ''Please. Will you take me to him? Will you permit that I ride back to your ranch, to speak with him?''

''Why do you want to?'' he asked shrewdly.

She shrugged and moved back. ''Because I am sorry for him, of course.''

''I'm glad. But that really won't do,'' he told her.

She lifted her eyes to his. ''Then, because I love him,'' she said gently.

He smiled. ''That was the reason I hoped to hear. Do you have a horse?''

''I will borrow Juliano's, my brother's!''

She ran to get it, her face radiant. Minutes later she was back, in the saddle, waiting for King.

He looked around as he got back on the horse. These people lived in the most appalling sort of poverty, but they seemed happy enough. They waved, along with the boy Maria had called Juliano, as they rode out.

''My papa was not happy about what he had done,'' Maria said as they went toward the border. ''He said that the past haunted him. It was for us that he did it. And it was for us, for his people, that he died, so that the authorities would stop persecuting us in their search for him.'' She glanced toward him. ''He was a great, and good, man, *señor*. I owe him my life, and so does Juliano. Whatever the gringos say about Rodriguez, he was no devil.''

''I had discovered that through Quinn. He is not the sort of man to love a devil,'' he told her. ''He has mourned Rodriguez.''

''Yes. As have we all. I was wrong to accuse Quinn. I hope that it is not too late to show him how much I care for him.''

King nodded. But privately, he hoped the same thing. Quinn had been belligerent and uncooperative on the way out to the ranch, and since. He spoke of Maria but not in any complimentary way.

Amelia was sitting on the porch when they arrived long after dark. She stood up with relief written all over her when they dismounted, leaving the horses with a ranch hand, and went into the house.

"I had no idea where you were," she told King irritably, and then ruined her angry stance by going into his arms and hugging him hungrily. "Where have you been!"

"Getting Maria," he said simply. "This is Maria," he added, introducing her. "Rodriguez's daughter."

Amelia smiled warmly. "I am happy to meet you at last. Our poor Quinn is very lonely without you."

Maria flushed. "It is the same for me. I was very cruel to him. I hope that he can forgive."

"I think you'll find that he's more than willing to meet you halfway. Come."

Amelia shot a loving look at her weary husband and led Maria down the hall to the guest room.

She opened the door, and Quinn, very hung over and headachy, looked up from where he was sitting, fully dressed, on the side of the bed.

"What the hell do you want?" he asked Maria coldly. "Another slice of my heart?"

She went forward, kneeling in front of him. "I am much too greedy, *señor*. I want all of it."

She smiled and held out her arms. With a rough cry, Quinn went into them, lifting and turning her roughly. He kissed her hungrily, and she answered his kisses without reserve.

Amelia chuckled softly to herself. She went out and left them, but she didn't close the door.

"Well?" King asked.

"I think we'll have another wedding very soon," was all she said. She took his hand, and they walked back toward the kitchen.

The elder Culhanes came home a week later to find incredible changes at Latigo. Alan was not with them, having gone to Beaumont, Texas, to work with his brother Callaway in the search for oil.

"I can't believe it," Enid said, laughing as she was introduced to Quinn's new wife. The newlyweds were living in a boardinghouse in El Paso, and Quinn had joined the El Paso police department, where he was working into a fairly decent deputy according to the sheriff.

King and Amelia were radiant and announced a little sheepishly that they were going to become parents. Enid took this revelation not without shock but also with a great deal of pleasure. Brant got out the brandy and began making toasts. It was a late night for all.

As they waved off Quinn and Maria, King circled Amelia's thickening waist with a long, powerful arm and pulled her close in the warm May evening. "They say we're going to have an eclipse of the sun soon," he remarked.

"A heavenly event," she agreed. She looked up at him. "But I have to tell you that the most heavenly event I know of will happen in just a little over six months."

King didn't realize what she was saying for a minute. When he did, he laughed so loudly that his father and mother came out on the porch to see what the noise was all about. The four of them, sharing the joke, looked out at the horizon where Quinn and Maria, in the buggy, were driving slowly back toward town.

"The beginning of a new generation," Brant remarked, clapping his son on the back. "I am glad that I have lived to see it."

"And think," King told him. "You can tell your grandchildren how you fought off Comanches and settled here with Mother when El Paso was barely a town. You will be a hero to them."

Brant thought about that and began to nod. "Why, so I will."

"Now see what you've done," Enid grumbled. "He'll strut for a week."

She followed him back into the house. Amelia snuggled close to King as they settled down in the porch swing to watch the clouds sail across the moon. She closed her eyes and sent a prayer upward for her poor father and her mother and little brothers, and even Rodriguez, none of whom would see the next generation that King had spoken of.

Somewhere in the darkness, a lone coyote began to howl, and the faint echo of it was hauntingly sad. But there was independence in it, and strength. It was, a dreaming Amelia thought pleasantly, a wild song for a fierce country that, like King, would never quite be tame. She nuzzled her face against his broad chest, and stronger than the lament of the coyote was the regular, firm beat of his heart at her ear.